The elder vampire had gone into a rage. One moment Jeanne was standing, arms clasped behind his back and his brow furrowed in concentration as he sought the perfect words to convey his meaning. The next he was flying through the air, stunned. Before he'd even hit the ground Montrovant was upon him, one hand holding him prone by the throat as if he were a child, or a recalcitrant mongrel. No matter how he'd struggled, he could not move, and Montrovant had slowly begun to compress his fingers in a crushing grip.

Face scant inches from Jeanne's own, Montrovant had spit his words like poison into his progeny's face.

"You will wish for nothing, Jeanne, that I do not wish for you. You will seek no other without my blessing, and you will not receive that blessing. I am apart from them, and you are of me."

There had been no way to answer with Montrovant's hand clenched over his throat. No words would have sufficed. Le Duc felt his hold on his new existence hanging in the balance, tipping gently one way, then the other on the fine point of Montrovant's temper. Then the moment had passed. Jeanne had said no more, and within the hour it was as if nothing had taken place. At least it was thus for Montrovant. That moment of uncertainty, where death had stared him in the face a second time, lines of finality etched across his face, would remain with le Duc as long as he walked the Earth.

I0545747

TO SPEAK WITH LIFELESS TONGUES

THE GRAILS COVENANT TRILOGY

BOOK 2

By David Niall Wilson

PART ONE

ONE

Evening dropped slowly over the walls of the Convent of Our Lady of Bitter Tears. Against the backdrop of orange sunlight and multi-hued clouds the structure stood silent, cresting a small rise with the huge expanse of the Cambrian Mountains rising up from behind. The last of the sunlight seeped over the tips of the peaks, slipping down at odd angles and sending huge, elongated shadows to grope at the old stone walls, as if trying to pry loose secrets long buried.

There was no movement in the gardens, and the bell in the small chapel was silent. The hour of meditation had arrived and transported the sisters to communion with their Lord. Each had taken to her quarters, waiting expectantly. Each expected that He or His servant might come to them. Each believed in her heart that it would be her time.

Behind the heavy oak doors of the Mother Superior's chambers the silence was broken by heavy, rasping breaths that wheezed and scratched their way free of one darkened corner of the room. The small table that sat before her window, commanding a view of the valley below, was set for a meal that had gone untouched. Flies buzzed lazily about the rotting remains of that meal and the sickly-sweet stench of rotted meat permeated the air. As the last of the light leaked from the room a chair creaked. Old bones crackled as limbs too long in one position were set in motion. A wracking cough, brittle and harsh, broke the silence followed by the grating sound of a flint being struck. The wick of a tallow candle came to life, wavering softly in the slight breeze from the window, and a thin, frightened face came into focus.

Mother Agnes sat with both hands cupped about the base of the candle, unmindful of the hot wax dribbling slowly down the sides toward her withered hands. She stared straight through the window into the black void beyond, waiting. As did the sisters who no longer took her counsel, she considered that He might come, and the thought chilled her to the center of her brittle, arthritic bones. There was no warmth in her anticipation. Death comes to all who wait in His own good time. Agnes felt that her time must be near. There was no other way to explain away the madness, and her God wasn't answering her prayers.

So many days had passed since He'd first come to them, so many dark and endless nights. Such beauty. Never, in all the years of her service to her savior had she felt drawn so completely to a man. She should have known then—should have felt that it was wrong. Nothing had mattered when he turned his eyes upon her. Nothing but pleasing him—not even her faith. He had taken that faith and twisted it, returning it only after it was worn away and useless.

Beyond the window a wolf howled, and a shiver shot through her weakened frame, nearly dropping her from her seat to the cold stone of the floor. What light there had been the night had swallowed whole. The moon had not yet risen to her throne of white light, leaving the world cloaked in black. A cloak of mourning. There was no way to know what might be out there, and yet Agnes knew. She felt it in her heart of hearts, the approach of eternity and the lack of light.

She prayed under her breath, a low, keening moan of words that were no more comprehensible to her mind than they would have been to any who listened. The verses were mismatched and random, blending and molding themselves to her grasping attempts at coherent thought. One anchor remained to her sanity and she clung to it with the patience of the damned and desperate.

The supply train would arrive soon. There would be contact with the villages below the mountain, and Father Joseph would be with them. He would arrive, God willing, by the light of day, and she would find some way to make her tongue function properly. She would gather the strength to go to him and to tell him of the Hell that had descended upon her convent. She would make him drive that evil forth, or they would all perish in the attempt, but it would happen in less than a day.

A whisper of cloth brushing against stone sounded beyond her window, and she cowered further into the shadows, willing her heartbeat to silence and clamping down on the suddenly raucous sound of her own breath. She felt the wood of her chair and the cool stone of the wall behind her, and she imagined herself a part of them, inanimate and uninteresting to whatever might be seeking her out. It was a vain hope. The shadow slipped across the sill of her window and came to rest, upright and towering above her, just within her chamber. She didn't have the energy left to scream.

The shadow figure stood suddenly at her side. She couldn't remember if He'd walked across that space, glided, or merely appeared at her shoulder, but He leaned forward and his lips brushed her ears as He spoke. She tried to pull away. The words of her prayers became more chaotic and meaningless, and the strength bled from her frame as she pressed against the stiff back of her chair, digging her fingernails into the wood until they broke from the pressure. She stared straight ahead, avoiding the sight of Him, but His words seeped through the wall of concentration she'd erected as easily as wind beneath an ill-fitting door. The taste of anticipation altered, but she continued her prayer.

"I have waited for this moment," the Dark One whispered, breathing the words into her ear and sending tingles of energy rippling down her arms, standing the soft hairs on end as it passed. She'd never been so intimately close to a man, not since her vows had removed her from the mainstream of life. She felt the magnetic pull of his flesh and nearly cried out in shame and desire at once.

"Leave me..." she rasped, surprising herself with the strength of her words. "Return to whatever shadow spawned you, leave me—us—in peace."

"I cannot do that, Agnes," the shadow continued smoothly. "You mean so very much to me now. I have learned from you, but I have shared so little. It is time for you to learn what I have to offer, as your little sisters have done. You want that, don't you, Agnes?"

She turned her head farther away, aware that the motion bared her throat, and tossed the graying locks of her hair aside in the same motion, though she knew it was not proper. There was no touch, not of breath or of pain. All that she sensed was His nearness, and it wore away at her control as he continued to speak.

"You pray to a savior who has been too long gone from the earth," he said. "You waste your life and your love on one who will see you only after you have fallen to dust, if ever. You were a beautiful woman, Agnes…full of life."

"I serve my Lord," she whispered desperately. "I will stand at his side in Glory, and this will be nothing but a dark moment in time—a nothingness without meaning."

"You are wrong," he said, laying one hand gently on her shoulder. "You will still be standing when he comes again, in the flesh that binds you now, and he will turn away."

Then the pain came, the bite of something sharp penetrating her throat, followed by wave upon wave of pleasure. She shuddered, and her arms dropped to her sides in sudden release, then returned to their grips on the chair. She felt the life draining swiftly from her aged frame, and she felt the faith of a lifetime being stolen away. It was too much.

A small flame still burned within her, a light that she could make out through the murky haze of sensations that began where the flesh of his hands gripped her frail shoulders and radiated out in waves that threatened to consume her humanity. Blanking her mind, she ceased her struggles and concentrated on that light.

There were other pressures. He assaulted her flesh, but he was attempting to violate her mind as well, her memories. He was seeking something, and the sudden knowledge that denial of that information would be the same as a victory gave her the focus to draw herself slowly toward the flame of her own being. He might have her blood—she knew that it was her blood he stole—but he would not have her soul. He would not drag her into the nightmare that was his own existence, and he would not find the answers he sought within her.

As her strength ebbed and the light grew to fill her mind, she felt a sudden influx of energy. He would not have her. Flesh was the cage that held her to the world, but within the light that grew and pulsed before her she felt the hands of her savior reaching out to draw her in.

He shifted her in his arms, drawing her up and out of her chair and tilting her back so that she faced the ceiling. His dark eyes filled her sight, threatening for a moment to blot out the light from within, then fading to a blur of shadow at the fringes of her consciousness. The world receded, but something was important about his actions. He held a wrist above her now, and he reached over almost casually with his free hand to slice at that wrist with a fingernail too long to be real, and too real to be pure. Her mouth opened, and she stared into the dark pits where his eyes should have been, but she did not see him.

His intent was clear, and as he raised the weeping wound above her, blood dripping in a steady stream down his forearm, she drew on the awesome strength of the light that called to her so strongly. She released herself from the world, wrenching herself from her flesh and soaring free.

From above and far away she saw her body convulse in the Dark One's arms. She saw the crimson flow of blood from the cut of his arm as it dribbled meaninglessly off over the lips of the shell that had housed her, but she felt no emotion at the sight. No disgust. No violation. No victory.

Her body was lost to her, but it was lost to him as well. She sensed that his words had not been metaphorical. There was an ageless quality in the glint of his eyes and a detached loneliness in the tones of his voice that hinted at knowledge beyond the scope of human years. There was hunger there as well, and not all of that hunger was directed at her blood, though that was a large part of it.

As she drifted away she sensed that he, too, fought his way through bondage. He sought answers, but the essence of his being forced other issues to the forefront of his mind and robbed him of time and concentration. He fed because he had to, but there was more that he'd wanted from Mother Agnes of the Convent of Our Lady of Bitter Tears. He would get nothing.

Other voices called out to her now, musical and inviting, and the light had grown so bright that all else disappeared from her thoughts. She slipped within that glow, and her essence co-mingled with the energy of the light. It was a true communion, a joining, and the voices became her own, or she became the voices. The chambers and the stone walls of the convent dropped away until nothing remained.

The dark figure felt the life slip from his aging victim's body, and he cursed. It was not directed at God, or at himself, but at eternity in general. Montrovant felt the rivulet of blood making its way down his flesh and cursed himself for not cramming the cut between the old one's lips before she could escape him. She was gone, and the blood that splattered and dribbled over her wrinkled, silent face was nothing but strength and sustenance wasted.

The wound healed quickly, and with a contemptuous toss he flung the husk that had been Mother Agnes across the room. Her bones shattered on impact with the stone of the wall, and her blood-drained flesh made a wet, smacking noise as it spread out on impact and fell to the floor, limp and empty. He hadn't meant to throw her so violently, but she'd been his best hope and now he would have to move on and try again.

Montrovant strode to the window, wiping his sleeve across his lips to clear away the last of the Mother Superior's blood. He'd shared enough of her thoughts before she escaped him to know that his time in the convent was at an end. That meant that he, or le Duc, would have to find an answer—any answer— this very night.

The supply train would arrive in the morning, or the next. It didn't matter. They would arrive soon, and that was enough. Montrovant knew that he and le Duc could take precautions that would lead those arriving off on false trails, away from the truth. They could make it look as if bandits had raided the convent for food and shelter, perhaps even for a taste of the virtue of the good sisters, but eventually there would be discoveries, information that didn't fit the motives or patterns of mountain bandits.

They would notice the wounds on the women's necks. They would notice the broken, blood-drained carcass of the Mother Superior and wonder what kind of man could perpetuate such violence with such disregard to their Lord. They would put the facts together, and they would know what to look for. He and le Duc had to be gone before the dawn, and they had to find a place that none would think to look for them, or it might be the last night of their existence.

He stared out into the darkness. He had vague ideas where the Brotherhood might have gone, where Kli Kodesh might have sent them, but it seemed a step beyond him to draw even with his prey. They always seemed a few miles ahead; or else they slipped away as he followed a false lead into one form of trouble or another. Montrovant had not been patient in life, and the virtue had not forced itself upon him as his mind matured and his body ignored time. Now this. Another delay.

He had purposely kept them as far from the cities as possible. The clans were beginning to grow in strength, and any hint of interference from outside forces drew unwanted attention. Montrovant had no patience for games of politics that involved the power of others. He had his own concerns.

He burned to find the treasure he sought...the Grail...to bring it back to his sire, to drink from that most powerful of cups and feel the power beyond anything he or any other had experienced...to rule. Surely one who drank the blood from such a cup would rule the world, and as long as he walked the earth, Montrovant would see to it that no other took that position. Perhaps even Eugenio would get a bit of a surprise, once the Grail was his.

He was tempted to go for le Duc that instant and leave the convent behind. They'd been lazy, staying too long and enjoying the solitude and the attention of the sisters, who'd come to view them as visiting angels or gods in human flesh. Only the Mother Superior had eluded Montrovant's control. It had been many years since he'd encountered such complete, unwavering faith in another. His faith was strong, but it was in darker gods and his unnatural instincts. Those instincts told him that it was time to change tactics.

He reached out with his mind and felt the subtle presence that was le Duc. It had been several years now since he'd Embraced the Frenchman, and though he missed having a living, breathing servant to care for his needs during the daylight hours, it was good to have a companion. Since beginning his quest, he'd been voluntarily cut off from Claudius and the rest of his clan. There had been communications, of course, reports back and forth, but he'd not seen any of the others since he'd left for Jerusalem decades prior. It seemed a lifetime, and even for one whose years had spanned several mortal lifetimes, it was a lonely burden.

Jeanne was feeding. For just an instant Montrovant maintained the link, savoring the beauty of the sensation—the joining. He knew Jeanne would pull free before the sister was gone completely, leaving her weak and trembling on her bed to wake with visions she'd never truly escape. Le Duc was more dramatic with the humans than Montrovant. Briefly, the elder Cainite wondered if he was becoming too jaded. There had been a time when he'd enjoyed the hunt and the kill as much as le Duc did now, but that was fading. His obsession was costing him his sanity.

He swept his arm across the table where the rancid meal still sat, untouched. The plates and garbage crashed to the floor, rotted meat and untouched wine splashed against the stone. Moving swiftly, he systematically ransacked the room. He removed a few valuables, a silver crucifix and several pieces of jewelry that spoke of an earlier time in Agnes's life. They were dainty, the sort of trinkets that a doting father might bestow upon his daughter.

Brief memories stolen from her as her lifeblood drained into him flitted through Montrovant's mind. An Agnes none of the sisters would recognize, dressed up for a party—waiting on the steps of a keep for her father's return from war. He caught glimpses of her mother, brothers who'd watched over her. An old woman who'd read to her and taught her to be a lady. None of it mattered now. The father had lost a daughter, the old woman a pupil.

Now that daughter lay in a heap of ruined flesh, her life

dedicated to pursuits that long-lost father would never have fully understood. Dedication such as hers was not a common human trait. Montrovant tucked the jewelry into a pouch on his belt and continued his destruction of the room. Somehow, he didn't want to leave anything of Agnes behind. She'd made her escape.

When the room was a shambles, he turned away, putting Mother Agnes and her life behind him. He strode purposefully into the hall and made his way toward the next floor of the convent, where the sisters' quarters lined two walls. The cells were small and severe, a single bunk for rest and a small table where each of the sisters could keep her personal effects. None was more elaborate than any other, and yet he knew from the experience of the past weeks that each had its own sensation. The flavor of the woman, her blood, her thoughts and her passions, seeped into the walls of cold stone.

Her name was Maria, a small pale woman, like a slender ghost with ringlets of blonde hair cascading over her shoulders. Her quarters had a delicate, frightened feel to them. Her thoughts were furtive, always seeking approval and fearing retribution. He'd spent one long evening just holding her, not feeding, not taking advantage, but pressing her trembling form tightly against his breast and letting the triphammer of her heartbeat flutter against him. She was possibly the most vulnerable human he'd ever encountered, and in her faith she sought an answer to that vulnerability, a protection that a cold, severe God would never grant her.

There were others, and Montrovant wished his time with them were not through. There was something new to be learned in each experience, and he'd built his strength considerably since he and le Duc had first appeared before the sisters.

An image of Eugenio rose unbidden to the forefront of his mind. For perhaps the first time since his sire had closeted himself away in a convent near Rome, he was beginning to understand the motivation behind that seclusion. The privacy and the security were temptations hard to resist in a world where one of his kind had to be constantly on their guard.

The last time Montrovant had visited Claudius, he'd left his sire standing on the ramparts of that monastery, staring off into the darkness. Montrovant had been in such a hurry to get away, to make a mark in the greater scheme of things and bring power and glory to their clan. It hardly seemed as if that clan still existed within the scope of his world. All his thoughts centered on the Brotherhood he sought, and the treasure they guarded... his treasure, the Grail. There had to be an end to it, and soon.

He turned a corner and le Duc was there, pulling one of the doors closed behind himself softly. He turned, smiling, and Montrovant found himself caught up in that smile.

"We must leave," he said quickly, not wanting to waste time.

Jeanne only nodded in answer. They'd been on the road together for so long that most thoughts seemed shared. Montrovant turned away, and le Duc followed as the tall, gaunt vampire led the way toward the front of the building. There was only one entrance to the convent, and it was there that Montrovant was heading. The two had not slept their days within those walls, and it would take a bit of time to gather their possessions for a long ride from the mountains where they'd kept them stashed.

"I'll go to the stables," Jeanne offered.

"I will be waiting," Montrovant answered. They moved through the huge wooden doors into the night, and Montrovant left those doors open wide.

The remaining sisters would recover eventually, and if they were lucky their supply train would arrive in time to nurse them back to health and to soothe their loss. Montrovant doubted that any of them would ever fully release his image, and the thought amused him. It was good to have left a mark on the world, however fleeting.

"Sleep well," he called over his shoulder. "Sleep well my ladies, and farewell."

Then he leaped into the air in one fluid motion and shifted to a smaller blur of darkness, spreading his arms as they collapsed into deeper darkness, a shadow, slipping among the shades. The night wind bore him upward toward the open face of the mountain, and his spirit soared. It was time to move on, and perhaps, with luck, their next stop would be the one.

TWO

Le Duc was making his way out of the stables leading two of the finest mounts the sisters had to offer when a soft, feminine voice drifted through the shadows to him.

"You are...leaving?" The voice was familiar, but it had a plaintive, whining tone to it that kept him from putting a face to it immediately. "Just as the other. You will go and never return."

Sister Madeline. He knew her now, and he shifted his gaze to the left, picking her form from the darker shadows. She stood watching him, her hands clasped before her and her eyes open so wide that it seemed he could see to the very depths of her soul.

"Other?" he asked, moving closer and stopping to stand only a few feet from the trembling girl.

"Yes," she said, breathing heavily. Her expression was the vacant, empty stare of one bereft of all hope. She did not seem concentrated on what she was saying, but instead let her words ramble wherever her thoughts carried her. Fascinated, le Duc did not interrupt.

"He came as you have come, in the hours of darkness. So beautiful. Sister Sarah said that he must be an angel, but to tell him so only made him laugh. His name was Owain. Will you follow him?"

"Owain?" Le Duc rolled the name about in his mind. Something was familiar about it, but he couldn't place it exactly.

"Owain," Madeline agreed. "You are not so tall as he," she continued, moving closer, "but you are more beautiful." She'd slid into his arms, drawn by some image created in her own mind...not truly seeing le Duc at all. Trembling with shame, she pressed her flesh wantonly against his and craned her neck as if to allow him easier access.

"I know what you want," she continued, trembling. "It was the same when he came to me. I will give it to you freely, if you will not leave me. I want to go with you."

He could see the battle waging beyond her eyes …could sense the tension. Years of piety and faith warring with stolen moments of darkness… dreams of adventures and other places and wilder hearts.

"That is not possible, love," le Duc said, pulling back slightly so he could meet her gaze. "Where we go, none may follow."

She would have protested further, but he leaned in then, clamping onto the softness of her throat and letting her warm blood spill over his lips. She had offered, and he would accept, despite the fact that he had no intention of agreeing to her terms. He would need strength for the time to come, and the scent of her so near had wakened the hunger. He wasted no time, draining her as quickly and completely as he dared, then carried her inert form gently to where a mound of hay lay in one corner and set her down atop it. She would remember little, another angel come and gone in the night. It wouldn't be until she saw Mother Agnes, or until the supply train arrived, that she would begin to realize the truth of what had become of her. Even then, Jeanne thought, she would remember him fondly. It was the way of his curse.

As he moved into the night with the horses in tow, he continued to wonder over this Owain. Odd that none of the sisters had mentioned him before now, especially to Montrovant, whose powers of persuasion caused Jeanne's own to pale to nothingness. He wondered if Owain could have anything to do with their search, or if it were just coincidence that another passing Cainite had made use of the readily available supply of blood in the convent. He had to hope that Montrovant would recognize the name as well, and that it would mean more to him than it did to le Duc himself.

He wound his way quickly up the mountainside toward the caves they'd shared these last weeks, deep in thought. He knew Montrovant would be ready, pacing before the doorway to the cave and fuming at the delay. He knew, also, that the scent of fresh blood would carry, and that the reasons for the delay would be clear. He was happy to have the news of another of the Damned with which to divert his sire's anger.

Long years on the road had not softened his sire's hard edges, but le Duc himself had matured considerably. He'd been an angry man, seeking something on which he couldn't quite focus. Others had distrusted him, including Hugues de Payen, who'd taken him into the fold of the Knights Templar long years past. That distrust had been well-founded, not because le Duc didn't respect de Payen, but because Montrovant was the stronger. There had been little choice in the decisions le Duc had made, but he regretted none of them. He was where he was because it was ordained to be so. That was what he believed. The fact that Montrovant scoffed at this logic deterred him not a whit from his belief.

Le Duc had been on his way to the Holy Land, part of a caravan. He and a few others, including his one-time ally Pierre, who'd been responsible in part for Jeanne's own induction into the Templars.

Turkish bandits had descended upon their group, trapping them against an outcropping of stone in the desert. Jeanne had fought wildly, his mind given over to the red haze that had ruled his youth and his arm, never tiring, sending one after another of their Saracen attackers to meet Allah.

In those days Jeanne had cared nothing for anyone but himself, but he'd lived for battle. When de Payen and his knights had stormed up and rescued them, Jeanne and Pierre had been the only two still putting up much of a fight. Later, after realizing who and what had become their savior, both men had made the commitment to join the ranks of those knights, each for his own reasons.

Pierre had been sincere. He was the sort of man who needed structure and rules. De Payen's order was nothing if not structured. Jeanne had wavered over the decision to go to de Payen when Montrovant had appeared to him from the shadows and all but coerced him into it. He'd become the man on the inside, Montrovant's agent within the temple.

The two of them, Montrovant and le Duc himself, had left Jerusalem behind when Montrovant realized that the treasures he sought, foremost of them the Holy Grail, had eluded him. The ancient one known only to le Duc as Santos had been driven from the tunnels beneath the Temple of Solomon, and Kli Kodesh, the most ancient vampire that Jeanne had yet encountered, had sent the treasures away with a group of his own followers, luring Montrovant back to the Holy City just long enough for the trail to become cold.

They had been searching ever since. Le Duc's own Embrace had come along the way, and it was that single experience he could reach back to in his mind and feel the completion of his destiny. He had always been a hunter, one who took what he needed from others without thought. Now that nature was realized more fully, his being centered on hunger and the hunt, and he owed that to Montrovant. Montrovant seemed to need something more, to seek completion. Jeanne had found himself in the Blood—he was content to follow Montrovant's lead.

He rounded the last curve in the trail and saw his companion, pacing as Jeanne had known he would be, his eyes blazing. Hurrying his pace, Jeanne led the horses the last few yards, trying to keep a grin from washing over his features.

"You should not have stopped," Montrovant said, his voice brittle with anger. "We have very little time to reach a place of safety—unless of course you'd like to take your chances with those who will find Mother Agnes's corpse?"

Le Duc ignored the verbal assault. He handed over the reins of one of the mounts and turned to the other in silence, grabbing his packed belongings from where Montrovant had placed them outside the entrance of the small cavern.

"I was gathering information," Jeanne said after a moment's silence. "Does the name Owain mean anything to you?"

"Ventrue." Montrovant's one word answer was filled with a mixture of complex emotions. Foremost was hatred. "Owain is Ventrue—very old. Why do you ask?"

"Madeline, the sister I spent the past few minutes with, spoke of him. She told me that he came here before we did— how long before, she didn't say. She said we were leaving her, just as Owain had done, like dark angels."

"Owain was here?" Montrovant's anger was sidetracked instantly by his curiosity. "Perhaps we aren't as far off our trail as I was beginning to fear. Owain has been seeking the old Christian secrets longer than I, though for vastly different reasons. If he was here..."

"But we have no idea where he went from here," le Duc pointed out, swinging into his saddle. "I wonder how the knowledge of his passing can help us?"

"It helps to be reminded of the world beyond our small circle," Montrovant replied, leaping onto his own mount in a single, graceful motion and spurring it up the trail, away from the convent. "I get so wrapped up in my own thoughts that at times I forget we are not alone here."

"I have not been alone a single night here," le Duc said, chancing a grin.

"You know what I mean," Montrovant replied. He tried to remain gruff, but for some reason his spirits had been buoyed by the news of Owain's passing.

"I know of several places Owain might have been headed. There is an abbey where I heard he stayed at one time—at Glastonbury. Perhaps we can pick up our trail again there. If not, at least we might find a way to contact Eugenio—to see if any have reported sightings of the order."

"Do you think that's wise?" le Duc asked cautiously. "Were we not to remain apart from the others?"

He waited anxiously for this answer. Though Montrovant was his sire, he felt the pull of their clan, as well, and for most of his time among the Damned he'd been forced to ignore that call. His road was separate from theirs, but he longed to know them. It wasn't something the two spoke of—not since the first time le Duc had brought it up.

Montrovant was usually an intriguing companion. His wit was honed by centuries of existence, and his mind was always questing after concepts and ideals beyond his present state. There were other times, when his innate cruelty shone through like a beacon and the bitter frustration of years on the road ripped away the veneer of control. Jeanne had broached the subject of the Clan Lasombra before. He wanted to travel among them, to meet others of his kind and to know the intrigues and emotions that drove them. It had seemed so natural, this urge, and he'd felt compelled to share that urge with Montrovant.

The elder vampire had gone into a rage. One moment Jeanne was standing, arms clasped behind his back and his brow furrowed in concentration as he sought the perfect words to convey his meaning. The next he was flying through the air, stunned. Before he'd even hit the ground Montrovant was upon him, one hand holding him prone by the throat as if he were a child, or a recalcitrant mongrel. No matter how he'd struggled, he could not move, and Montrovant had slowly begun to compress his fingers in a crushing grip.

Face scant inches from Jeanne's own, Montrovant had spit his words like poison into his progeny's face.

"You will wish for nothing, Jeanne, that I do not wish for you. You will seek no other without my blessing, and you will not receive that blessing. I am apart from them, and you are of me."

There had been no way to answer with Montrovant's hand clenched over his throat. No words would have sufficed. Le Duc felt his hold on his new existence hanging in the balance, tipping gently one way, then the other on the fine point of Montrovant's temper. Then the moment had passed. Jeanne had said no more, and within the hour it was as if nothing had taken place. At least it was thus for Montrovant. That moment of uncertainty, where death had stared him in the face a second time, lines of finality etched across his face, would remain with le Duc as long as he walked the Earth.

"We can chance contact," Montrovant answered slowly, unaware of Jeanne's musing, "but we will have to be discreet. The cities are not as they once were. I used to walk those streets without fear. The dangers were there, of course, but only for the unwary. We kept to ourselves, the others did the same. It has changed. Glastonbury is a Ventrue city—there are those of our kind present, but they are not in power, and it will do us well to remember that we are walking onto dangerous ground."

"What would be the charm in a safe, boring existence?" le

Duc asked, arching an eyebrow. To himself he wondered what advantage or disadvantage this new turn of events might prove to his own situation. He'd spent little enough time in the cities since his Embrace—even less in a city where they planned to stay for more than an hour or two. For Montrovant it would be old, but for Jeanne it was a new experience.

"Let us waste no more time," Montrovant said with finality. Wheeling his mount, he spurred it up the trail.

The moon was nearly full, and the mountainside glowed with a luminescence that bordered on the brilliance of the day, though the colors were muted to silvers and grays. It was a good night to be on the road. It occurred to Jeanne that they had indeed spent too much time at the convent. Their focus had been lost, temporarily, but now it had been returned to them.

They made their way up the mountain in silence, lost in separate worlds and content to remain that way. The road narrowed as they climbed, and it was obviously less traveled, but Montrovant hardly slowed his pace, passing over rocky crags and leaping cracks in the road at breakneck speed. They did not need the horses to carry them. They would make better time without them, in fact. It was for the sake of appearances that they rode, and Montrovant was not concerned enough with those appearances to worry over the health of his mount. It would move with sure-footed grace, or it would fall. If it fell, he would leave it. Le Duc knew this from experience.

He wasn't as gifted as his sire at taking other forms, but he could move very quickly when the need arose. They neared the peak of the first crag, and Montrovant reined in, turning to stare back the way they'd come.

"I don't want to climb farther than this. We should be far enough ahead of them that they can't catch up before nightfall— not allowing time for them to discover what we have left behind. There was a village here once—there."

He pointed down the steep side of the mountain toward an indistinct grouping of shadows. Le Duc could make out the shapes of crumbled buildings, but there was no sign of life. He turned back to Montrovant quizzically.

"There are safe places for us there," Montrovant said simply.

"I have stayed there before—long years ago. We will camp."

Le Duc was surprised. There were still many hours before the sunrise would crest the mountain, and he'd thought Montrovant would want as many miles as possible between them and the convent before he sought shelter.

They turned from the road and began the slippery trek down the mountain. Jeanne felt his mount flounder once, sliding and whinnying sharply, but it regained its balance, and thus its life. He followed Montrovant, still silent, but suddenly full of questions. There had to be something of significance in the ruins they now approached. The question was, how did he broach the subject without knowing the nature of his sire's emotional attachment to the place? He had no desire to be attacked again.

The ground evened out and they moved along what must once have been another road, though it was covered over by sliding rock and gravel. It led straight into the center of the ruined village, and Montrovant rode through the crumbled square without once glancing to the right or the left. He moved to the center of the square and stopped, looking around slowly as if he saw things that were not there.

"It was different last time I saw it," he said softly. "I came here with Eugenio once, before he locked himself away and became prince. We spent a lot of time on the road in those days— nothing like you and I have done—but more often than not we found ourselves between homes. We came here one evening, to an inn that stood beyond those trees." Montrovant gestured to the left of the road.

"There was a woman—Gwendolyn—who came to me that first evening we were there. Something was different about her, I saw it from the start, but I couldn't quite make the connection. She knew me immediately as one of the Damned, and yet she was not one of us. The blood pumping through her veins was as red and hot as any I've tasted, and it was her own. Her eyes were what set her apart from the others.

"She couldn't have seen more than twenty summers, and yet those eyes drank me in as if she'd known my spirit for eternity."

"What did Eugenio think?" le Duc asked softly. "Did he approve?"

"Eugenio was much wilder in those days. He saw none of this. If he was aware of her, and I have to believe that he was, he did not care that she was present. If she had no intention of revealing us to the mortals of the village, then Claudius was content to leave her, and me, to our own devices."

Le Duc was truly intrigued. This was certainly a side of Montrovant he'd never expected to see, though he knew he should have suspected it.

"Who was she?"

"I never found out," Montrovant sighed. "I spent most of a single night in her company, dancing, talking. She knew what I wanted of her, and I was arrogant enough to believe that I would just take her when the time was right. It became one of those moments that Claudius is so fond of throwing up in my face when he gets onto one of his sermons on caution."

"Do you want to tell me the story?" Montrovant spun in his saddle, smiling slightly.

"I thought I already was."

They dismounted, and Montrovant led the way to the remnants of what must have been a stable. Enough remained of the walls to conceal their mounts and to shelter them if the weather grew bad.

Next Montrovant moved down one of the side streets and came up near the rear of what must have been the inn he'd spoken of earlier. There was an opening leading downward, broken steps and the scent of stale, damp earth. Montrovant didn't hesitate, and le Duc followed. Moments later they were swallowed in comfortable darkness and they passed more deeply inward until they reached a door.

It was odd. The door stood, even after all the years since Montrovant had claimed he was last in the village. Wrought of stone, the door had a wrought-iron handle in the shape of a great ring. It looked as though it would take two large men to pull it aside, though le Duc had no such concerns about Montrovant's ability.

To his consternation, however, Montrovant grabbed the ring with a single finger and pulled. There was no sound save a soft, sibilant hiss, and the stone slid aside smoothly. Turning to face

Jeanne once again, Montrovant grinned widely.

"This is where she brought me, Jeanne. It is here that the story truly begins."

Jeanne ducked inside, taking in the stone benches that lined the walls and the torches embedded in the walls. There were racks that must once have held hundreds of bottles of wine and there were one or two smaller alcoves that might have been for the storage of supplies, but the main room looked like the ruined, rotting memory of someone's private chambers.

Montrovant pulled the door shut once again, slipping a metal bar into a bracket beside the door that secured it effectively. Taking a seat on one of the stone benches, he crossed his legs, glancing up with a gleam in his eye that was different from any Jeanne had seen.

Jeanne seated himself as well, waiting, and after a few moments, Montrovant spoke.

THREE

Montrovant was vaguely aware of Jeanne leaning back to listen, but his mind was a thousand miles and a hundred years away. He could still paint the images of the village over the remnants. The walls and buildings, streets and squares had not been crumbling ruins then—they had lived and breathed, and he'd stumbled into the midst of it like a drunken prince. He spoke, and the words washed the present into the recesses at the back of his mind.

Claudius had known of the inn they approached from some earlier time. Dwelling on his past was not something Montrovant's sire was known for, and he looked even less kindly on those who would try to force the issue. To Montrovant it hadn't mattered. He was content to live the present and let the bones and shadows bury themselves.

For whatever reason, he had no idea that the inn would be anything more than what it appeared to be, a gathering place for mountain peasants who wanted a deep tankard of ale and an even deeper measure of cheer. The sounds of song and laughter had carried beyond the village to the road, and Montrovant drank it in like a prince might enjoy a fine wine. Life. He could sense them, could pick up their scents on the wind, each subtly different, each magnificent.

Claudius was in rare form himself. His pace had picked up steadily as they drew near to the inn, and there was a gleam in his eye that Montrovant had not seen in months. He was actually looking forward to rubbing elbows with these mortals, and Montrovant found this more fascinating even than the prospect of the hunt. Claudius was a creature of habit, and this night he seemed bent on breaking his own rules.

"We must be cautious," Claudius warned as they entered the village square. "They will be drunk, and they will all be stumbling away from this place through the shadows...but they are not stupid people. They know the kinds of dangers those shadows hold all too well, and they will jump before there is even a reason to do so...you must watch them. They will know if something is seriously amiss, and we must be careful that they don't realize it is so until we are gone from here, the memory of our passing nothing more than mist on the grass."

Montrovant nodded. He knew all of this as well as he knew his own mind. It was not like Claudius to instruct him, but Montrovant knew better than to question it. His sire had an air of distraction about him that made Montrovant nervous. He wanted no ill words between them until he knew exactly what was going on.

Light spilled from the windows of the inn, and the bloodscent permeated the night. The two were met near the entrance by an old man who took the reins of their mounts. His grin was lopsided, and the left side of his face did not function properly, falling slack and lifeless. His expressions lacked completion. He was half-grinning as he took Montrovant's reins.

"I'll take good care of 'em, masters," he slurred through a nearly ruined mouth. "Take fine care of 'em, that's what. You go on in and have a drink or two—best thing for a night like this one. Best thing for a night like any."

The man's cackling laughter floated after the two as they made their way to the door of the inn and entered. The light from the fire was bright, and it took Montrovant a moment to adjust his senses. He moved quickly toward the back of the room, ignoring the sudden silence and the stares of the locals. Claudius followed more slowly.

As the two slid into a booth near the back of the inn the sound picked up slowly. It was clear that they weren't going to prove immediately entertaining, so for the moment they'd been appraised and forgotten. Montrovant knew that his sire had worked toward that end, making the two of them as inconspicuous as possible and clouding them in the eyes of those they passed.

It was a necessary precaution. Montrovant stood nearly six foot five, gaunt and thin but at the same time wiry and powerful. Claudius had long, flowing gray hair and eyes that could steal one's soul. The two made an imposing sight, one not the usual fare for such an establishment. If they were to draw no attention to themselves, it was necessary that they sacrifice a bit in style.

A few moments after they'd seated themselves, a thin, waifish girl sauntered over to the table. She couldn't have been more than sixteen, but the wink in her eye and the swish of her hip told other stories about her experience.

"What'll you have?" she asked, tossing her hair over one shoulder and letting her gaze linger a bit longer than necessary over Montrovant's eyes. She clearly intended herself as a menu item, and Montrovant had to fight to hide the grin that threatened to surface. Claudius had no such problems.

"We will have wine, mulled and hot. We will also have privacy. You will leave us, and you will not return, except to bring our wine. Do you understand?"

It wasn't a true question. The girl had no more choice in the matter than the wine. They would not drink it, of course, but they could savor the aroma and dream, and the sight of the drinks in their hands, emptied discreetly now and then to be refilled, would serve their anonymity.

She turned, but not before taking another instant to stare at Montrovant longingly. She sensed something in him. He drew her and she flitted around the flame that was his essence like a trapped and helpless moth. Eugenio snapped her mind free and sent her scurrying toward the bar with a glance. Glaring at Montrovant, the elder vampire almost snarled.

"I told you to be careful. She is the innkeeper's daughter. Too many would miss her presence. She is not for us."

Montrovant was shocked. He'd enjoyed the moment of control with the girl, but he'd not meant to follow that road. He could sense her mind as well as his sire could. He'd already removed her name from the menu. What in Hell was bothering Eugenio?

"I am not a child," Montrovant grated at last, aware of the possible mistake he was making but unable to keep his silence.

"I know what is safe and what is not. What I don't know is why you have so suddenly forgotten my knowledge of these things, and why you would insult me when I have done nothing to deserve it."

Claudius half rose from his seat, then sank back down. The anger drained from his features as quickly as it had risen, but Montrovant was pinned to his seat by the remnant of the fear that short moment had generated. Scenes from his past he'd not thought of in decades had surfaced, and he'd contemplated, just for a second, what it might mean to truly die. The moment passed.

"I am here on business," Claudius said at last. "It is a tricky thing, and I am not certain how it will go. This place is not exactly what it seems. It would serve you well if you could learn to look at every new place in that fashion. I have to talk to an old acquaintance, and you will be on your own."

"Acquaintance? One of the clan?"

"No," Claudius said almost too fast. "I will tell you more when we are a safe distance from this place. Suffice it to say that our roads may never be the same after this night."

"You are afraid." Montrovant didn't ask it as a question, he stated it in disbelief.

"I am not afraid," Claudius snapped. "I am nervous. There is a difference."

Montrovant snorted once, but he held his silence. He knew he'd pushed the boundaries of good sense already, and he knew when to retreat. He already had enough to mull over in his mind; no sense in agitating Claudius further.

"I'll be fine," Montrovant assured his sire. "I'm certain I can behave myself for a few hours on my own, and I'm equally certain I can provide my own meal without causing undue stress to your meeting, whatever it might be. Dismiss me from your thoughts."

Claudius had glared at him for what seemed an eternity. Montrovant knew that the elder vampire was weighing the dangers of their situation. If Claudius knew that things were not as they seemed, that meant he also had a good idea what things were. Montrovant wondered what test he was passing or failing in the mind's eye of his maker.

"Just be careful," Claudius said at last. "It is an important night."

It was then that the girl returned with their wine. She also had a small bit of parchment which she nervously placed before Claudius. She stood staring at him, as if waiting to see if he would reveal his secrets in her presence.

Impulsively, Montrovant reached out and took her hand in his own, meeting her gaze with a smile. He watched Claudius out of the corner of his eye. The response was sudden and final. The girl clutched her hand to her breast, ripping it free of Montrovant's own and whirling in sudden fear. Claudius only smiled after her, then turned for an instant to meet Montrovant's gaze. There were volumes of anger and promises of pain in that gaze, but Montrovant met it steadily. He tried to keep his own smile cold and unreadable.

"I hope that everything goes...well." he said softly.

Claudius turned to the parchment and unfurled it hurriedly, scanning the single page quickly, then rolling it and tucking it beneath his robes. Montrovant waited, as had the girl, but he got no more response than she, and finally he feigned a loss of interest to let his eyes rove about the room. "You will know more than you care to soon enough," Claudius whispered, suddenly so close to his ear that the soft exhalation of air behind the words tickled Montrovant's ear. "For once, trust that I am serious and act accordingly."

Before Montrovant could answer, he was alone. He glanced quickly about the room, but none seemed to have noticed Claudius's passing.

A fight broke out momentarily at one end of the bar, but a well-aimed swipe of one huge arm from the beefy innkeeper, catching one on the chin and the other across the throat, sent both assailants crashing into a wall. Montrovant stared, caught by surprise for the first time in decades.

"That'll be enough out of the both of you," the innkeeper growled. "Next time I won't be so easy on you." Neither of the two assailants was rising, though one of them was shaking his head groggily and trying to roll over to his back. The power behind that blow had been incredible.

Turning to Montrovant slowly, the innkeeper caught his eye for just a second. The man winked, nodding ever so slightly at the two on the floor and giving a quick shrug of his shoulders.

This place is not exactly what it seems.

Eugenio's words came back to him in an instant, and Montrovant scanned the room more cautiously, but with renewed interest. Most of the attention, for the moment, was drawn toward the short scuffle, so he was able to take in each patron in turn without fear of being caught at it. In remote places such as this, it was best not to show any undue interest in the affairs of strangers.

There were three men at the corner booth, small and swarthy and dressed in the rough clothing of farmers. They kept to themselves, each nursing a mug of ale. They talked in low voices, dark eyes locked on their drinks and the table. Montrovant probed more deeply, exerting just the slightest bit of mental energy, but there was nothing there.

He slid around to the next booth. A man and a woman sat opposite one another. He was tall and thin, blonde hair sweeping back over his shoulders and a hat pulled close over one eye. He leaned so far across the table that his chest was flat against the surface and his hair dangled dangerously near his drink. She was shorter, but equally fair of complexion. She did not lean forward as he did, but neither did she lean back. She hung on his every word, and he laid it on thicker and deeper as the moment progressed.

Before Montrovant was able to probe further, the man stopped speaking suddenly and turned. Montrovant lowered his gaze to the table before him barely in time. They knew he watched them. More to contemplate, more danger to avoid. He waited until he heard the faint murmur of the man's voice again, then continued to scan the room.

Nothing caught his interest among the others. A pair of hunters, two guardsmen on leave from the service of a Welsh lord. Talk of the wars in the East, rumors from France and the British Isles. Nothing new or even slightly captivating. He was about to return his mind to contemplation of just what might be going on in such a place when a whisper of silk and the scent of jasmine ushered a slender figure into the seat opposite him. "I hope you won't think me rash," the woman said, smiling. Her voice was deep and husky... sensual. She leaned back so that the folds of her robe revealed a subtle curve of breast. Her heart pulsed brazenly, just beneath the surface.

Montrovant didn't speak immediately. He drank in her lithe, well-muscled frame, clearly visible despite the loose-fitting garments. She had a playful grin splashed across her face and her eyes made promises he doubted any mortal could keep.

"Beautiful," he said, whispering the word softly so that it would not carry. He wanted her to hear him, but he did not want the others in the room to be aware. Too many of them had already proven more than they seemed. He had no intention of giving them a reason to pay attention to him.

He shifted his gaze quickly about the room. None of the other patrons seemed aware that she had joined him. Either that or they were too caught up in their own concerns to worry over it. Montrovant returned his attention to his new companion.

"Do you make a habit of joining strangers at their table?"

"I make a habit of doing what pleases me," she replied so quickly that it nearly startled him.

"That is an interesting habit," he replied at last. "It will not prolong your life, I'm afraid, but it will make it so very much more enjoyable."

Smiling, the woman raised her glass, which he noticed for the first time was full of wine, just as his own. He picked his own glass up reflexively and raised it to meet hers above the table.

"To interesting times," she said, taking a quick sip. Montrovant nodded, raising the glass to his own lips and letting the warm wine rest against the surface of his lips before setting it back on the table. He feigned a swallow, but he didn't know if she bought it. It didn't matter. He'd been looking for the perfect victim, and she'd dropped herself at his table without even an invitation. He only hoped that whatever business had drawn Claudius to the inn was going as smoothly.

"It's warm in here," she said, drawing her robes a bit farther apart. Montrovant gripped the table to calm himself. She'd turned her head, allowing him full sight of her pale throat. A wave of dizziness passed through him, and it took longer than he would have liked to regain control of his voice.

"Would you like to go for a walk?" he rasped, cursing himself inwardly for the break in his voice. "I'd like that," she answered, reaching for his hand, "if we were walking to my quarters..."

Montrovant rose without a further word. He placed some coins on the table and met the innkeeper's eyes a last time. The man wore an expression of indifference, but Montrovant would have sworn he'd seen something more dancing in the depths of those eyes. It was as if the innkeeper were laughing inwardly at some earthshaking joke the rest of the world was not aware of. Perhaps he was. Perhaps they all were.

He allowed himself to be led past the scattered tables and into the night beyond, barely aware of the buzz of conversation that rose momentarily at his departure. The sound was cut off by the clatter of the door swinging closed behind him. It was like walking into a different world.

She wrapped her arm about his waist, and he allowed it. The warmth of her was fascinating, and the tantalizing closeness of her fresh, sweet blood was dizzying. He let the sensations sweep him away. Claudius had abandoned him for the evening, and he'd not get a better invitation than this one. None in the bar had shown her the slightest attention, and there had been no protest when she left the establishment in the company of a complete stranger. Apparently it was a habit of hers. He knew he would be gone before any noted her absence the following evening, if indeed any noticed it at all. Alarm bells sounded deep within his mind, but his mind had little to do with what was happening to him. His hunger had supplanted all pretense at coherent thought. The beast within him was rising to the surface, and it would not be denied.

She seemed unaware of the change taking place within him, but Montrovant was no fool. The slight tightening of her arm about his waist, the hurrying of her steps, these indicated that she was aware that something was different. Even with the bloodscent blurring reality, he knew that something was—different. Victims did not hurry to bring the wolf to their home. Victims struggled, and bled, but they did not smile, nuzzling into their assailant's neck and whispering endearments into his ear. Victims did not do anything he did not dictate to them, and this woman was doing whatever she pleased.

The woman seemed more impatient for them to reach their destination than he himself, and that was the thing that finally reached him. She was eager. She knew the danger he presented—possibly even his nature—and yet she dragged him onward as if it were she, not he, who was doing the stalking. He dragged his pace a bit, fighting to regain control of his senses. He fully intended to go through with his plans, regardless of what this woman thought she might be out to accomplish, but he needed to do so with his mind alert.

She hesitated for a second, turning to search his eyes. He allowed the glazed expression to return—leaning in a bit closer to her and leaning on her strength. She seemed satisfied, and moments later she was stumbling down a set of stairs behind the inn toward the cellars, giggling and dragging at his arm as if she were nothing but a young girl with a new love. He let her drag him downward. The darkness would serve him better than it would her. Now that he was making a conscious effort to sort things out for himself, something had begun to itch at the back of his thoughts. He tried to brush it aside, but whatever it was would not release him once it had his attention. There was something familiar about the girl at his side, something in her scent, or her eyes. He couldn't imagine what could be of such importance in a mortal, but he knew now that he would have to find out.

She had ideas of her own. She fumbled open the lock on the door and the two of them tumbled into the shadows beyond. Montrovant's vision wasn't hindered by the lack of light, but he forced himself to trip over an empty bottle on the floor, maintaining what might remain of his facade of humanity. She only turned and looked at him oddly. There was no hesitation to her steps, and though she closed the door behind them immediately, she did not look away from his eyes. She could see as well as he. The games had begun.

"Who are you?" he asked, sliding a few feet away from her and bracing his back against the wall. He must have looked in some way comical, because she covered her mouth with one slender hand and giggled at him, offering no answer. She took a slow step toward him, loosening her shirt another notch. Her gaze was locked on his. He exerted his will, expecting her to break the contact, or at least to struggle. She leaned into the draw of his mind, releasing herself and slipping across the stone floor into his arms in a rush.

He was assaulted at once by the heat of her flesh and the wanton offering of her throat. She'd turned her head to one side as she moved forward, nearly impaling her soft skin on the tips of his fangs before he could snap his jaws shut and push her away. She was quick. Before he could disengage her from his arms she was pressing forward again, speaking softly.

"Please," she murmured, sliding back into his embrace. "Please. You want it—I know you want the blood. Take it. Make me as you. I burn for it. My nights are consumed. Make me as you, and I will serve you for eternity...I will hunt for you. I will entertain you..."

Montrovant ducked beneath her arm and crossed the room like a streak of dark lightning. She followed, but he moved away again, staying far enough away that the hot pulse of her blood was not clouding his thoughts.

She knew. That was the first and most important thing that stabbed into his fogged mind. She knew, and he could never let her leave this room with that knowledge. She was also right. He wanted her—badly. It was more than just the blood—he could have returned to the shadows beyond the inn and found a more suitable meal. He did not want that; he wanted her. Forever.

It was a sensation that had not plagued him since his Embrace. He'd never thought to bring another under the shadow. Eugenio was his companion and sire; how could he have sought another? Certainly none had ever begged him for that Embrace. Damn her, how could she know? There had to be something he was missing, something that set her apart in a way that he could understand.

She moved toward him again, tentatively. She knew he

could evade her if he wished, so she tried a different tack. She lowered her head, letting the dark locks of her hair fall forward across slender shoulders and moved toward him, never looking up to see if he still waited or if he'd gone. Her hands she held out before her, crossing them submissively. "Take me," she said softly. "Oh, please take me..."

His resolve was crumbling. Her bare skin fairly glowed with the life that flowed through her veins. Her movements were sensual, graceful to a degree that escaped most mortals. The scent of her blood blended with the aromas of a hundred years of wines, ale long aged in wooden casks, and a hundred dried spices lining the shelves of the small room.

"Who are you?" he mumbled a final time as she reached him, kneeling and dropping her hair in a cascade across his boots. She did not speak, and he found that he no longer cared for the answer.

With a roar of desire and frustration, he grabbed her, drawing her up to him and twisting her head roughly to the side.

"Oh!" she cried. He thought she might be coming to a realization of what her reckless plunge into his arms would truly mean, but as her eyes passed his, as her face turned away, all he saw in her eyes was delight—delight and triumph. It fueled his hunger, and he dropped his lips to her soft throat. He never touched her flesh. There was a sound from above, then a rush of wind, and he felt himself yanked off his feet. He was tossed across the room like a sack of grain, and though he rolled aside with a quick grunt as he crashed into the cellar wall, he wasn't quick enough. Strong hands held him by his throat, pinning him to the floor, and he found himself thinking of the girl's blood. It was a worthy final thought. "Alphonse!"

The word broke the silence like ice shattering on stone. It was Claudius's voice, and the grip on Montrovant's throat was released as quickly as it had taken hold.

"Claudius, he is mine. He would have taken her
—would have taken her soul."

"You know the truth of this, Alphonse. I will not ask you twice to leave him be."

Montrovant rolled to one side. He could see a thin, wiry figure crouched a few feet away from him, and Claudius's tall form framed by the doorway, backlit by the moonlight from outside. Gwendolyn had crawled into a corner and was sitting with her knees clasped before her. She did not seem concerned with the scenario playing out before her. If Montrovant had had to put a guess to her thoughts and expression, he'd have said she was pouting. What in Hell was going on?

"She is not for you," the thin Cainite spat, turning to face Montrovant. He made no further advance, but neither did he back away, even though Claudius had taken the last few steps into the cellar and stood between them.

"I thought you told me you could look after yourself?" Claudius said softly. The tone of his voice belied his calm. "I told you what I was doing was important—couldn't you have gone to the fields and found a peasant?"

"She found me," Montrovant said, wishing momentarily for better control of his own tongue. "She knew me."

"Of course she knew you," Alphonse growled. "Gwendolyn is my daughter. She has tasted my blood—it was necessary for her own protection. You—you would have Embraced her."

Montrovant said nothing, but he turned to where Gwendolyn sat alone in the corner.

"I would have shared his Embrace, if I could," she said, finally raising her eyes. "You tantalize me, show me your powers, then deny me. You claim you love me, but you torture me daily and nightly, and there is no escape. If I cannot be as you, I wish I were dead."

Claudius paid no attention to her. His eyes were cold with anger, but there was a distraction to his movements that spoke of other concerns. "Come," he said at last.

Montrovant followed his sire out of the cellar. Behind him he could hear the girl's voice rising to a screech of anger. He pictured her launching herself at her father, scratching futilely at his eyes, begging and receiving everything except that which she desired. It was a dangerous situation. If she ever gave up on getting her way, she might turn on him. Better if, as she suggested, Alphonse allow her to die.

"You have disappointed me," Claudius spat, "but I have no time for it. Great forces are at work, historic events at hand, and it seems that we are to play our part in them. At least I must...

"Grondin has passed. There are few as ancient as I, and the balance of Clan power is shifting."

Montrovant stopped in his tracks. He'd known his sire was old, but he'd never stopped to wonder just how old.

"My words were clear enough," Claudius snapped. "You will have decisions to make in the days to come. I will not be free to travel, and I would not hold you in one place. You must decide your own fate from now on."

Smiling darkly now..."You will be fine, my dark one, I call you that because even under my control you are arrogant; in the face of sanity you spit and turn away. Where others would not go, you travel freely and without fear. It will bring you the eternal death, but that is now your choice."

Montrovant didn't trust himself to speak. Too much had already happened for one night. Freedom. He'd dreamed of it, talked of it—yearned for it. Now, in the face of realizations Gwendolyn had brought to the surface of his mind, he knew it for what it also meant. Separation. Solitude. Eternity loomed dark and endless.

"Come," Claudius said, turning and taking to the air in a rush of wind and shadow. "Let us feed. Tomorrow at sunset we leave for France."

Le Duc was mesmerized. It wasn't until the familiar weight of the sun rising to the sky beyond the walls that protected them had settled firmly over him that he realized just how long Montrovant had talked. He'd never heard his sire go on at such length about anything in the past.

Montrovant shook his head suddenly, as if he were just becoming aware of how much he'd said. "You must have thought a lot about this Gwendolyn," Jeanne said softly. "To remember that time so vividly."

"She was nothing," Montrovant replied quickly, rising and moving to the base of the steps leading to the surface. "Help me check the seal on the door. We will have to move fast once the sun drops."

Le Duc didn't press the issue, but he smiled at Montrovant's back. A sensitive side? Not likely, but interesting. He rose quickly and joined Montrovant in his careful checks of the light seal. It was only an empty gesture, something to defuse the tension that had followed Montrovant's tale.

'We will follow Owain," Montrovant said at last, breaking the silence. "It is possible that such a course will take us nowhere, but it is as good as any. A great deal of information passes through the streets of Holywell. There are those who will share that information with us—others that can be coerced."

"And the rest?" Jeanne asked.

"We will see about them when we get there," Montrovant replied. He made his way to one of the cots lining the walls and lay back in silence.

Le Duc followed his example. He had a great deal to think about, but it could wait for the night. The sun was rising, and his mind was slipping into cool, protected darkness.

Beyond the sealed entrance to the wine cellar, daylight crept slowly across the ruins of the village. Shadows shortened. Through those shadows, a single figure moved slowly closer to the remnant of the inn. The wind caught in her hair and caused it to dance about her softly. Her lithe, slender figure was complemented by tight leather leggings and a long robe of deep green material that shimmered in the growing light. Her eyes were hidden deep within the folds of the robe, but a smile twitched at the corners of her mouth.

She noted where Montrovant and le Duc had tethered their horses. With a quick whistle she summoned her own mount and calmly secured it with the others. There were a lot of hours before sunset, and she needed to find some shade and get to sleep. The sunlight didn't have the same kind of terror for her that it would for those below, but it wasn't pleasant, either. She preferred the light of the moon and the caress of shadow.

There was a ruined home nearby that still had three of its four walls and a bit of roof left to it, and it was there that she headed. Her pack would make a fine pillow, and she had a drape to string across the area where she would sleep. It would block the worst of the sun and her natural desire to sleep during the daylight hours would take care of the rest. She hadn't yet been able to shake the draw of the earth, as her sire had assured her that she would. He had, of course, several centuries of experience over her.

Gwendolyn lay back with a smile and closed her eyes. It was going to be an interesting reunion. A night to remember. She reached impulsively into her pack and pulled free the letter, sealed in wax and imprinted with her sire's mark. She clutched it to her breast. It had been a long time since she'd seen Montrovant, and he'd failed her that night, but it would be good to see what the years had done with him. One thing her sire had told her had proven true. In the face of eternity, it was best to keep things interesting.

FOUR

When they rose and exited the wine cellar, she was waiting for them, seated on a slab of stone that had once been the lower corner of one of the houses. Her head was lowered, so her eyes were not visible. Montrovant stopped short, holding up a hand to stop Jeanne as well. No normal woman could have crept up on them so easily. They would have heard her, smelled her, sensed her in a thousand different ways. Montrovant felt a tingle of something familiar, but he couldn't quite grasp it. When she raised her head and her eyes met his, the silence grew tense. She was smiling, but if there was any humor present in that gaze, it was not near the surface. She did not so much look at them, as through them...at something far away.

"It has been a long time," Montrovant said at last. "You have not changed much—you must have found another more willing than I soon after we left."

She didn't answer at first, and Jeanne was about to break his own silence and ask his sire just what the hell was going on, when she spoke.

"He found me. That is why I am here. He has sent me, and I am to bring you a message."

Montrovant watched her, and Jeanne saw that he frowned. Something was wrong.

"Gwendolyn," Montrovant said softly, "what has happened to you?"

As the realization of who they faced surfaced suddenly in Jeanne's mind, along with a thousand questions he'd have liked to ask on his own, the first spark of emotion leaped into her eyes and she rose in a sudden, liquid motion.

"You know full well, and yet you did not warn me." Her words were cold, distant. "You would have done this to me yourself, wouldn't you? You would have let me become—this—without thought of anything but sating your own desires and hungers.

You have a poor memory," Montrovant answered quickly. "I offered you nothing. You asked.

I would not have Embraced you—I would have fed and left you."

"You lie," she said without passion. She was mouthing the words, but there seemed to be nothing behind them. All emotion, even the sudden spark of anger that had filled her so completely a moment before, was gone.

"I have no need to lie," Montrovant replied softly. "What would I gain by it? Who has done this to you, and why does he not keep you close by his side?"

She turned away, but she continued to speak. "He has no real need of companionship from one such as I. He took me because it interested him for the moment. His one fear is boredom."

"Boredom?" Montrovant had grown very still, and the word rang out like a clap of thunder.

She turned to him, the slightest touch of curiosity burning in the deadened depths of her eyes.

"Kli Kodesh," Jeanne breathed. Montrovant had said nothing. He had needed no words to convey the weight of emotion, anger, hatred and desire that the ancient's name could invoke.

Gwendolyn was looking at Jeanne now, and the tiny spark of curiosity had been fanned to a flame.

"How do you know that name?"

"'Our greatest enemy,'" Montrovant recited from memory, "'is boredom. We must strive to keep things...interesting.' So, Kli Kodesh has sent you to me. Does he know of our past? Was sending you here, to this very place, an amusing side note—a moment's diversion? Have you truly fallen to that level?"

"I came because I wanted to," she snapped, rising quickly to stand before Montrovant fearlessly.

"He has many others he could have sent. I knew it was you,

and I asked that he let the message come through me. I did not know I would find you here, but I hoped it might be so."

"Why?" Montrovant asked coolly. "All that happened here was a near mistake—something that was never meant to be. Why would you return to drag that bit of both of our pasts to the surfaces to haunt us?"

"I was fascinated with you then. I still am—haunted by the memory of you," she answered truthfully. "You were a handsome creature, Montrovant. You still are. I thought that perhaps, if I came back here where it almost began for me, I could recapture some of whatever it was that made me pursue you in the first place."

Feeling bold, Jeanne spoke up quickly. "Quite the coincidence, don't you think? It is hard to believe that we just last night found ourselves drawn to this place, and you knew you would find us here. You must have waited here a long time?"

Montrovant turned a scathing glare on le Duc, but the point had been made. It was too much of a coincidence, and now the issue required clarification.

"I called you," she said at last. "I sent images of that time, memories to draw you closer. He knows me, Montrovant. He owns me, and he knows me in ways no other ever has. He knew you would come, and he was right. He wanted us to meet here."

"Because it was more interesting," Montrovant finished, gritting his teeth so tightly that the sound of bone on bone was audible throughout the ruined city. "Always because it is more interesting."

Gwendolyn let her chin fall to her chest, not denying it. Once again, it seemed, Kli Kodesh had manipulated Montrovant's life, and consequently le Duc's as well. Once again he had drawn them back into a game in which they couldn't even discern the elder's stake.

"Give me the message." Montrovant's voice was cold and distant, and le Duc watched him anxiously. Without a word she rose, moving closer and reaching beneath the folds of her robe. She drew forth a rolled parchment, very official looking. Montrovant took it, staring at it as if it were a serpent, poised to strike. It was obvious that he didn't want to read it. It was equally obvious that he could not resist the urge.

With a sudden snarl he ripped free the ribbon that bound it and unrolled it before him. Le Duc watched Montrovant's face for signs of what the message contained, but his sire's features revealed nothing. Not the slightest hint of emotion transited his face. He scanned the contents of the scroll quickly, returned his gaze to the top and read it all again slowly. Without speaking, he rerolled the parchment and tucked it absently under his belt.

Le Duc stole a glance at Gwendolyn. She was paying no attention to Montrovant, lost in her own world of depression and disappointment. He could read nothing there. Perhaps she didn't even know what message she carried, or care. He returned his gaze to Montrovant.

"There will be a slight change in our plans," Montrovant said suddenly. "We will be traveling to France. It seems that old obligations beckon to us both."

The questions must have risen to Jeanne's eyes, because Montrovant continued immediately.

"It is from Kli Kodesh. De Molay is in trouble—the Church has declared some sort of holy war on the Templars—they've been outlawed."

"Why the sudden concern for our 'brethren'?" Jeanne asked. "We've traveled long years without mentioning them at all. I thought when we left de Payen and the others behind, that it would be the end of it."

"As did I," Montrovant agreed, turning to stare off into the shadows. "It seems that others have not been as lax in their relations with the Temple. Kli Kodesh tells me that certain treasures—artifacts once kept beneath the ruins of the Temple of Solomon—have been moved into de Molay's Keep. They are in danger of falling into the hands of the king's men, or worse, the Church. Once again, he has turned to me in a time when he cannot reach what he seeks."

"Cannot," Jeanne mused, "or finds it more amusing not to? Can you trust him?"

"I cannot afford not to trust him. We have no leads. If we must return to the Templars to complete our journey, so be it. I formed them, and I should be there at the end."

"There are others." Gwendolyn spoke up softly, but she grabbed their attention with her words. "You are not the only ones. The knights you left in Jerusalem are not the knights you will find in France."

"What do you mean?" Jeanne asked quickly.

"They are dark. There are those among them who meddle with powers they have no business seeking. It is part of why they are being destroyed. They brought it on themselves."

Montrovant frowned. He tried to imagine the tall, powerful Hugues de Payen, or the slight, angular Pierre, who had been his companion, engaged in dark rites. The image would not come, it was too preposterous.

Guessing his thoughts, Gwendolyn continued. "They are not the men you knew, Montrovant. They are generations beyond, and they have taken in teachers to aid them. The Church did not hold the answers they sought."

"So many years," le Duc mused. "Could it have all changed so very much?"

"Change is the only constant in the universe," Montrovant replied. To Gwendolyn he said, "If what you speak is the truth, then there is less time than I first suspected. We must move out now. Are you planning on traveling back with us, or are you just a messenger these days?"

Her eyes blazed. "I do as I wish. Perhaps I will travel with you for a while. I want to see what it is that I've been missing all these years."

Montrovant held his silence, moving to ready his mount. Le Duc watched Gwendolyn for a moment longer. Her gaze trailed after Montrovant's retreating form, and for just an instant, he thought he saw a deep, haunting longing in the depths of her eyes. As the moon rose to her full splendor in the sky, three shadowed forms disappeared down the side of the mountain and into the plain beyond. The darkness swallowed them slowly, and the ruined village was left to its silence and its solitude.

PART TWO

FIVE

The walls of the keep of Jacques de Molay, Grand Master of the Knights Templar, stretched up toward the mountain at its back. The towers were manned and the ramparts patrolled incessantly. No hostile force had yet made an advance on the keep, but it was only a matter of time and death: the death of their brothers.

Those on the wall had heard the tales. There were others joining their ranks daily, refugees from the cities and provinces beyond their own. The stories were grim, mumbled and cursed through trembling lips or cried angrily over too many flagons of wine.

King Philip had ordered them all to be seized. They were to be tried as heretics and devil-worshipers and tortured until they confessed. There was talk of demons and secret orders within their ranks, but to most of those not closely associated with de Molay and his advisors, the stories were insanity. They were a holy order, dedicated to Christ. They had fought and died from France to the Holy Land and back. If any were insane, the refugees muttered into their drinks, it was Philip and his men.

There were those in the Church who resented the Templars for various reasons: their wealth, their influence. The arm of the order was far-reaching and quick to react to political and economic changes. This had won them a great deal of power, but it had earned an equal part of enemies, and it would appear those enemies were more powerful than any of them had imagined.

Philip in particular had resented their power, and it was

his resentment, in the end, that had become their undoing. The Church had turned on them as well. In the beginning the two entities, Templars and Church, had complemented one another perfectly. The Vatican had wanted an army of its own, one that was beholden to no particular lord or king save Christ. This was the order that Hugues de Payen had envisioned, warrior monks dedicating their lives to keeping the Holy Lands free and protecting the followers of Christ. A noble intent.

Things had changed. As the refugees continued to arrive, the stories that had driven them from their homes took on new and frightening proportions. Dark figures prowled the passageways of the keep, and there were chambers and passages in the tunnels below that were off limits to all but the Grand Master and his most trusted aides. An aura of dread, of ancient evil and corruption, rested just beneath the surface of the place. Whispered rumors fluttered among the ranks like phantom birds, never quite coming to rest in reality, but watching and hovering just out of reach.

Once-proud warriors tracked the movements of trusted comrades warily. Sullen stares replaced ready smiles. Their lives crumbled about them, and the rot that ate them away appeared strongest at the core.

Along with the refugees, the treasure of the order had piled into de Molay's vaults. As secretly as possible, and more quickly than the nobles of the combined empires of Europe could have imagined, the exodus unfolded. Documents, gold, jewels, objects of power, everything and anything that contributed to the infrastructure of power that was the Templars had been gathered in one place, leaving only husks and questions behind for those who came to destroy and desecrate. They had been ordered to disband, but there was no way that the spirit of something so grand could be wiped easily or completely from the Earth.

They would endure. Through secret meetings and traditions they would survive, possibly to see both Church and empire in ashes. The question in many of their minds, as they assimilated the situation in the keep and searched for their own answers, was what would survive. What were the secrets being sought so desperately by their leaders, and would they ultimately improve, or corrupt? Who was to say? For the moment they were stuck with time alone as a companion and mystery for a bedfellow. Jacques de Molay could have answered their questions, and there were others who might as well, but none were speaking, and Philip drew nearer every day, death in his heart and the Church at his back. It was a time of darkness, and the word that spread was despair.

The chamber was dark, so dark that the only way that the men gathered before Santos could see to find their places in the room was by following whoever was directly in front of them, and by staring into the indistinct shadows thrown by a single candle. The candle flickered just out of sight in an alcove, its eerie dancing light reflecting dully off the rough surface of the stone. There were no missed steps, despite the close quarters and lack of light. It was a practiced ritual—a bonding of the energy of many to the will of a single man.

Santos watched them in grim silence, waiting for someone to make a mistake. He was particularly fond of torturing those who erred in the ritual. It had been some time since he'd had that pleasure. Behind him the altar stood, covered in black velvet carefully embroidered with symbols and designs only he fully understood. He'd taught secrets to a select few of his followers, but none of them had enough knowledge to make them any real danger to any but themselves. Santos had been more careful here than anywhere else he'd called home in the long years of his existence. In those previous years, he'd carried out his duties, providing the service he'd been created to provide. He'd had no reason to be bitter.

Things had changed. He had not laid eyes on the treasures he was created to guard in far too many years…had not held them or traced their ancient lines with his withered fingers. Despite his best efforts and the powers and tools available to him, the ancient known as Kli Kodesh had managed to evade him. He had found it necessary to take steps that would set wheels in motion, and such steps were never without danger. He'd lived for many years in a great many places, and there were those who would recognize his hand in this if he weren't careful.

Now the men gathered before him knelt in silence. Each wore a brown robe that rose to cover his head with a copious hood. Each moved in careful, precise motions. Energy was precious. That lesson they had all learned. It was never to be wasted. Only so much energy was allotted to each of them, and the wise use of that energy was the only worthy task that lay before them. To waste it would be a sin.

It was amazing how easily these men had allowed their understanding of sin to be manipulated and warped. If asked, each would claim to be a God-fearing man. As a unit, they were the most awesome fighting force in Europe: the Poor Knights of the Temple of Solomon, the Templars.

Santos allowed himself the briefest flicker of a smile. If Bernard, the fiery-speaking, weak-armed "saint" who'd organized them into an army could see them now, it would be a sight worth traveling for. If Montrovant, whose actions were so different from others of his kind...more enigmatic, more arrogant, even, than the elders Santos had known—so different that even his own brothers called him the Dark One, whose meddling had caused the loss of everything that Santos held dear—if that one could see them, he'd be equally shocked, though probably less displeased. It was a singular point of satisfaction to come to this place and warp what they'd created. It was poor revenge for the loss he'd suffered, but at least it was something to concentrate on.

Before him, nearly prostrate, knelt Jacques de Molay. Of them all, de Molay was most eager to learn. It was de Molay who had fought for Santos's admission to the order as a teacher and counselor. It was de Molay who had shielded Santos's actions, and later his own and those of his followers, from the Church. De Molay bought Santos time, and though time was not something Santos was in dire need of, the peace and quiet that accompanied it were a welcome respite.

Santos had rebuilt his strength and renewed his search for what Kli Kodesh had stolen from him. He now had the resources of the Templars in his hands, given to him in return for certain teachings and small powers, insignificant, but impressive to the uninitiated. So quickly they forgot. He'd not even changed his name, though he'd dropped the "Father" in the name of good sense. As Father Santos, he'd come close to ending their order before it had truly been launched. It hadn't been that many generations since those events, and yet it seemed that the newer members of the order knew nothing of him, and those old enough to remember had forgotten, or did not care. Montrovant had left them, and de Payen was dead. Power was something they all sought, and Santos was able to provide it, albeit at his own pace.

He shook off the weight of memory and closed his eyes, bringing his hands up before him and clasping them tightly. He let his head fall back until his long dark hair brushed the back of his robe and his eyes pointed directly to the heavens. His lips opened, and he began to chant, softly at first, but gaining in volume and intensity as each syllable rolled out over the room.

Other voices joined his almost immediately. None of them knew the entire chant, but each had his own part to resonate, echoing words and cadences. Hands clapped in subtle rhythms that integrated themselves into the whole of the sound. They were not ready yet, but soon. He only had a few more lessons to teach, and they would be able to complete the ritual. It had been many years since that portal of energy and knowledge had been open to him, and he felt the elation building within him. So much power to have been denied.

Images crowded his mind suddenly, images from his past. He saw the tunnels beneath the Temple of Solomon in quick flashes. He saw Montrovant's burning, arrogant eyes and the steadfast, righteous countenance of Hugues de Payen. Other faces surfaced. The confrontation beneath the city with the Nosferatu, Kli Kodesh and his insolent, insane smirk. The treasures, now lost, all but one. He saw the Earth as it had been, falling away from him. He heard the true name of the buzzard as it had rung through his mind, felt the powerful wings that had borne him upward, the head clutched tightly in talons that gripped like steel clamps. He saw Montrovant, his puny shadow form fluttering helplessly behind. Too late and too slow to prevent Santos's escape. An ending, and a beginning.

Santos shook his head violently, returning his concentration to the chant. It was enough that those he worked with required so much of his time to learn their parts without causing the ritual to fail on his own. There was a time and a place for everything, and the time for revenge would come soon enough. For the moment he needed to build his strength and to train his followers. The Templars were about to fall, and he needed to be certain that he and those he chose to keep would be prepared to make it out in one piece. He needed to be free and with the means to carry on the search that dragged him onward.

Santos required no companionship. Ancient tomes, secrets long buried and others yet to be discovered, these were his bedfellows. He needed no conversation, nor did he require respect or friendship. He had dedicated a long existence to a single purpose, and he had failed at that purpose. It was too late to redeem that failure, but it was not too late to rectify the situation.

He needed to recover what was rightfully his. The secrets he'd been entrusted with were not his possessions, but the position of guardian was his alone. It was his right, and his responsibility. Without that responsibility, he was nothing, and that reality had spun its web of bitterness over him slowly and certainly. The darkness that had swallowed his reason at times was more constant since he'd been run out of Jerusalem, and he needed to regain the control it was costing him to hold it at bay.

There had been a time when he'd considered certain of his followers students. He'd even thought of teaching them secrets that might have given them a semblance of his own power, his "gifts." These before him he held in nothing but contempt, though he was careful not to let this show. To them he was the "Dark Master." They believed that he would lead them to the spiritual purity and strength that their puny, disorganized Church had not been able to provide.

He felt nothing for them. They were tools to be used toward his goal, and the deadening of his heart told him that it would always be so. He had trusted others too much in the past, and they had failed him. Though he hadn't been stripped of everything in his flight from the Holy Land, he'd lost more than he cared to admit. That defeat had taken something he'd clung to for centuries—the last remnant of his humanity.

Behind him he could feel the cold, lifeless stare of glassy eyes. They bored through him to the core of his being, calling out to be freed. He did not flinch from that call. Soon it would be time, and answers would be his. When he had that information, these fools would be tossed to the King of France as bait, and he and a very few others would depart on the greatest adventure of a long, long life. He would regain what had been stolen, and he would find a way to make Kli Kodesh pay. If the ancient could not be killed, nothing said that unlife had to be bearable.

With a deep breath to steady his nerves, Santos returned himself fully to the task at hand. The others swayed back and forth to the rhythm of the chant and he let himself be swept away by that motion. Releasing his mind, he slipped free, riding the current of sound generated by the ancient words. Close. He was very close to his goal. It would not be long before it was over.

SIX

The night was nearly ended when Jacques made his way to the upper levels of the keep, avoiding contact with the few others who were about and staggering into his quarters. He was spent, heart and soul. No energy remained for balance, and the bruises on his legs and shoulders from banging against walls and door frames were witness to this. He'd sent the servants away before slipping below to meet with Santos, so there were none present to witness his weakened state. His mind whirled with images and strange words, rhythms and incantations only half understood. Jacques did not have full control of the power they were unleashing, but he could feel it just the same. He knew when something grand was knocking, and he meant to find a way to open that door.

The pungent aroma of incense had embedded itself in his hair and clothing, and his eyes were red pits of exhaustion. He stumbled across his chamber to the table beside his bed and reached immediately for the bottle in its center. Hands trembling, he dribbled a cup full of the rich, red wine into a goblet and gulped it down. The drink burned his parched throat, but he ignored the pain, pouring a second and downing it with equal disregard.

After a third cup had disappeared, the trembling dissipated, and he was able to stand up straighter. Jacques moved to the window, where the light of dawn was just beginning to seep over the horizon, and he stared down at the road leading up to the keep. No sign of Philip. No one was moving on that road at all, in fact, and that was a sobering thought. Nothing was the same. Nothing would ever be the same again. Jacques looked out over the land that was his by right, by birth and blood. His remaining time as ruler could be measured in heartbeats, he knew, and there was one, and only one, resolution. The dark stranger inhabiting the lower levels of his keep was the key. Santos was many things, mage, savant, teacher, but Jacques had never fooled himself on one point. The man was evil. He represented power, but it was not the pure power of the spirit.

If Jacques was to find a way to save his knights, and his life, it would be through that power. The tremble threatened to return to his hands, and he doused it with yet another mug of wine. His thoughts were beginning to fog, but he fought for a few more coherent moments. He wanted those moments for himself. Santos had begun to leak up from the dungeons into his daily affairs, his thoughts and his dreams. Jacques did not like the sensation of another controlling his actions.

There was a soft knock on his door, and he contemplated sending whoever it was away with a gruff shout. He needed to rest. He could not fight Philip, or Santos's control, if he couldn't keep his eyes open and his mind sharp. Too many nights had been spent in darkness and shadows with too little result, and he needed to shut down his overworked mind before it fell apart completely.

"Who is it?" he called.

"Louis," came the quick reply. With a grunt, Jacques stumbled away from the window sill, managing somehow to grab the wine bottle as he turned.

"Come in," he said.

Louis de Chaunvier entered quickly, pushing the door closed firmly behind himself. He showed many of the same signs of fatigue as his lord, but somehow his dark good looks hid the bags beneath his eyes more easily. Though the fatigue was obvious in his expression, the fire in his eyes burned brightly. Too brightly.

"What is it, Louis?" Jacques asked.

"I cannot sleep, Jacques. I cannot think. What is to become of us, do you think?"

"I do not know, my friend," Jacques replied, lurching forward to slap the shorter man's shoulder drunkenly. The wine combined rapidly with his exhaustion to steal his reason. "We will find a way through this. I swear it. It has always been so, and it will remain so."

"That may be true," Louis frowned, "but it has never truly been like this." He shook his head and walked across to the table for another glass. Guiltily, Jacques filled his own glass while his friend's back was turned. The bottle was getting low.

Turning back quickly, Louis added, "There has never been one like him."

"If you believe the chronicles, there has," Jacques argued. "The very foundations of our order rest on legend. Hugues de Payen himself spoke, when he'd had enough wine, of a man he called only Montrovant. This man had powers beyond anyone's understanding. There are others. Do not make a fool of yourself through naiveté, Louis. Santos may not be all that he claims, but he is more than we believe.

Your words make no sense," Louis snapped. He snatched the bottle and poured the last of its contents into the mug he now held. "You speak of legends and ghosts when the very walls of your own keep are to be assaulted by an army. That army is very real, Jacques, and very large. I do not believe that Philip will be in any mood to negotiate."

"You have seen Santos," Jacques whispered hoarsely, tossing back the last of his wine. He brushed the unruly locks of his hair aside so that he could make eye contact with his friend. "You have seen what he can do, felt what he can bring forth in a man. How can you deny that?"

"I deny nothing," Louis replied. "but I fail to see how he will help us. Has he given you a plan? Has he explained to you how these 'great secrets' will win our salvation from the fate that awaits us? No. I see it in your eyes, and I know it in my heart. He offers nothing, and he eats our very souls. We must ready ourselves for war, Jacques, and we must rid ourselves of this dark burden."

"No." Jacques turned away so that Louis could not read the fear that was rising quickly, fear that he would be denied what Santos had promised, fear that there might be nothing to the dark stranger's words after all. Fear that he'd cast himself and all that followed him onto a dark path that led to roads he had no desire to travel.

"Jacques..." Louis started toward him, but Jacques held up a hand to warn him back.

"It is beyond our control now, Louis. You know it is. I cannot send him away. I have to know what he offers, to know it fully. We are doomed men whether he stays or goes. We allowed him within our walls and our minds. The only way to be rid of him is to understand him, and we have little time left to gain that understanding."

"I don't even understand you any longer," Louis snapped, downing his wine in a quick gulp.

De Molay didn't answer. He teetered between anger and unconsciousness, and he used the last of his remaining strength to lurch toward his bed. Jacques fell face forward across the mattress and Louis only stood, watching, waiting for him to rise. When it became obvious that he would not, Louis whirled to the window, sending his mug through the opening and out to the courtyard beyond with a loud curse.

Spinning on one heel, he slammed back through the door and left de Molay to his silence and his rest. As he passed from the chamber, he spotted Jacques's servants huddled nearby, waiting anxiously with a tray of food and drink. There was a single bottle of wine in the center of the tray, and he snatched it from the startled serving girl as he passed.

"He won't be needing it," he explained, "or you. Not for several hours. I believe the 'master' has passed out again."

Louis turned away and marched off toward his quarters, the bottle clutched tightly in one hand. He did not look back.

One of the servants was a young man with a piercing gaze and hair so blond that it glistened like spun silver. He slipped back along the wall the way they'd come as soon as de Chaunvier had passed from sight. The others were whispering among themselves, still wondering if they should go to de Molay and check on him, or leave him alone. They did not miss the blond youth as he drifted along the wall, silent as a puff of smoke, and slipped around the corner.

Once out of sight, Ferdinand wasted no time. He followed the curving stair to the main level of the keep and made his way to the south wing. He kept his eyes to the ground and his movements were smooth. All around him others were beginning their day, making their way to prayer or meals, talking in small groups and wondering what the next few hours would bring.

There was none among those gathered, knights and servants alike, who did not fear that the next day might bring their last few hours on the Earth. De Molay had put forth no plan, no means by which they might escape the fate that Philip planned for them. The only hope lay in casting aside their pride and their beliefs, and slinking off into the shadows. Surprisingly few of them took advantage of this means of prolonging life.

Ferdinand did not understand their motivations. He knew they would die. His master, Father Kodesh, had seen it and proclaimed it. Of course, the father had not proclaimed it to de Molay, or to the other knights. To them he was a simple priest.

He recited the mass when it pleased him and took confession for those who had the inclination. He blessed their weapons and their hearts and sent them on their way. He played with them like pieces on a grand chess board, waiting eagerly for some counter-move that would bring him the challenge he so craved. That was why Kodesh fascinated Ferdinand...drawing him like a needy, hungry moth to a flame.

None of those in the keep held any meaning for Father Kodesh. He came to them as an emissary of the Church, but he could have as easily come to them as the focus of a nightmare. Ferdinand knew this. He'd seen both sides of his master, dark and light. He'd been singed by both, and yet he could not bring himself to draw away.

He rounded a final corner and entered the small chapel that bordered the south side of the keep. The interior was dark. Only the muted glow of the early morning sun leaked through the arched windows to lap at the edges of shadow. He knew he would find Father Kodesh there. It was in these moments, lost between darkness and light, dusk and dawn, that the father walked most freely. Ferdinand knew he would want to hear what he had to say, though at times he wondered why the priest didn't just reach out with his mind and take the knowledge he sought. Another part of the elaborate game that was Father Kodesh's life.

"Good morning, Ferdinand." Father Kodesh leaked from the shadows, never registering at the periphery of Ferdinand's vision, and yet there before him as if he'd been thus all along. Kneeling, Ferdinand lowered his eyes.

"Good morning Father."

"I trust you have found something of interest for me?"

Ferdinand nodded, rising slowly and keeping his eyes downcast. It was only partly from respect. He'd been captivated by the depths of his master's eyes often enough to know the dangers that lurked there. Better to chance a surprise blow to the head than a lost soul.

"De Molay has returned from the dungeons, Father. He returned to his quarters over an hour ago, and since then he has finished a bottle of wine and passed out."

"That is all?"

Before the level of dismay in Father Kodesh's voice could rise to dangerous levels, Ferdinand added, "Louis de Chaunvier was with him. He stormed out, taking the wine from de Molay's breakfast and muttering about how de Molay would need nothing for some hours to come. He did not look pleased."

"And well he should not," Father Kodesh replied, twining the long, slender fingers of his hands behind his back and turning away to walk slowly toward the altar at the front of the chapel. "De Molay is weakening. His hold on this keep, and on his knights, is dwindling. It will not be much longer that he is able to hold this place."

"He has the darkness wrapped about him like a cloak," Ferdinand observed, watching carefully to see how his words would register with the priest. "He is so caught up in his spells and the dark one below that he cannot see the wolf slipping up to swallow him whole." Then, suddenly realizing his boldness, the boy fell silent, eyes downcast and face flushed.

"Do not underestimate de Molay," Father Kodesh said quickly, spinning and lifting Ferdinand's chin with one long, slender nail, forcing the young servant to meet his gaze. This time the young man was not quick enough to avoid the other's eyes. "That mistake has been made with these knights in the past, and that is why the Dark One has had to come a second time. It is not perhaps the second coming that the Church would have me teach, but it is significant. De Molay is more aware of what is happening here than any give him credit for. His chosen method of delivering his order might be flawed, but his heart is strong. It is going to be a most interesting confrontation."

Ferdinand felt the words he'd longed to speak hurtling to the surface of his mind, and he was not able to bite them off. This time the curiosity got the better of him. "Father, who are you? Really? I need to know who it is that I serve."

Trembling, Ferdinand dropped to his knees on the stone floor. He'd dreaded this moment, dreaded the time when his own resolve would crumble. He'd not even seen it coming.

There was no immediate flash of pain, nor did Father Kodesh raise his voice in anger. At first there was no reaction at all. Then came the laughter. It was like the crackling of ice on a lake when the sun's rays hit full force. Ferdinand didn't dare to raise his eyes from the stone. Not until he heard Father Kodesh speaking to him softly.

He raised his head slowly, and he found that the old priest wasn't watching him at all. That thin, haunted face was turned away. The words were very softly spoken, so soft that—despite his fear—Ferdinand was forced to crawl closer to make them out.

"I will tell you a story," Father Kodesh began. "It is a story of love and hate, betrayal and salvation. It is the story of a bargain and a curse. I will tell you my story, and when I have finished, you will sit with me and help me to decide whether I must kill you for the knowledge."

Ferdinand grew very still at that moment. Father Kodesh had grown momentarily silent as he gathered and sorted his thoughts. Ferdinand heard his heart echoing dully in his chest, and for a moment he thought it would pound its way free. There was a great rushing sound in his ears, and his sight grew red and hazy. He found it difficult to breathe. None of this mattered. He pushed away from the concerns of his body. He tipped forward for an instant that lasted an eternity, then righted himself and raised his eyes to meet his master's.

Father Kodesh looked deeply into his eyes, then nodded as if he'd found whatever it was he sought. Without further hesitation, he began to speak, and as he did so his hands moved to the pouch that he always wore at his side, absently undoing the leather strips that bound it as he spoke.

"I knew a man who was once king," Father Kodesh began. "He gave me many things: a family that I'd never had, a purpose that would serve me for eternity, and a love I never asked for. These things he gave me because it was his nature to give. I would not have taken them. I was not as you see me now—nothing is ever twice as you've seen it once. Remember that, Ferdinand, it is an important lesson."

As he spoke, his fingers drew forth objects from within the leather-bound pouch. As Ferdinand watched, trapped by the powerful voice and the magic of the moment, Father Kodesh dropped a single silver coin on the floor between them.

With a toss of his head that sent his silvery gray hair dancing over his shoulders, he smiled down at Ferdinand without humor. "This is my story.

"There were great men such as this world may never know again in the days of my youth. Men of purpose. Men of honor. There were darker powers, as well, and it was to those that I fell as a young man. I had been warned away from certain ruins. My parents had told me the legends, but I was strong and fierce—born to be a warrior. I would listen to no one who told me there were things I might not do. Because of this, I died for the first time a great many years ago—so many that your ancestors spoke a different language and lived in a far-off land when I was born.

"That does not matter. I went to the ruins one day while hunting. I told myself it was because I'd seen game in that area, and that the legends would keep the other boys away. I told myself it was only so that I might bring meat to my family and honor to myself. It was not. It was for foolish pride and the satisfaction of boyish curiosity. Satisfaction, from that point on, became a very subjective matter.

"I could have gone there by morning. I could have taken a friend, or a dozen friends, but I went alone. It was late afternoon when I strayed to that side of the mountain, and I knew that if I did not turn back soon, it would be too late—that I would have to make a camp and wait for the morning. Rumors or not, there were other more natural dangers about by night, and I had sense enough—or so it seemed—to fear those. I made my choice, spurring my mount toward the ruins while the light was still bright.

"It was a magical place. There were stone towers half torn to the ground by time, and the greedy seeking secrets buried deep within those walls.

Those walls were eaten away from the top and covered in clinging vines. There were places where windows and doors still opened onto shadowed secrets. Not much of interest to a man, but for a boy it was a treasure trove of adventure.

"I made my way to the largest of the structures that remained erect. It must have been the main building, for there were stairs stretching beneath it and many of the rooms had kept at least three of their walls, providing some shelter. I found a nook that was particularly well-preserved. There was a fireplace that had not seen use in many years, and a section of roof still remained to break the worst of the wind and to provide shelter if it was to rain. Perfect.

"While the daylight remained, there was little to fear. I placed what supplies and equipment I carried within my chosen camp and gathered wood quickly. This done, I set out to do the hunting that had been my original purpose. It was not late, and the area was well populated with deer. I remember very clearly the buck I brought down that evening. Somehow the taking of that magnificent beast's life touched me. I dragged it back to the clearing—the light fading rapidly around me—and managed to hang it from a tree near my camp. I gutted it quickly and left it to drain as I started a fire among the twigs and logs I'd gathered, thinking back on it's death.

"I still carry that image embedded in my mind. I found the buck on the slope of the mountain. It had stopped on an outcropping of rock, its chest pulled up proudly and its nose raised to the wind as if it sensed something was wrong. I carried only a short bow, but I was skilled. I watched it longer than I should have, captivated by that sight. Somewhere in that time I pulled back the string and let the arrow fly. I have no idea how long I stood there, before or after the shot. All I could see was the buck, outlined against the sky—the arrow in flight—the buck rearing up and crashing, the expression in its eyes holding my gaze captive as it fell to its death. I'm not certain I had a coherent thought between that moment and the moment I lit the fire. So many things happened that night that I'm not certain I remember any of them clearly.

"As I cooked a portion of that meat, I watched the stairway that opened through what had once been a doorway a few feet to one side of the fireplace. The dark hole was mesmerizing as I sat, gazing through the dancing flames. I remember that, despite the fire, I felt a chill in the air. I moved as close to the heat as was safe, and when the weariness finally overtook my nervous fear, I turned my eyes away from the doorway and drifted into fitful sleep.

"I dreamed of red eyes and screaming stags, of shadows that fell from the walls around me and blocked the fire from my sight. They moved about me, touched me, whispered to me and toyed with my senses and my mind. I was never truly brought out of that sleep, and yet I knew that what I saw was truly happening, no dream, and as I lay helpless—they fed. They touched their foul lips to my throat and drank from me as though I were a full wineskin. They did not take all I had to offer, just a little. I know now that they probably did not even need it. Something in me called out to them.

"I woke as alone as I'd been the night before, but everything had changed. The light was harsh on my eyes and my head pounded as if I'd been drunk for a week and only just woken. I staggered to my feet and took my bearings, remembering almost at once where I was and what I'd done. The stag still hung from the tree outside the walls of the ruins, pale and limp—somehow appearing more dead than it had when I'd hung it. I saw as I approached that there was no blood. Gone. Drained. The embers of my fire still glowed brightly in the ancient fireplace. There was no sign of the shadows, and yet, as I've said, everything had changed.

"I stared long and hard at the entrance to the cellars below. I wanted very badly to turn and to run and never to return, but something in me wouldn't allow it. Neither did I mount that stair. It was a standoff, of sorts, or so I allowed myself to believe. I turned and left, taking the meat back to my family and accepting their praise without attention. Nothing mattered, though the meat was heavenly when my mother served it that night for dinner.

"I was waiting for something, you see. That something did not come for a very long time, but the knowledge that it would come was enough to mark me as odd. I spent long periods of time alone, took walks beneath the moon when my family slept. I volunteered for night guards and hunts that kept me away for weeks at a time.

"It became too much for me when I was nearing my twenty-seventh year. I'd been too long at home, and the ache was burning within me to return to those ruins. I did not go to hunt—the memory of that stag, of its blood and those eyes, boring through to my soul—had removed any taste I had for that. I took my pack, a blanket, and nothing more. I told no one where I was going—they would only have protested, and I knew somehow that this was something I would never be able to explain.

"The ruins stood much as I remembered them from years before. The remains of my fire had been blown away by the wind, but the stairway still loomed, and the walls and roof remained in place as if they were waiting for me.

"I made my fire quickly and settled in, brewing some of the herb tea my mother had mixed for me and letting my mind wander. I had no idea why I had come back, what I expected. I knew that my life of hunting and chasing women in the society of my family was growing less and less entertaining, and even then that tendency toward boredom was a factor in my being. It was a different time, a different place—and yet it was me, and I was unhappy. "Flashes of my first night in those ruins had haunted my nights. I dreamed of red, glowing eyes and flitting shadows. I dreamed of a doorway into a darkness I could not penetrate, but that called to me just the same. I sat, sipping tea and waiting, wondering what would become of me.

"They came as I was nearly ready to drift off. They came openly this time, one at a time, exiting the doorway and forming a moving circle around me. I did not rise, it would have been pointless. I did not desire to flee, though my heart pounded wildly and my gaze swept over them rapidly—waiting, searching. They would never have let me go. I'd made my choice, though they had called to me. I'd come back, and I was theirs.

"There were no words. Perhaps they talked within their minds, or perhaps they'd been so long in the darkness, so long one unit, that they'd forsaken the spoken word altogether. I will never know. One of them, perhaps the leader, knelt in front of me, cupping my face in his hands and tilting his head to one side, curious—searching my eyes. I tried at first to meet that gaze, then I tried in vain to pull free. I felt my energy drained, felt the lethargy falling over me.

"They moved in closer then, brushing hands and lips over me. I was punctured so many times that I felt my blood would drain away into the soil and restore me to unity with the Earth Mother. It was not to be. They wasted no precious drop of that blood. I grew weaker with each sharp caress, but the images grew clearer, the beauty of their eyes and pale, luminescent skin overwhelmed me.

"I awoke alone once more, but this time to darkness. It was cold—colder than any place I've ever been—and yet the cold seemed somehow natural. Though it was dark, I could see clearly, and the bottom of a stairway beckoned to me. I rose, as though in a trance, and staggered toward that stair. I sensed the sunlight streaming down from above, and I smiled. All would be clear once I was out in the daylight.

I took one step, then another, and my strength seemed to be returning. It was on the third step that my leg passed through the light of the sun. The searing pain was incredible, and my leg collapsed, sending me crashing back to the stone floor. I clutched my leg against my chest, then scuttled back into the shadows like a crab, panicked. I stayed that way until the unbelievable weight of the sun pressing down on my heart dropped me into blessed darkness, and I lay still."

Ferdinand had been sitting, rapt, his eyes locked on Father Kodesh's features. As the words faded, and the odd priest grew silent, the air left the younger man in a long slow breath. "Vampire," he breathed.

Father Kodesh's eyes were far away, but his words were chilling and sharp as shards of ice. "You will not use that word. You will not acknowledge that I am anything but what I appear to be. If you do, I will know. If you betray me, remember that only I shall live. We will speak more of this."

Ferdinand gulped down the words he'd meant to say. He couldn't vocalize what he felt, and somehow he knew it wasn't necessary that he do so.

"Leave me," Father Kodesh said softly. "Leave me to think on what we must do next."

Nodding, Ferdinand nearly leaped to his feet, rushing from the room. Kli Kodesh watched him go, wondering at the folly he'd just committed. It had been too long since he'd had anyone to talk with—anyone who cared to listen, in any case. Far too long. For just an instant he let his mind wander to Gwendolyn and her quest. He hoped she managed to complete the task he'd set her before King Philip came through and leveled the keep. It would be so much more—interesting—that way.

SEVEN

The city of Holywell was not large, nor was it particularly prosperous, but Jeanne could sense an aura of antiquity that was both sobering and intriguing. He knew there were others like himself within the city walls, others who would know him for who and what he was. He also knew that they might not be welcome, particularly in the company of one such as Gwendolyn. Kli Kodesh was known to all, and it would not take long for any with the sight to mark her as one of the ancient one's chosen.

He'd noticed that despite her initial despondence she'd moved closer and closer to Montrovant's side during their ride. Now Jeanne was forced to bring up the rear as the other two conversed in low tones. He'd have been jealous, but it didn't serve his best interests. If there was going to be trouble with Gwendolyn, he knew he was the one who would have to keep his eyes open for it. Montrovant was distracted by his quest, and by Gwendolyn.

It was not like Montrovant to enter any situation with his mind clouded, and that worried Jeanne most of all. Once or twice he was on the verge of saying something, then pulled back. There were things to be learned from Gwendolyn, as well, and it was interesting to have another companion, even if she were concentrating most of her attentions on his sire.

It also meant that Jeanne was more free to explore things on his own. That was more of a blessing than he'd dreamed. He knew that the impression that Montrovant was giving of inattention was likely a false one, but it was pleasant to feel, if only for a while, that he controlled a part of his own destiny.

There would be a time in the future when that destiny would have to be addressed, but that time was not yet near.

They entered the city just after dusk. The merchants and vendors were just finishing the stowing of carts and goods against the coming darkness, and the denizens of the darker hours were seeping from the shadows. Loud shouts and cat-calls rang out through the night, women laughed and sang. The music and lifeblood of the inns and taverns echoed through the cool night air. Torches lit small portions of the shadows, and children scurried about, some on their way home, others sneaking off for fun and adventure away from their parents' watchful eyes. Jeanne was caught up immediately in the sounds and scents, lights and parade of humanity—the rhythmic pulse of blood through warm veins. He was several steps beyond the door of the Weeping Violet before he noticed that Montrovant and Gwendolyn had slipped inside.

Cursing, he spun on his heel and backtracked, pushing aside the heavy curtain that draped the door and moving silently into the dimly lit interior. He spotted his companions almost immediately.

Montrovant was deep in conversation with a short, squat man behind the bar, and Gwendolyn was playing the part of his woman very well for one who had claimed to have no interest in him. She hung on Montrovant, draped over his shoulder, one arm dangling around his neck and dangling down across his chest. Her head rested in the crook of his neck at a pert angle, her hair washing over him like a silken waterfall.

They were the most astounding couple le Duc had ever seen, and yet he couldn't keep his attention on them. He'd been near the sisters in the convent, but that had been a moment under his own control. He'd been with others, but only to take them, to feed. Not since his Embrace had he been deluged with the variety and intensity of sensations that assaulted him in the crowded tavern. He stumbled, righting himself with difficulty and bumping violently into a large man with ragged black hair and a patch covering one eye. He tried to form the words of an apology, but his tongue was thick and heavy. In any case, the man gave him no chance.

He spun to face Jeanne, and as he moved—suddenly—his dagger was in his hand and level with Jeanne's chest. The man's one good eye glittered dangerously.

The scene shifted off kilter, and everything slowed strangely. Jeanne saw the other patrons of the bar turning to the disturbance, the men grinning broadly but making no move to interfere, the few women present crying out in delight. His attacker's arm jerked in a cruel arc toward his face and he reached out calmly and gracefully, catching the wrist beyond the blade and stopping it cold. There was no thought involved. It happened so quickly that the entire room came to shocked silence. The expected blood did not flow.

Jeanne stood there for a long moment, holding the man immobile by his arm, then he released his grip and stepped back.

"I was about to say I was sorry, friend," he said softly. The one-eyed man stepped forward as if his mind couldn't comprehend what had happened and he wanted another go. It was then that Montrovant stepped in.

"I believe my friend apologized," he said. His voice was like ice. "I also believe he will kill you if you don't put that fool's toy away and let it go. If he doesn't, I most certainly will."

One-eye had had enough. He turned, glanced at his companions, who had stood a few paces behind him until le Duc grabbed his arm and who now had moved a safe distance back. They turned their heads as if they'd never seen him before, and he bolted for the door. Laughter followed on his heels: loud, derisive laughter. It seemed that the mood had shifted. Those who'd so recently wanted Jeanne's blood to drench the floor had turned their amusement on his assailant.

Montrovant grabbed Jeanne's arm and dragged him to a booth in the back of the room, trying to slide out of the center of the tavern without further incident, but the damage was done. Gwendolyn nodded toward the back entrance and Jeanne noted the passing of a darker patch of shadow into the night. Any hope they'd had of a quick, silent entrance to the city had been shattered.

"What did you imagine you were doing, you fool?"

Montrovant hissed, holding his lips very near to Jeanne's ear so no other would hear. "You have made a spectacle of yourself that these men will not easily forget. What were you thinking, that you'd kill and feed on the man right in the middle of the tavern?"

Jeanne shook his head. In truth, he had no idea what he'd thought he would do. He had no memory of any thoughts at all. One thing was certain: whatever had motivated him had not been well-conceived. He still felt a bit overwhelmed, but he was beginning to get a tentative hold on his emotions. His first emotion was anger. Montrovant had kept these sensations from him, all of this—the incredible rush of blood, the interaction with others—and for so long. How could he not have anticipated the effect it would have?

"Have you never been in a tavern before?" Gwendolyn chimed in, her eyes glittering, delighted. Apparently her understanding of the moment was deeper than Montrovant's, or deeper than he allowed to show. "You nearly took that man's arm off."

"He attacked me," Jeanne said softly. "I couldn't very well let him stab me, then walk away from it like nothing had happened."

"You have much to learn," Gwendolyn said, laughing. "Have you kept him so shielded from the world, then, Montrovant? Is this what I would have had to look forward to, then?"

Montrovant would not be drawn into their banter. He was deep in thought, and his gaze followed the movements of the squat man behind the bar. After a few moments Montrovant leaned close between Jeanne and Gwendolyn, the incident of moments before seemingly forgotten, and whispered to them hoarsely.

"That is Bertrand. He serves Bastian, and he has been running this tavern, in one form or another, for as long as there has been a Holywell. They are Brujah, and Bastian is very old. He will not take well to your little display, Jeanne, once Bertrand reports it. He works very hard to keep this place neutral."

"I'm sorry," Jeanne said simply. "I have never experienced anything so—overpowering. You could have warned me."

Montrovant spun on him, nearly raising an arm to cuff him on the side of the head, then stopped. He stared at Jeanne for a long moment, then suddenly his face transformed and he burst into raucous laughter. He clapped Jeanne on the back hard enough to make the smaller man stagger, then turned back to the bar.

"That I could—that I could. Sometimes I forget myself. Another round for my friend," he called out more loudly, waving to the bartender who glared at him darkly.

Bertrand moved down the bar toward them, a flagon of wine in his hand. He moved slowly and precisely, as if each motion had been thought through carefully. He leaned over the bar as Montrovant passed him the necessary payment.

"Another incident like the one earlier, and you'll never leave this city. Am I understood?"

Montrovant was not intimidated, but he nodded without speaking.

"At dawn be in the stables. There will be safe lodging and we will find a moment to talk, I think. There is more than just a social call involved here, and I will have no business transacted on these premises without my knowledge."

"Of course," Montrovant agreed, extending one huge hand across the bar. Bertrand took it reluctantly, studying Montrovant carefully. There was a tension in the air that even the more mundane customers must have witnessed, but it passed, and the bartender actually smiled.

He didn't speak, but the tension was broken. As the shorter man turned away, Montrovant did so as well. He nodded toward the back of the bar and headed for the door where they'd seen the shadowy figure exit earlier. Jeanne breathed a sigh of relief as they came out into the fresh night air.

They stood in a narrow alley. At one end, a few feet away, was the street through which they'd entered on. The alley extended in the other direction until it curved between two ancient stone buildings. Debris littered the ground, and there was a prone figure propped against the wall just beyond the fringe of shadow.

Montrovant moved easily into the shadows, Jeanne and

Gwendolyn at his heels. The figure leaning on the wall didn't move or acknowledge their presence, but Jeanne sensed that the man—it was a man—was alive and awake.

"So, the wandering cub returns to civilization," a gravelly voice rose, echoing eerily in the confined space. "Has Eugenio tightened the leash, or are you sniffing about on your own?"

Montrovant lunged forward suddenly, and seconds later he had the man dangling from one huge hand, held aloft by the throat. Their faces were very close, and yet the man showed no real fear. Jeanne decided he was either dangerously insane or blind.

"It will be a cold day in your master's afterworld when I answer to the likes of you," Montrovant said at last, letting the man slip from his grip to fall in a heap at his feet. "I trust that you've informed all those who need to know of my presence—along with those who do not?"

"I tell no one a thing without a price being paid," the man replied, rising and dusting himself off carefully. He was slender, not young, but not exactly old, either. There was a gray, timeless quality about him that told Jeanne there was more to him than met the eye. "I waited here to see if your price might be better than the others," he continued.

Montrovant stared at him for a moment, then shook his head, grinning ruefully. "I know you too well to pay you not to talk, Michel," he said softly. "I might as well pay you not to breathe—I would get equal value for my coin."

"You do me injustice," Michel replied, also grinning. "It is good to see you again, Dark One. The city has not been as entertaining since your last, shall we say, overly hasty departure."

Jeanne was truly confused now. Montrovant must have known the man would be waiting for them.

Now, after nearly taking the fool's head off by way of greeting, he was carrying on a conversation like they were the best of friends.

"What did he do?" Gwendolyn had moved forward, eyes shining with interest. Jeanne watched in amazement.

"Tell her nothing," Montrovant said quickly. "Those days are behind me."

"That isn't all that was behind him," Michel grinned. "Half the Duke's private guard was behind him as he rode out of town. They were bitter, too. It has taken fifteen years to raise a new princess...

Princess?" Gwendolyn's eyebrow arched, and

Jeanne turned to Montrovant with a grin.

"Enough," Montrovant said. "We have more important things to do here than the recounting of my past mistakes."

"Oh, they have been recounted many times since you left," Michel added, his grin still wider. "Sondra came back, you know. Quite the event that was."

"Sondra?" Jeanne asked.

"The princess, of course," Michel laughed. "Or, she was the princess when our friend here met her. She was somewhat more than that when she returned, and she was not happy to see how her father had forgotten her and elevated her younger, bastard sister to legitimacy."

"He recognized Seline?" Montrovant asked, suddenly interested. "Despite my warning?"

"No one paid much attention to your warnings after you'd been gone a year or so, my friend," Michel said ruefully. "They might be frightened of you, but they are certainly not long of memory. Once things calmed down, they were pretty quick to start chasing their own interests again."

"But Seline?"

"Yes, Seline, and you can imagine the stir that raised. He was without an heir, and she was the only remaining hope with the bloodlines to keep the house intact."

"And did she?" Montrovant asked.

Jeanne was fascinated, watching the interaction between the two and trying to piece together the fragments of what they said into a decipherable whole. Montrovant was getting caught up in the story, and that in itself was entertaining.

"Of course not," Michel laughed out loud. "She might have pulled it off, though. She was one of the finer wenches of the palace, as you will recall. If Sondra hadn't come back—who knows?"

Turning to Jeanne and Gwendolyn, his expression

apologetic, Montrovant explained. "Sondra was the daughter of a man I had a—problem—with. She was infatuated with me, and I'm afraid I might have let the passion of the moment carry me away."

"You Embraced her?" Gwendolyn's voice was sharp, and Jeanne moved a step back.

"I did it for revenge." Montrovant met her stare evenly. "She did not beg me, but her father did me a disservice. She was beautiful, and young, and vital, and she was there when I hungered. A very convenient way to even an old and tiring score."

Gwendolyn didn't respond, but it was clear that the issue was far from resolved.

"Sondra came back almost a year to the day of her own—transformation" Michel continued, taking up the story again eagerly when Montrovant hesitated. His eyes were animated, amused and the dim light glittered off them brightly. It was obvious that he'd caught the interchange between Montrovant and Gwendolyn and put two and two very quickly into four.

"She visited her father first. He was sick for weeks. Every time the doctors thought he was on the road to recovery, he'd grow pale and weak."

"She killed him?" Jeanne asked, unable to contain his curiosity.

"No," Michel said, grinning, "the doctors did. They determined that he had a poison within him and that they needed to bleed it out. They did that. They bled everything out of him. The physicians were found dead the day after he died, and I suspect that Sondra did that out of anger over the waste.

She is still here, then?" Montrovant asked.

"Sondra, I mean."

Gwendolyn moved closer, as if she would protest his interest, but suddenly all humor had drained from Michel's face, and she held herself back.

"No. She is dead, and that is why I must warn you. The Brujah, they have taken this city for their own. There are those of other blood-lines who come here, but only with Bastian's approval."

"Then Syd is no longer here?" Montrovant demanded. "I have come a long way to speak with him.

Oh, he is here," Michel answered quickly. "He has always been here. Even Bastian hasn't made any sort of move in that direction. Syd leaves Bastian alone, Bastian pretends Syd couldn't kill him whenever he might decide. Pretty precarious, but somehow it works."

Such intrigue. Jeanne had been used to this sort of thing in mortal life—it was the way of noble blood. This was different, somehow—deeper. The powers involved had been there for so long, and the roots of the "families" had had time to grow very deep. There was more involved than a younger son putting his sibling to death, or a duke poisoning the legal heir.

"This Sondra," le Duc cut in. "You say she is dead—she was killed by another Damned?"

"You sound surprised," Michel observed. "The Dark One must truly have kept you sheltered. A hundred years ago a question like yours might have brought a frown to my grandfather's face, as well. Now it is common. The Brujah breach no challenge to their supremacy here without a confrontation. Bastian has all but proclaimed himself ruler of this city, and he is no slouch at tactics.

"Only those who are truly old stand against him, and, as I said, those he leaves alone."

"I must see Syd," Montrovant repeated. "Michel, can you lead me to him?"

"You know the price that would put on my head," Michel countered, meeting Montrovant's gaze levelly.

"I will make it worth your while," Montrovant continued. "I will also offer what protection the three of us can offer. I may not have Syd's age, but I know a few tricks. Bastian is not so old he couldn't be brought down a notch."

Michel hesitated. He seemed to be weighing the consequences against the entertainment value, and Jeanne thought suddenly of Kli Kodesh, waiting somewhere ahead on a road they'd only begun to travel. Who was this Michel, and how was it that he spoke so freely and with such knowledge? It was becoming painfully clear that Montrovant had kept certain things from him very carefully. Another thing to concentrate on. Jeanne almost wished they were back on the road where things were much simpler. Almost.

"You may be right, my friend," Michel said at last, nodding curtly. "I will take you as close as I dare, and I will direct you the rest of the way in. I'm not certain how Syd will feel about seeing you again—it will draw attention to him, as well."

"That is a road I will travel when I reach it," Montrovant replied. "Syd will see me. There is no way he could not. If he is not happy to see me, well, I will have to find a way to cheer him up, won't I?

You have worked that magic on me," Michel said, grinning. "I can't remember the last night that promised so much of interest. It is good to see you, old friend. You spend far too much time roaming around. One like yourself could make things very hot for Bastian and his minions."

"You know that, of my kind, I am the only one for whom the city is not home. The Dark One…called by the hunt, the wolves…something not quite right in my blood," Montrovant countered. "I have my own roads to travel. I will leave Bastian to his sedentary life. Eugenio as well."

As Montrovant spoke, Michel turned away and trotted quickly up the alley away from the street. Jeanne was just about to voice a question as to their destination when the man took a miraculous leap, clearing a fifteen-foot stone wall to his left and taking to the rooftops without a slip.

Montrovant followed easily, as though he'd expected the move, and Gwendolyn wasn't far behind, though Jeanne heard her cursing softly as she corrected her balance and scaled the wall clumsily. Again he was several steps down the alley before his mind completely registered that the others were gone.

Another lesson. Michel might be human, but he was not one to be trifled with. Jeanne let out a soft growl and leaped to the rooftop, taking off as swiftly as possible in pursuit of the three shadows disappearing in the distance. As he caught up with his companions, a cloud slid across the moon, plunging the city into total darkness. A darkness that swallowed them without a ripple.

EIGHT

Michel led them quickly over several rooftops, down through a second alley, and came up short at the rear entrance to a stable on the southern border of the city. Montrovant didn't bother with questions, and they moved with such speed and purpose that le Duc was hard-pressed just to keep up. He trailed along behind Montrovant, at Gwendolyn's side, lost in his own thoughts. He knew he'd need to ask some questions about Michel at a later time. For the moment he focused on their breakneck journey across Holywell, and on watching their backs as best he could.

He had a lot to learn about the politics of the city, but already he understood that they had inherent enemies. Best to keep his wits about him and his eyes and ears open in directions Montrovant's were not. Michel huddled immediately against the rear wall of the stable, as if concentrating, and Montrovant stood silently beside him. Gwendolyn stood at Montrovant's other elbow, watching. She paid no attention whatsoever to Michel, nor did she watch le Duc. Only Montrovant captivated her. Another reason to keep the watch—another responsibility. It seemed as though, youngest or not, he was the only one with any common sense left. Michel peeled himself away from the wall. Jeanne couldn't tell if he'd been listening, or sensing by some other means, but he was apparently satisfied. He turned to face Montrovant once more. "The way is clear, for the moment. This is as far as I go, old friend."

"You will not take me to Syd?" Montrovant asked quickly.

"I have done so, you just don't know it yet," Michel said softly. "I must go, Dark One, but I will see you again soon—you will owe me, you know.

That may be true, my slippery friend, but what
I will owe you remains to be seen," Montrovant answered.

Without a word, Michel leaped to the rooftops again and
headed off at an angle from the way they'd come. Le Duc moved
as if to follow, but Montrovant stayed him with a hand on his
shoulder.

"Wait," he said softly. Jeanne was going to protest, but he
saw Gwendolyn stiffen suddenly and back against the wall. It
was only seconds later that he felt them. Not that it mattered.
They were completely surrounded.

"You have come a long way," a sibilant voice floated out to
them through the shadows.

They stood alone, looking about themselves in alarm, and
then he was there. Tall, slender to the point of emaciation, eyes
glowing with a deep golden fire. Le Duc took a step back, but
Montrovant held his ground.

"Hello, Syd," he said softly. "You seem to have been
expecting us, despite the long journey."

"It isn't a large city," Syd replied. "Word travels quickly in
certain circles. I, and mine, travel in all of those circles."

"So it would seem. You have saved us the trouble of finding
you."

"You have made an error, Montrovant," Syd replied quickly.
"You were told to stay clear of all of us—not to drag us into your
little game. You have chosen to ignore this, and you have chosen
the wrong time and place to make that mistake."

"Is this any way to greet an old friend?" Montrovant replied
smoothly.

Le Duc caught the slight edge in his sire's voice. The air was
so charged with tension that every movement, every intake of
breath and every word spoken was unnaturally immediate.
They were immortal, all of them, to a point. That point was a
fine line they were walking, and the straight-edged blade of
that point was sliding softly across Jeanne's spine. "Friend."
Syd spoke the word as if it were unfamiliar, as if it were an
unpleasant taste passing over his tongue. "Friends do not
endanger one another," he continued. "Friends do not travel
hundreds of miles to drop their troubles in the lap of another.

Friends do not ignore the instructions of their elders."

"I have ignored nothing," Montrovant replied. "I have come to you for answers, but I have done nothing to endanger you."

"You have no understanding of how things are now," Syd replied. "You come wandering in from Hell knows where, dragging a bitch and a pup behind, asking questions and leaping across buildings in the middle of the night, and you tell me you have done nothing to endanger me. Things are not as they were. The Damned are not all solitary powers any longer—clans have gathered in some of the great cities, and rumor carries of others. There are places where groups of our own have taken control. Do you know who is in control here, Montrovant? Do you care?"

"I know more than you believe," Montrovant said, taking a step forward. "I know that Bastian calls orders and others in this city jump, and it shames me. You are here. You are both older and stronger than he, and yet you cower in the shadows and threaten your own."

"You are not my own."

"You were Embraced by Eugenio, as was I," Montrovant stated. "You are my brother. If you choose to deny this, that is your decision, but it is also a fact."

Le Duc felt the tension growing, and he knew that the next words spoken would not be as friendly. Montrovant was arrogant, and that wasn't always the best way to approach a would-be ally. As it turned out, it didn't matter. The air around them erupted in sudden sound, and dark shadows dropped from the walls and slipped from the streets and alleys. Bastian was upon them.

"You have led them to me," Syd gasped.

"If you think that then you are a bigger fool than I had believed," Montrovant spat, spinning toward the nearest of their attackers. He flipped his hand out in an almost careless gesture, and there was a howl of outrage and pain from the shadow.

Jeanne moved without thinking. He was young to the Blood, but his mind was the mind of a warrior. The red haze had not abandoned him in his Embrace. The world slowed, and his blade was suddenly in his hand as he backed toward the wall. It was an instinctive motion, protecting his back as he swept the blade in a quick arc to clear the area near him.

He noted that Gwendolyn was gone. He'd not seen her go, nor did he believe she'd been taken down so swiftly. Another question for later, assuming that later existed.

They were surrounded, but there weren't as many as he'd originally thought. Syd's followers had melted from the shadows at the first sign of trouble, and Montrovant had entered the battle like an avenging angel. The odds had evened and turned in the blink of an eye. A short, squat form leaped from the shadows, moving in an odd, sidewise gait toward Montrovant's back. Jeanne levered himself off of the wall without thought, leaping at the shorter vampire and swinging his blade in a vicious arc.

His target moved in odd, disjointed motions. Jeanne adjusted mid-leap, angling the blade lower and tighter. There was a snarl as he was spotted, and he felt the air rush past his throat as long, knife-sharp nails raked upward, barely grazing his skin. He saw feral, yellowed eyes glowing brightly, then spinning away at a crazy angle as his blade separated head from neck. Montrovant whirled, ducked as Jeanne flew past, and grinned ferociously. It was over moments later.

Jeanne came back to the reality of the moment slowly. He was aware that the battle had ended. He was aware that there were others moving about him, speaking in low, hurried tones. He leaned against the wall and waited for the haze to clear. He prayed that no one would come to him, that none would touch him. He'd kill them, and it would be a shame to waste the second life offered in a single existence. The red slipped from his eyes. The voices became coherent. He felt someone drawing near and steeled himself for the touch that never came.

"You fought well." It was Gwendolyn. He turned slowly, staggering slightly as he removed himself from the protective surface of the stone wall. He was surprised once more.

"Where did you go?" he managed to reply. "They came, and you were gone. Where did you go?"

"I was here," she said, smiling enigmatically. "There are a few tricks you don't know yet, my friend. I didn't know who or what they were. I thought it might be better if one of us were— less obvious."

Jeanne stared at her for a long moment, assessing the emotions he saw warring in her eyes. Trying to decide whether to call her a coward or applaud her ingenuity. Neither option was available a second later when Syd appeared at their side.

His eyes were brighter than when they'd first seen him. His motions were quicker, more certain. He was smiling, and the transformation of his features was amazing.

"You are all right?" Syd asked. Though the words were friendly, there was a bright glitter in the elder vampire's eyes that made Jeanne wonder if there were any point in answering.

"I'm fine," Gwendolyn answered immediately. Jeanne was only able to nod. His mind still lingered on that fine edge between red and reality. It had been a long time since he'd been caught up in a moment of battle. It had never been like this. More lessons. More that Montrovant might have told him, but hadn't. Had he known?

"We must move," Syd was saying. "We must get out of sight before Bastian realizes you weren't alone. These were sent after you, not me. Not enough of them—not by a long shot."

He turned and Jeanne followed. Gwendolyn had insinuated herself close against his side, and he allowed her to support him slightly for the first few steps, aiming him in the right direction.

"You will have to tell me about this place inside your mind, the place you go when you fight," she whispered as they began to move through the door into the stables. "There are many things you can tell me, I think."

He didn't reply, but he knew the conversation was far from over. Syd led them into the stables quickly. Montrovant had entered well ahead of them, not even bothering to turn and offer reassurances. The door closed behind them with a decisive, final thud.

They moved through the center aisle of the stable in a silent, single-file column. The animals shied away, snorting and stamping in disapproval, but did not raise more of a disturbance than that. It was apparent that this wasn't the first such late-night, blood-scented entourage to pass this way. Most animals would have been in a frenzy.

A dark passage opened in the wall ahead, and Jeanne

watched with interest as those ahead of him disappeared through it. When he and Gwendolyn reached that hole he hesitated for a long moment, adjusting his eyes to what lay beyond, then mounted the stairs that appeared before him and started down. Those behind made their way onto the stairs as well, and the portal was closed behind them.

As they moved down the shadowed passageway, Jeanne felt the weight of eyes upon them. No one was visible, but there was no doubt that they were watched. There was no warmth in that surveillance.

"Stick close," Jeanne whispered, leaning forward to place his lips close to Gwendolyn's ear. "Just because they've invited us in doesn't mean they aren't going to kill us."

She nodded almost imperceptibly in answer. She needed no warning from him, but it had made him feel better—more in control—to voice his concern. Almost immediately he began to wonder if anyone else had heard. Cursing himself under his breath he continued into the darkness.

The first thing he saw when he returned to the light was Montrovant's face, illuminated by flickering candle-flame. He stood before Syd, whose back was to the door, a thin, ethereal figure against the backdrop of Montrovant's vast height and broad shoulders. The lines of Montrovant's face were relaxed, and Jeanne breathed easier. They might not be completely safe, but if Montrovant was willing to take the chance, odds were he had reason to believe he could get them out of whatever was to come.

"You were still wrong to come," Syd was saying. "The more years pass, the more important it becomes that we hide our nature from mortals. We hide from one another now, and it won't be so long before the younger ones start coveting your own blood. Things are different now."

"That is all the more reason to aid me," Montrovant responded quickly. "What I'm doing, what I will be able to offer to you, and to the others—it is worth the risk."

"To you, everything is worth the risk," Syd replied, shaking his head. He turned toward the wall, unwilling to meet Montrovant's eyes.

"There are stories," Syd continued. "I will share what I know. I will offer you no aid, nor will I give you any sort of blessing, but after wrongly accusing you of leading Bastian's filth to me—and after the—entertainment—they provided, I feel I owe you this. Besides, I know little of your knights beyond what you might hear on the street."

Montrovant took half a step forward, as though he'd protest, but stopped when Syd turned back to him.

"Do not press it, Dark One," he whispered. "I know of your ways...I know of your mind, more than you would believe. Be happy with what I offer. You are not so dark as all that."

For a long moment the two stood, facing off in silence, then Montrovant smiled. He didn't drop his eyes, nor did he look back, but the smile carried all the answer he needed. Syd returned it.

"It has been too long after all, Dark One."

They both broke into sudden laughter, some understanding passing through their taut gaze, and the tension in the room eased several notches. Others appeared from shadowed alcoves and dropped from perches nearer the ceiling of the cavern—for that was what it was: a huge, hollowed cathedral in the stomach of the mountain.

Now that the boundaries of the encounter had been set by the leaders, Jeanne was able to take a moment to scan the room. It was an impressive sight. Tapestries lined the walls, and upon closer observation, dark passages branched out in all directions. It was a massive, labyrinthine maze of the damned. They swarmed around the small group in the center of the room, forming in smaller groups and watching. Apparently they didn't get many visitors. Not that moved under their own power and had an option of leaving, in any case.

"So," Syd said at last, after less formal greetings had been exchanged, "you chased that dog Santos from the Holy Land, and now you follow the Grail to the stronghold of these knights, knights whose very order is a result of your own machinations. What makes you believe they have found what you seek?"

Montrovant reached beneath his cloak and pulled free the letter. He spoke no word, but handed the paper over to Syd and waited for the other's reaction. It wasn't long in coming.

"Damn him," Syd spat, scanning the letter quickly. "How can he continue to mock us like this?

He is very old," Montrovant replied, "and it would appear that he has the luck of the gods on his side."

"There are no gods," Syd replied, handing the paper back. "If there were they could never stand by for such treachery."

Jeanne was surprised by the violence of Syd's reaction. Kli Kodesh's actions were difficult to understand—insane in some instances—but treachery? What could the old one possibly owe to Syd that would cause such depth of emotion?

Gwendolyn had moved back to stand more closely by his side.

"He doesn't appear to be very fond of my sire," she whispered.

Jeanne nodded in agreement. Apparently Syd had heard her, as well, though she'd kept her voice subdued. He turned to face her then, studying her features intently, then returned his gaze to Montrovant.

"She is not one of ours," he said. "Why is she with you?"

"She was sent to me," Montrovant replied calmly. "The two of us have—a history. It was another message from Kli Kodesh."

"I thought I recognized the scent of that blood," Syd nodded. He was trembling. "Why have you brought her here, Dark One? There can be nothing good between their kind and ours. Nothing. And look at her! It is his blood. She is Nosferatu, and yet she shows only small sign of the twisting, of the scarring. She is not for you."

"There is more between us than you understand," Montrovant replied quickly. "She travels under my protection."

"None could protect any of you if it were not my will," Syd said softly. "You will walk from these halls with my blessing, or not at all. It would serve you well to keep that in mind."

"I am well aware of the situation," Montrovant replied, still smiling. "I wish that you could have spoken with the ancient one last time I was in his company. He had some interesting things to say about Eugenio—things that might change your opinion of what we all have in common."

Syd moved so quickly that Jeanne saw only a blur. The slender vampire took Montrovant's throat in his grasp and actually began to lift Jeanne's sire from the ground before it became clear that he had not been quite as quick as he'd thought. Montrovant's own hand held a dagger poised over Syd's heart.

"You will not speak in that manner of our sire in my presence," Syd said, trembling. It was obvious that he was fighting the urge to squeeze Montrovant with all his strength and take his chances. "I will speak at any time and any place in the manner that I wish," Montrovant grated, forcing the words past Syd's grip on his throat and pushing the blade forward, backing Syd away.

Jeanne moved closer, and Gwendolyn followed, but Montrovant waved them back. "You have invited us into your safe-haven," he continued. "You have offered me information, and for that I thank you. Do not mar that by foolish pride. Eugenio is no saint, and you yourself would not even know the name Kli Kodesh if you'd not heard him speak it first."

"I do not care for the truth," Syd spat. "I care for family. That was not such an issue when you and I were young. I tell you again, these are different times."

"Different times have the same history, my friend," Montrovant replied, easing back from the other's grip and lowering his blade. "There is no better teacher than your past."

"You will find Philip's army on the road," Syd said softly. "They left to lay siege to de Molay several days ago. Many of the knights have given themselves up, renouncing their vows and returning to the safety of the Church. I doubt their sincerity, truly, but the renouncement of the order is all that is asked of them. Those in the temple are not so easily swayed. Another warning. They are not your knights. De Payen was their founder, but others joined him after you departed, and not all of them were exactly as they seemed."

"What do you mean?" Montrovant asked, suddenly serious.

"There are rumors of three knights who came to the temple after you departed, knights with particular abilities. Magi, they called themselves, and if the stories are true they had abilities that would have come too close to those of your friend Santos for my taste. You will find a different sort of order upon your return. I don't want you to ride in unaware."

"Suddenly you seem very concerned with my welfare," Montrovant grinned. "I will have to learn what I can from those on the road, then, and change my approach appropriately. At the very least I will discard the notion of riding up in full Templar regalia."

"That would make for an interesting battle, if nothing else," Syd replied, smiling back at him thinly. "No doubt Philip would be amused to find something outside the walls of the keep to vent his anger on."

"No doubt." Montrovant began to pace. "Now we have to find our way out of this place safely—get our things and get back on the road without another incident with Bastian. If I'd known things were so bad here, I'd never have entered his inn."

"Your things will be fine if you make it back to them," Syd said softly. "The one rule that Bastian has created which even he abides by carefully is the neutrality of the inn. It is a way station, nothing more. If you make it there, and you intend to leave, you will be fine. I would not take him up on those quarters, if I were you. That is another matter altogether. You may stay here until the nightfall."

Montrovant reached out his hand and clasped Syd's. "You won't regret this, my friend," he said. "I will do as I have set out to do, and Eugenio will know that he was right to put his trust in me—as will you."

"We do not put any trust in you, Dark One," Syd said grinning more broadly. "We just hasten you along to get you as far away from us as possible before you bring the world down upon your shoulders.

You will miss out on some very interesting times, then," Montrovant concluded. "I manage to keep things entertaining."

Syd motioned to one of his followers, a dark woman in robes of deep green. Her eyes were deep-set and haunting, and she gestured for Montrovant, Gwendolyn, and Jeanne to follow. Montrovant exchanged a few more words with Syd, his voice lowered so that only the two of them knew what he said, then released the other's hand and followed the woman's lead.

Jeanne looked hesitantly over at Gwendolyn, who watched
Montrovant intently. She didn't hesitate to follow, and Jeanne
took up the rear once more, his mind reeling with all he'd
seen and heard. New knights? Magi? Not words normally
bandied about in casual conversation. What were they letting
themselves in for, and how much did Kli Kodesh have to do
with it? He was half-tempted to ask Gwendolyn, but he knew
that she wouldn't answer...not truthfully. No more than he
could betray Montrovant.

They wound through shadowy passageways until they
came to a series of doorways opening off of the main corridor.
The woman opened a door and beckoned for them to enter.
They walked into a suite of two rooms. There was no light.
Along one wall was a table with four crude chairs. There were,
of course, no windows. A single cot hung from the wall by
chains.

Jeanne moved to the doorway leading to the second
chamber. It was more lavish. There was a single sleeping
surface in the center, large enough for a group if the need arose.
There were books lining the walls, their spines showing from
the shelves. There were musical instruments, covered in the
dust of long disuse.

"We have other visitors occasionally," the woman spoke
for the first time. "This was the quarters of a traveling band of
Damned musicians...a flame-haired woman and her followers.
I hope you will find it comfortable."

"It will be perfect," Montrovant assured her. She watched
him a moment longer, sizing him up, then spun on her heel
and departed, leaving the three of them alone for the first time
since they'd burst into the alley behind the Weeping Violet.

"You trust him?" Jeanne spoke up quickly.

Montrovant looked at him for a long moment as though he
might get angry, then grinned fiercely. "Of course not. We'll be
safe enough for the moment, though. He has nothing to gain by
harming us, and he does owe us one for the help with Bastian."

"Well," Gwendolyn chimed in, "I guess we'll be here for the
night—any thoughts on who will rest where?" She had moved
a step closer to Montrovant, putting a hand possessively on his

shoulder and letting her gaze slide to the large bed in the center of the second room.

"I have it all worked out," Montrovant replied.

As Jeanne felt the sluggish hold of the sun seeping down through the earth to cloud his thoughts, he sensed Montrovant on the surface beside him. From the other room he imagined he could feel Gwendolyn fuming. Entertaining. Always.

NINE

As it turned out, Syd lived up to his word. When the sun began to set, the same dark-clad woman appeared at their door, and though they were ready for whatever form of treachery might occur, they were led back through the tunnels and deposited in exactly the same place they'd first found Syd.

"I wouldn't linger here long," the woman advised. "Bastian will not take what happened last night lightly."

"Nor do I," Montrovant agreed. "Let's go."

He leaped to the rooftop nearest him and disappeared, leaving Jeanne and Gwendolyn to scramble after him. They had no trouble matching his pace once they recovered, but he'd robbed them of their opportunity to depart in grace. Ahead they heard his deep, throaty chuckle.

Jeanne hadn't asked what their plans were. It had seemed a bit too obvious for that. Get their things and get out without Bastian ending their unlives. Possibly not an easy task, but not complex, either.

He couldn't make out much of their surroundings as they passed—they moved far too swiftly. Montrovant was taking a great chance so early after dark, moving openly with such speed. If mortals saw them there would be an uproar. If Bastian, or even Syd, were to catch wind of it, they would be furious at the risk to their own security. It bothered Montrovant not at all. They slid across the last of the buildings like a shadow and dropped into the alley behind the inn in silence.

Again there was no hesitation. Jeanne would have liked a moment to collect his thoughts, and to ask what they planned to do once inside, but Montrovant was not in any mood for caution.

They entered so quickly that their sudden appearance from the back brought the room to a complete and uncomfortably heavy silence. All eyes turned in their direction, then slowly back to whatever had amused them moments before. All but Bernard's.

"You did not sleep?" he asked softly, polishing the wood of his bar with an old rag. "I sent someone to wake you, but you were nowhere to be found."

"Visiting old friends," Montrovant answered smoothly. "Sorry if it caused you any—inconvenience. We will be leaving tonight. I will pay for the room, of course, though we did not use it."

"Of course," Bernard replied.

"If you could be so kind as to have someone fetch our things," Montrovant continued, "we would be most grateful. I have a sudden aversion to closed-in places. I suppose I've been too long on the road.

That much is certain," Bernard replied, his control nearly cracking. "You know too little of the ways of this world, I think. I will have your things brought in, and you will leave. If you so much as look back over your shoulder, you will leave more than my inn—you will leave the Earth."

Montrovant's smile broadened. "We understand one another well enough, then," he replied. "There is little here to look back to, and I for one will be happy to be back on the road."

They glared at one another for a few more moments, but neither could think of anything more to say. Bernard broke the stare first, motioning for one of the girls waiting tables to come closer. He sent her for their supplies and baggage, then turned away without a further word. Jeanne watched him carefully, but with the exception of the tension in the innkeeper's muscles, there was no indication that he even remembered Montrovant and his companions were present.

"We will have to watch our backs, I think," Gwendolyn whispered, drawing Jeanne and Montrovant closer. "The girl went for our packs, but two others left as well—Cainites, and with Bastian's stink oozing from them. I sensed them the moment we came in. I doubt it is coincidence they left the moment he sent her out."

"I saw them," Montrovant replied. "Probably just to make certain we leave as promised, but you are right. Nothing can be left to chance now. It would appear that I have a lot to learn about the world I'm about to enter, despite the fact that I have walked its roads for centuries."

"There is nothing constant but change," Jeanne commented dryly. "Here comes our girl now."

They looked up and saw that he was right. The girl had returned, staggering under the weight of all of their possessions. Montrovant took a small pile of coins from his pouch and laid them on the bar without a word. Turning to Jeanne, he nodded in the direction of the girl and they started moving. Bastian never turned once, not even to be certain the correct amount had been paid.

Jeanne grabbed his things, smiling brightly at the girl as he took them in hand. She was trembling, a human girl who sensed herself on the verge of knowledge she did not wish for. Then they were moving again, and Jeanne followed Montrovant toward the door. Gwendolyn was bringing up the rear this time, and she looked even more nervous than Jeanne felt. If this was what city life was like these days, then he wished they'd never left the mountains. If he'd wanted this kind of intrigue he never would have left home for the holy land in the first place.

Their mounts were waiting for them at the stable and they were in the saddle and riding hard for the city gates before the stable-master was fully aware of their presence. There was no sign of movement in the darkness surrounding them, and Jeanne spread his senses as wide and thin as possible, but came up empty. Odd, but it seemed that the city's inhabitants had cleared out to make way for them. Did they sense danger, or had Bernard spread the word?

The silence meant nothing, he knew. Montrovant was the one to watch, the one who would know. The problem was that Montrovant wouldn't tell them until the last moment, because if he gave away what he knew—they would know as well. So they rode on in silence, the three horses side by side, tearing down the road at breakneck speed.

Montrovant rode easily, his form bonded with that of his

mount so closely that their silhouette against the bright light of the moon was that of a single dark entity. Such rhythm and power.

They rounded a corner, and suddenly Jeanne sensed the others. They crouched beside the road in a small copse of shrubs and low-slung trees. Montrovant veered suddenly, riding straight at them, and with a shrug, Jeanne followed. Jeanne's own instincts told him that the men were only there to watch them leave, but who was he to argue with Montrovant's actions?

There was an intense burst of fear from the direction of the shrubs, and two dark forms darted suddenly from the shadows beneath the trees. Montrovant drew his blade and rode in close to the first without allowing his mount to break stride. He swung his arm in a lazy arc, severing the vampire's head from his shoulders cleanly before he had a chance to turn or defend himself.

The other met an equally swift end. Gwendolyn rode him down, not hesitating as the hooves of her mount made contact with the man's heels, then his head. She wheeled and returned, causing her horse to rear and bringing it down solidly on the vampire's back. He lay, twitching and moaning wildly in the mud.

Jeanne leaped from the saddle and drew his own blade. As Gwendolyn backed away, trying to calm her horse, he lashed out and removed the second head. It rolled a few feet away and stopped, dead eyes glaring back at him accusingly.

"Do you think two such as these would have dared to attack us?" Jeanne asked softly. "It would not have been...prudent."

"They were only meant to make certain we left," Montrovant said. "I want to send a message back to Bastian."

"This should serve," Jeanne replied, sheathing his blade and leaping back into his own saddle. "Assuming these were the only ones he sent."

"There are no others." There was no way to tell for certain how Montrovant knew this, but Jeanne shrugged and returned to his mount, swinging into the shadow.

"Remind me to make no travel plans in this area," Jeanne said with a grin. "Somehow I doubt we will be welcome here again."

"Don't forget Syd so easily," Montrovant replied grimly. "I

think we may have given him just the taste of victory he needed to stir him to action. If we were to return, I think we would find a very different city indeed. Syd and I may not agree on many things, but the blood running through those veins is old and strong."

Montrovant turned away, and Jeanne could tell that memories were flashing through his sire's mind. He yearned to share them, to ask the questions that seethed and snatched at his own thoughts, but he knew better than to push. Time was not a commodity they lacked. Montrovant would tell him what he needed to know when he was ready. He always had.

Gwendolyn was not so easily put off.

"How do you know him?" she asked, spurring her mount until she came up beside Montrovant. "I heard you say Eugenio was his sire?"

"Eugenio is very old," Montrovant said, brushing her off brusquely. "I am not the first he Embraced, or the last."

"Perhaps the most difficult, though...?" she persisted.

Montrovant smiled grimly, but he didn't answer.

Gwendolyn finally caught the mood of the moment. They rode on in silence, more slowly, but still at a gallop. Holywell became a dim glow on the horizon, then faded completely from sight.

Montrovant rode on without further comment, and Jeanne fell in behind him. Gwendolyn rode at the Dark One's side for a while, then dropped back with Jeanne. They covered ground steadily but not with particular haste, and it was several hours before dawn when Montrovant pulled over and beckoned for them to follow.

"Shouldn't we get farther away before we stop?" Gwendolyn asked quickly. "You didn't exactly send a friendly message back to Bastian..."

"He won't follow," Montrovant stated, waving his hand in dismissal. "He doesn't have the time to spare for such pursuits now that we've stirred up his own hornet's nest. We have other matters to discuss."

Montrovant slid from the saddle easily and led his mount to a small copse of trees off to one side of the road. At first it seemed only a good place for a moment's rest, but as they drew closer, Jeanne saw that beyond the trees there was an opening into the side of the mountain itself. The trees grew around the opening of the cavern, disguising it from view. "You knew of this place." Jeanne stated the obvious, not really questioning.

"I have been here before," Montrovant agreed. "Our people have traveled these roads for centuries. Do you think they have done it openly, walking in the daylight and waving to the crowds?" Jeanne didn't answer. None was expected.

"You could have mentioned this place," Gwendolyn tossed off with her usual candor. "You may lord it over your progeny all you care to, Dark One, but do not presume so much with me. I am not so much your junior, and my sire is—ancient." Montrovant stiffened and turned. The air in the small clearing dropped several degrees in temperature, and Jeanne cringed inside. Then the tension dissipated, and Montrovant actually laughed. "You make me forget the seriousness of the moment. Come. I have some questions for you, and I think it is time that I got my answers."

They secured their horses carefully outside the cave, tying them off with the best cover available. Jeanne brought up the rear, sending a final questing thought behind them. There was nothing, as Montrovant had said there would be. It just made him feel better to check.

The cavern was deep and evenly cut. It was obvious after a few steps inside that it was not a natural cavern. The walls were too straight, too perfect. There were niches carved in the stone for torches, but Montrovant ignored them, plunging headlong into the gloom.

They moved through a narrow corridor and entered a larger, darker chamber. Montrovant moved toward the center of this, then stopped in front of a series of stone benches.

"I haven't been here," he mused, "since I came this way with Eugenio. I wasn't certain that it would all be intact."

There were signs that they were not the first to use the chamber, but at the same time there was no indication that any earlier inhabitants had been through recently. Dust coated everything with a fine veneer, and the air had a stale, stagnant taste. It reminded Jeanne, not unpleasantly, of a tomb. He searched the shadows. There were small heaps of clothing piled in the corners, the remnants of a couple of fires—which seemed bit out of place—but most of all there was darkness and shadow.

"This is a safe haven, one of the way-stations we set up in the old days. It is a place where the sunlight will never reach us. Did you notice the curves as we came in? They were cut so that the light would be trapped before it reached this chamber. We will be safe here until morning."

"Bastian doesn't know of this place?" Jeanne asked quickly.

"Of course he does," Montrovant answered, gazing at his progeny steadily. "You doubt, then, my telling you that he will not follow?"

There was a moment of silent tension, then Jeanne looked away. "Of course not," he said softly. "I just worry."

"It is your nature," Montrovant agreed. "He will not follow, Jeanne, there is nothing to be gained in it—that is why we have nothing to fear. There will be times in the days to come when we will not be safe, but we are now."

Jeanne nodded, not trusting himself to speak. Gwendolyn never questioned Montrovant's word. She seemed content to unpack her things and pick one of the stone benches for her own. Jeanne suspected that she had known the cavern was there as well. It made him feel isolated and alone. He erased the sensation from his mind.

Turning to Gwendolyn, Montrovant smiled again. "Now, my fine lady, you will tell us a bit more about just what in the name of the seven levels of Hell is going on at de Molay's keep, why your sire wants me there, and we will see if we can form a useful plan." She stared at him defiantly for a long moment, and Jeanne ducked back a step. She might have been talking out of place when she spoke of her own age, and that of Montrovant, or not. Certainly she was older than he, and the energy crackling through the chamber was ancient and potent. Had Montrovant presumed too much this time?

"You will get your answers, Dark One, but not because you order it. I have not been instructed to withhold information from you, and so I shall not. You forget that I am not overly fond of Kli Kodesh, even though he granted me what you denied."

"Of course, the old one will know that, as well," Jeanne noted bleakly.

Gwendolyn glared at him darkly, but did not reply. "There are dark powers at work in the keep of

Jacques de Molay, Montrovant. There are things there that even Kli Kodesh himself cannot control, though he does not fear them."

"I would have thought that the knights would have had their fill of dark powers dealing with Santos and his ilk," Jeanne cut in again.

"Santos?" Gwendolyn spun to face him. "Where do you know that name from?"

Jeanne stared at her, shocked by her sudden outburst, but Montrovant was on his feet and had her by the shoulders, turning her back to face him roughly.

"Where is he?" The words dripped malice and poison. "If you know where that son of a dog has gone, I will have the answer."

"You will have that answer soon enough, in any case," she replied, studying him intently. "He consorts with de Molay as we speak. It is Santos who led the Grand Master down the path that has led to Philip's attack."

Montrovant released her, turning away quickly. "Does he still walk in the robes of a priest, groveling in underground tunnels with his cowled rats?

He lives below, yes," Gwendolyn replied. "But he is no priest. He walks in the shadows. He takes what he wants without asking, and de Molay brings him more. Others have complained, all but a few who are close to de Molay fear what is happening, but none has the courage or strength to challenge.

Now it is too late."

"What do you mean?" Montrovant asked quickly. "It is never too late."

"It is too late for de Molay," Gwendolyn replied, turning away. "He will not let go of his dark dreams. He and Santos have brought Philip's wrath down on the heads of the Templars, and they will bring down the order before they are done. It is all or nothing with that one—I have felt it deep within him. I have fed from him, Dark One." She spun to face him again, moved closer so that their faces were scant inches apart. "I know his heart. He believes that the only way through what is to come is a portal of darkness, and he means to open it."

Montrovant stared at her for long moments before he spoke. He searched her eyes—Jeanne wondered if he might be searching even deeper.

"There was a head," Montrovant said softly. "Have you heard anything about a disembodied head?"

"They worship such an image," Gwendolyn said softly. "They have painted symbols and diagrams of such a thing, and they claim that it will bring them answers. It is said that a head will lead them to the truth."

"He has them as he had his other followers in Jerusalem," Montrovant said. "He will drive them toward the ritual, and they will get answers, but the answers will be to Santos's own questions. He seeks the same things that I seek, and he will stop at nothing to possess them."

"Then we must stop him," Jeanne said.

"You know as well as I how difficult that will be," Montrovant said, turning to face his progeny with a dark, brooding expression painted across his face. "And Kli Kodesh knows as well. Santos is the only being I have faced that I believe might be more ancient. If the treasures I am led to believe are where your sire claims them to be," Montrovant turned back to Gwendolyn, "then he has arranged for another round of entertainment. They are right under Santos's nose."

Montrovant grew silent then, and Jeanne took the moment to study him. This was the moment they'd been waiting for since they'd left the Holy Land behind, but certainly not the situation they'd dreamed of. Santos and the Knights Templar were behind them, or so they'd thought. Now both loomed on their horizon, the one a faded memory, the other a recurring nightmare. So many miles, so many years, all of it to come full circle and face the same challenge they'd faced at the beginning. At least it had been the beginning for Jeanne.

Montrovant's memories were deeper. They carried

generations and decades beyond Jeanne's earliest recollection, and the bits and pieces he'd heard over the years had only made a sketchy backdrop against which to paint the coming encounter. "We will be prepared this time," Montrovant said at last. "I have no power that can withstand Santos if he reaches his goal, but we have some time left to us, and we have Philip. The army on the horizon will distract de Molay. His followers will be in a panic. He will have to expend more energy than he wants to keep them in check. Santos will suck at his soul, but there is only so much that he can do to hurry things. He races against Philip, and now against us as well."

"At least we will have surprise on our side," Jeanne said, not really believing his own words.

Montrovant grinned at him. "You think he won't know we are there? How did we find out he was up to his old tricks?" He spun quickly to Gwendolyn. "Your sire will be certain to drop some hints, I'm afraid. It is all a game to him—everything is a game."

"He has no contact with Santos," Gwendolyn retorted hotly. "He would not."

"You have no idea from whence you come," Montrovant said, cutting her off. His voice had dropped an octave, and there was an odd energy in the air. Jeanne felt himself removed from it, but it crackled around him.

"You trust no one," Gwendolyn accused.

"You will not exist as long as I if you do not learn that lesson," the Dark One replied. "Kli Kodesh may be amused by you now, but he is not easily entertained, nor for long. He will sell us all out for a midnight show. We must plan with him in mind as well. If we are to get into de Molay's keep, get what I seek, and get out without being destroyed, then we will have to make this the best effort of our second lives. Are you prepared for that?"

He swept his gaze from Jeanne to Gwendolyn, back to Jeanne. Gwendolyn wasn't really included, but there was the question hanging in the air. When the time came, could they count on her? Would she be with them, or would Kli Kodesh yank her by the hidden, subtle ties that bound her, and cause her to betray them?

"The most important thing," Montrovant went on, "is that we get to de Molay as quickly as possible. We may have to leave our mounts behind. I don't want to be riding down some dusty country road when Philip takes the keep and hands over the treasure to the Church, or to his own coffers."

"We might be spotted," Jeanne pointed out. "We might die any number of horrible deaths, or be staked by mindless mortal fools, or burn in the light of the sun," Montrovant countered, eyes blazing. "But if we cower in fear in the face of challenge, we might as well be dust."

No one spoke after that. They moved among the cots, each of them choosing a place to rest, and they lay back to await the encroaching weight of the sun's light. Montrovant had made their choices, and neither of them had disagreed. When darkness fell, they would fly, fast and free. Though Montrovant had listed the walls that stood between them and their goals, the tone of his voice had fired Jeanne's mind. It was time to see what fate would pit against them. As comfortable as he'd been on the road, it could never replace the red mask he wore to battle. The darkness held only questions, but the answers hovered on the periphery of his mind. He met unconsciousness with a smile.

TEN

Mordecai watched the sun set from the parapet of his keep. Despite the years since Kli Kodesh had gifted him with blood that lessened the pain brought on by the light of day, he still could not get over the wonder of such a simple thing—to watch a sunset. He wasn't comfortable in bright sunlight, but in those quiet hours between day and night, he felt as though he ruled the world. Free of death, and less inhibited by the restrictions of his kind. Free of everything save responsibility, and that responsibility gave him a purpose to drive him—another gift.

The others rarely joined him for his evening vigil. They were a quiet bunch, loyal and true, but not much in the way of imagination. When Mordecai and his old brood had Embraced them, they had been on their way to the Holy Land to lend their lives to God. Now they did that same thing, after a fashion, though the lives they would have given were long behind them.

"It is nearly time to go," a voice floated to him through the growing shadows. Gustav stood a few feet inside the doorway.

Mordecai nodded. "In a moment. The night is just now upon us, and we haven't so far to travel." Mordecai stood at the wall, the wind whipping at the wispy remnants of his hair. His skin was so pale that it seemed translucent, glowing faintly from within. His disfigured face, long beak of a nose and ears tapering to sharp points somehow failed to mar the austere beauty of his features. He was Nosferatu, but he was more, as well. He was of the blood of Kli Kodesh.

He spun from the wall and entered the tower. The steep stairs wound away below him and he followed their mesmerizing spiral toward the lower levels. He knew Gustav would have the others ready in the stable. They would be mounted, awaiting his word.

At times like these, Mordecai wished more than anything in the world for another to talk with, one who knew the places and times he'd known, one who would look upon him as an equal. That was, after all, the cost of his gift. He could not truly go among men, though he walked nearer to the light, earlier and later than almost any other Cainite he'd encountered. He could not go among his own kind, either. The blood in his veins was too valuable, too important. Mordecai hadn't fed on human blood since he'd left the Holy Land, and the hunger, behind him.

He entered the stable and strode directly to his horse. Gustav stood beside the animal, one hand holding the reins, the other soothing the beast as he spoke to it in hushed tones. Mordecai took the reins and levered himself into the saddle in one smooth, quick motion. Gustav was mounted before Mordecai could wheel his snorting stallion. Without a word, they moved out.

The doors to the stable closed behind them as they passed through the portal and into the night. Not all of his followers would join them on the road: the tower had to be guarded. That which had been entrusted to them had been spread across the land in small pockets, but not all of it had passed from their hands. Certain treasures, certain secrets—these mortals were not yet ready to know, if ever they would be. These had to be kept safe.

"Did the master tell you what it is we seek?" Gustav asked, pulling his mount alongside Mordecai's. "It must be something powerful indeed if he wants us so directly involved."

Mordecai didn't answer immediately. Then, "I know only that the Templars have gathered an abundance of relics and treasure into their coffers over the years. Among that hoard there were bound to be things better left hidden. Santos has come to them."

Gustav's eyes sparkled. "Santos? You have spoken to us of that one, but I never expected to see him alive and sniffing around our business again."

"The guardian is not so easily driven away," Mordecai

replied. "He is ancient, and he can sense objects of power more readily than you can trace the lines across the palm of your hand. His presence verifies what the master has told me. We must be there before Philip puts the castle to the torch, and we must find a way to get in and out with whatever they have found."

Gustav didn't reply, but Mordecai sensed the questions hanging between them. It was one thing to guard secrets carefully in a tower, tucked away from the sight and intrusion of the world. It was quite another to go wandering into the midst of a war, sneak into a heavily guarded keep and make off with the thing those inside coveted most. Even ignoring all of that, there was Santos to consider, and he alone would make it a risky endeavor.

Mordecai was thankful for the silence. He had no answers to offer, and he preferred not to dwell on the impossibility of what was to come. The Master would not summon them if there were no hope, or plan. They would just have to wait until the time came when that plan could be revealed.

They wore heavy robes with deep cowls to hide their ravaged features, and the wind from their horses' speed whipped the cloth back behind them like huge wings. The road to their tower was not often traveled, and time was wasted as their mounts worked across the rough footing, but none would see them pass. No one came near the tower. Dark legends surrounded the forest skirting those stone walls, legends that had been old when Mordecai first led them down that road with their wagon dragging behind them and the dust of Jerusalem on their sandals.

Kli Kodesh had sent him to the tower. Kli Kodesh knew the legends—for all Mordecai knew, the ancient was the cause of the legends. Whoever or whatever was behind them, they were powerful. No more than a dozen travelers had made their way to those gates since Mordecai first strode through them, and none of these had returned. It is not difficult for the Damned to provide substance to legends. In fact, those moments had proven immensely entertaining. Mordecai was beginning to understand the ancient's love of entertainment.

The tower disappeared behind them, and the road stretched ahead. Miles and miles to travel, hours to think and wonder, plan and pray. Odd, that last, but after so many years with Gustav and the others, Mordecai wasn't beyond the notion that someone might be listening—even to the Damned.

ELEVEN

Jacques woke with his head throbbing madly and his eyes half-focused into blinding, invasive light. He wrenched to the side, burying his face in the sheets, but the damage was done. Pain lanced through his brain and dragged him back to consciousness. With a groan he rolled over and sat up, letting his head fall into his hands.

The light told him he'd slept too long again. The cries of vendors and steady clip! clop! of horses' hooves were signs that the rest of the inhabitants of the keep had met the new day when it was truly that. He wondered for a moment what time it was, just as quickly forgot the question. Not important. What was important was to stop the pounding in his head and to find Santos. There was something about the daylight hours that diminished the dread the smaller man could instill. Now was the time to confront him, and for Jacques to find his answers. There was a quick knock on his door. The servants must have heard him stirring. He imagined them standing there, huddled against the door, waiting for the moment he would finally rise and require their services. He ran his hands quickly back through his hair and sat up straighter. "Yes?"

"We have food, your lordship. Food and wine…

Bring me water in place of the wine," he growled, regretting the sound as it vibrated through his skull. "I will take the food now."

The door opened and a young girl, no more than fifteen years behind her, scurried into the room with a platter in her hand. Hushed voices echoed in the passageway, and the retreating footsteps of the others as they rushed off after the water. Gritting his teeth against the pain, Jacques scowled at the girl and nodded curtly in dismissal. She launched herself back through the opening as if her dress were on fire, and he almost managed a smile. Louis. As soon as he thought of his friend, the memories seeped back, dim candle-light flickering this way and that, shadows and chanted words in languages spoken in tones that reverberated in some strange, unnatural way. Following Santos in the circle, shuffling, then dancing, leaping and throwing themselves about in a frenzy of dark emotion and anticipated power. Louis had shared those moments, and yet he didn't quite grasp what Jacques knew deep within his heart. Santos was the key.

There was nothing concrete that he could lay a finger on, but he knew he was right. With Philip only days away on the road, leading an army with the might and righteousness of the Church behind it, nothing short of a miracle could save them. There were miracles both dark and light, and Jacques had felt curiously alienated from things that leaned toward God and daylight since he'd begun his studies.

Not all of that learning had come from Santos. There were secrets that had been passed down through generations of Templars, powers granted to those with the sight and spiritual power to recognize and use them. These were his by right of birth and office. He was Grand Master of the Knights of the Temple, and that was no small thing. Neither was it enough to stop Philip.

The faithful gathered around him now. Many of them had never been near the central keep. There were those who still lived and died by the creed—no possessions, no purpose but to serve the temple, the Church, and their lord. There were others whom Jacques doubted had ever stood within the walls of any temple for fear of burning to ashes on the spot. The order had grown out of all proportion, and far beyond his complete control. Like all empires do eventually, it was failing. The only thing that had kept Jacques and his followers on their feet for this long was the fact that half the rulers in Europe owed them money.

Louis was among those who would rather fight and die than

fall into the debt of one such as Santos. Louis had the power, as Jacques himself, but with Louis it was more a question of honor. Jacques wanted knowledge to bring himself to a higher level, to find answers for himself. Louis wanted the answers for the order. It was a difference of opinion that had slowly driven them apart since Santos had arrived at their door, and now it was driving them all to destruction.

Unless he was right.

He staggered to his feet and wolfed down the fruit, leaning heavily on the table and closing his eyes against the stabbing pain in his head. The girl returned moments later with a pitcher of water and poured him a goblet. He took it from her trembling hand, smiling again, and upended the glass over his head.

"My Lord..." she backed away a step, nearly dropping the pitcher to the stone floor, and he grinned at her, the water pouring from his hair and dribbling down his chin.

"Much better," he said. Then he laughed. "Pour me another."

With a timid smile in return, the girl did as he asked, and once more he tossed it down over his head, feeling the chill as it shocked him from his lethargy. He set the goblet on the table and ran his fingers back through the long, damp tangles of his hair.

"Do you want me to fetch a comb, Lord?" the girl asked.

"A comb?" he stared at her dumbly for a moment, then grinned. "Oh, I don't think that will be necessary," he answered her. "I have much to do." He reached for the water again, pouring a third goblet full, and she stepped back away from him, eyes wide with wonderment and confusion.

Jacques threw back his head and roared with laughter. Then he turned the cup up and drained it, letting the cool water flow down his throat and wash away the sensation of swallowing sand that the wine had left him with. He slammed the goblet onto the table and turned away, looking for his sword. He found it leaning against the table beside his bed and grabbed it, belting it in place. At least he'd not been too drunk to take care of his weapons.

The girl scampered back into the hall as he turned, and Jacques allowed himself to drop his head into the palm of one hand a final time to concentrate on ignoring the pain. He might fool the servants and save himself a bit of unnecessary scandal, but he couldn't fool the pain away.

With a final regretful glance at his bed, he turned toward the door and strode purposefully into the hall. One of the servants, a boy of about sixteen, still stood waiting in case he needed anything.

"Go and find Louis de Chaunvier," he ordered tersely. "Tell him that I have gone below, and that I require his company."

The boy nodded, dropping his eyes to the floor. Jacques waited, and the boy bolted suddenly like a frightened deer. Jacques turned away and continued toward the stairs. He looked neither right nor left, nor did he scan the passage behind him to be certain that the boy was doing as he'd asked. He was already fixated on what lay ahead and below, and there was no room for mundane concerns between the throbbing bursts of pain that were his blood pounding through his temples.

Santos heard footsteps approaching. He knew it would be de Molay. Only one of his own would dare to come to him at such an hour—alone. He smiled into the shadows. Time was slipping away from them, and it was good that the Templar leader was growing impatient. It would make the next few days' events go more smoothly. Santos had to finish what he'd begun, and it would have to happen before Philip's arrival. In his present state, de Molay would be malleable, open to more radical suggestions than he might otherwise have been.

Behind him, lost in the shadows of the chamber he'd claimed as his own, sat a short wooden table. Atop that table rested the head, silent and staring—watching his every move with comprehension beyond time and physical dimensions. Waiting with all the answers he needed and sought, waiting for the ritual. Only the perfect blend of sound and scent, rhythm and meter could invoke that power. It had been a long time since he'd had the resources at his disposal, and that last time had ended in disaster.

A mortal. A half-Damned mortal had walked into his chambers and prevented him from completing his ritual. He'd sought only a name. He'd not been careful, letting arrogance rule his actions, and he'd failed. That mortal had cost him everything, and he meant to restore all that had been stripped from him. One power still in his possession could grant him that, and it stared blankly at him with the wisdom of the universe captured behind blind eyes and a silent tongue.

A knock on the door startled Santos back to the moment, and he pulled the door wide. De Molay stood just outside, glaring at him. The lack of sleep and wealth of wine that had been the Templar leader's night shone forth from the overly bright glitter in his eyes and the slight slump of his shoulders, despite the tension with which he held himself.

"Enter," Santos said, beckoning Jacques closer. "I have been expecting you."

"None of your dark lies today, Santos," Jacques grated, stepping quickly into the room. "We have listened to you, done as you asked, learned—but too slowly. Philip marches on the castle not a week away from our gates. Give me an answer, a way through this."

"All the answers you require reside within you," Santos replied, turning away. He measured his steps, knowing that de Molay's anger would only be fueled by such a cryptic response.

"You mock me," Jacques said softly. "You mock me, and you laugh behind my back, and it will end. You will tell me the secrets I need to know to save my order, my holdings and my life, or I swear you will regret it for the rest of your unnatural existence."

Santos spun, eyes blazing, and strode toward de Molay defiantly. "You would do well to watch the tone of your voice," he said softly. "You will also do well to remember what you have seen, and with whom. You are dust beneath my feet, Jacques—a moment's diversion in years beyond your comprehension. I don't need you, but you need me. Perhaps this has slipped your mind?"

He was close now, so close that he could feel the slight tremor that rippled through de Molay's frame. Close enough to see the light of fear, coupled with the madness of total despair, that kept the man standing before him, defiant despite the consequences.

"You will share what you know with me," de Molay continued with a great effort, "or I will tell them all who and what you are. I will admit to every dark thing we've done or contemplated, and I will see to it that they drag you out into the sunlight you seem to hate and stake you to burn."

Santos stopped short. No one had spoken to him in such a manner for centuries. Even Kli Kodesh, that fool of an ancient, who had stripped him of that which he'd been charged to safeguard and spirited it off into the night, had not been so bold. The instant temptation to kill de Molay and just walk away was nearly overpowering. Nearly. He lowered his eyes and concentrated, then he spoke.

"I will show you a thing you have not expected," he said at last. "I will show you the answer to your problems, and mine, and we will find those answers together. All of our training thus far has been leading you toward the completion of the required ritual. We are as ready now as we will ever be, and if we don't act, we will be destroyed."

"Show me," Jacques said softly. "Show me this answer. I knew that you possessed it, and yet I doubted. Louis thinks me a fool for listening to you at all."

"Your friend de Chaunvier is not a visionary," Santos said, his voice suddenly soothing and sibilant at once. "He lacks your vision, and he lacks your power. You will be remembered as a great man, Jacques de Molay."

As he spoke, Santos ushered his guest toward the back of the room. As they came to a stop facing the table, de Molay stopped short, his face awash in confusion.

"This is a joke? You have brought me here to show me a head that has been sliced from some poor fool's body, and you offer it to me as an answer to an army at my doorstep?"

De Molay's hand was on the hilt of his sword in an instant, but somehow Santos was at his side, pressing down on that hand and holding it in place, not allowing the blade to free the scabbard.

"You will listen to me, you fool," Santos hissed, "and you will not interrupt me again. You have done nothing to deserve the answers I will give you. You have corrupted a once-great order and it crumbles around your ears. Your only value is that I cannot perform this ritual alone. You will be grateful, and you will bow down before me," Santos had turned so that the full impact of his eyes washed over de Molay's suddenly retreating form, "and you will do as I instruct. You will do this, or you will die. Do you doubt me?"

De Molay stood still for an instant, and Santos was forced, grudgingly, to admire the man's courage. He didn't answer at once, weighing the probabilities on both sides—thinking it through. Lesser men had withered beneath his glare. Weaker men had fallen at his feet and begged for their miserable lives.

"I will do as you ask," de Molay said at last. "I will help you to find your answers, and mine. I will bring the others, and we will drive Philip back to his palace. All these things I will do, but know this: I fall at no man's feet. Suggest that again, and we will see if your power is a match for cold steel. I would rather die here, in the shadows and deceiving my followers, than submit to such dishonor."

Santos met de Molay's gaze for a moment longer, then nodded slightly. What he'd said earlier had been only partially true. While he could continue his existence indefinitely despite what de Molay might do, his immediate needs included the knight and his followers in a very direct manner. They were at somewhat of a standoff, and for some odd reason it was refreshing not to be immediately looked upon as superior.

"The head is more powerful than you could imagine," he said at last. "You see an amputated bit of some long-dead body, but you see only the surface. The head has not known a body for centuries, and yet it is preserved as well as yours or mine. The eyes are blind, the mouth silent, but this is not always the case. The mind within? I'm not even certain that it is a mind, or that it is embodied in the head itself, but it knows all, and it will talk. We must bring it to life, you and I, and we must do it now, before we are overrun."

"I am glad that you begin to understand this as a possibility," de Molay said softly. "There are a great number of men, women and children in the keep above our heads. They may not know of you, or care what you do, but they depend on me for their very survival. I do not intend to let that faith be wasted on me. I want to see them through this."

"I will not promise you foolishly that I know we will make it through what is to come," Santos replied. "I do know that if there is a way—if there is a bit of truth that can shift things in your favor, or even turn the tide and calm Philip, the head will know."

Jacques nodded. He'd heard enough of what he needed to hear to bolster his failing confidence, and already the implications of what Santos had revealed to him were beginning to sink in. He turned toward the head and gazed at the closed lids of its cold, dead eyes. Nothing. He sensed nothing of the power Santos hinted at, and yet he knew that it was true. There was something itching at him from just beneath the surface—something that would not be ignored, like a voice whispering from just far enough away that the words could not be made out clearly.

"I will bring the others as soon as the light begins to fail," he said at last. "Tonight must be the night."

"If we are not ready," Santos cautioned, "if we go into this unprepared, we may perish to the man.

If we do not, we will surely do so," de Molay countered. "My scouts place Philip three days from here. I will give you two of those to finish our preparations. We will meet again tonight."

Santos nodded, and de Molay turned away, heading directly for the stairs that would lead him back to the upper levels—to his people—his knights. He had neglected them for too long, and it was time for answers, whatever they might be. He had been dwelling for too long in a world of doubts and questions. Jacques felt Santos's eyes burning into his back as he walked away, but he wouldn't give the man the satisfaction of turning back. Let him gloat. He would have his moment, and if he provided everything he claimed that he could, perhaps de Molay would not kill him for suggesting he bow down beneath his own keep. The order was not without those of power, and though that power was of little use to him in his present situation, it might prove more difficult to ignore than Santos believed. Jacques did not lack power, he lacked the knowledge that might make that power come to his aid. As he stepped onto the main floor of the keep, Jacques' first thoughts were of Louis. The Templar leader needed his friend to support him in what was to come more than any other. They had been through life and love together, and Jacques could think of no other he might turn to. He needed the other man's earthy, well-grounded common sense for a fresh perspective.

Besides, the two of them would be able to reach the others twice as quickly. There was no time to waste if they were to spread the word as widely and discreetly as necessary. There could be no surprises. They would need every moment of time, and every ounce of concentration to memorize the chants and the steps of the dance. The two days seemed like a matter of short hours as he contemplated the cost of failure.

He rounded a corner, and ahead he saw Louis's tall form towering over another man in one of the small interior gardens. Jacques walked more rapidly. A greeting was on his lips when he bit it back. Louis's words floated across the scant yards that separated them—words Jacques was never meant to hear.

"You will not speak of Jacques de Molay in such a manner while I walk these halls," Louis said heatedly. "You have no idea the pressure that presses down upon him."

"I have no idea?" the man fairly whined. "Philip is on the road to put us all to the flame, and you tell me I have no idea of the pressure? We all know the pressure, and what I want to know is just what the hell you, and your precious Jacques, plan to do about it."

Louis's face reddened, and he slammed his fist backhanded across the man's face, sending him sprawling. Jacques stood still for a moment, stunned, then moved forward again more rapidly. Louis was advancing, towering over his fallen adversary with storm-clouds shifting across his brow.

"Louis," de Molay called out. "Louis, wait."

His friend looked up, startled, and backed off a half-step, though it was obvious from his expression and the set of his shoulders that he did not wish to be distracted.

"Jacques," he said softly, "I…"

"I know, old friend, I know," Jacques said quickly. "It is not the way to our goal. You know this. Don't let the frustration drive you to actions that do not become you."

"This from you?" Louis replied suddenly, and with venom. "Why don't you go cower in your shadows and prove them all right, then."

Jacques stopped for a long moment, fighting to control his temper. He knew there was a measure of truth in Louis's words, but he was not accustomed to being confronted by his own men —particularly not with others present to carry the word of it to his followers.

Turning to the man Louis had backhanded, who was just rising from the ground, one hand clamped across his rapidly swelling jaw, Jacques forced a thin smile. "I would suggest that you find another place to offer your opinions," he said softly.

The man was going to speak—Jacques felt it—then he stopped. Something in the eyes he faced, or the feel of Jacques's eyes on his own—or the fear of Louis—stopped him. He nodded quickly and turned away, scurrying out of the garden and returning to the depths of the keep.

"He will say nothing good of this," Louis growled. "We can't afford more rumors of our weakness.

Let him talk," Jacques replied quickly. "We have more important things to discuss."

He moved closer to remove the likelihood of anyone overhearing what he said. "I have seen Santos," he began. Though Louis frowned at the mention of their dark mentor's name, he kept his silence. Jacques plowed onward. He told Louis of the head, and he told him of the words that had been exchanged that morning. Nothing in his friend's countenance suggested that he approved, but he did not interrupt, and it was a long time after Jacques grew silent before he spoke.

"We have opened Pandora's Box, my friend," Louis said at last. "We have no choice but to see this through, or to stand here and wait for our deaths. I have to confess that I'm tempted to wait—but my heart tells me we must try. Whatever the cost to our souls, whatever the weaknesses that Santos will exploit, we have to do what we can."

"Then you will help me gather the others?"

Louis stared into his eyes, searching for something that he obviously found.

"I will help you," he said. "How could I not?" The two of them turned back toward the keep, separating at the door. It would be another sleepless night, but what else remained to them? Nothing. They didn't look back at one another as they parted, but both men had the nagging sensation of laughter from beneath their feet.

TWELVE

Ferdinand hurried his steps, moving toward the chapel with his head lowered and his ears burning, as though the Devil had caught him at something and was following on his heels. He'd been outside the chambers of Louis de Chaunvier, and he'd overheard the heated exchange that had gone on within. Before de Molay could exit the room, he'd turned and run, fearful of being caught. It was not odd for him to be waiting outside in case something was needed. He knew it was a needless fear—none would suspect a poor servant of treachery. Not unless the fool didn't have the good sense not to run. Though his mind cried out for him to slow down and be cautious, he couldn't force his body to comply. He was long gone from de Chaunvier's chamber door, but his heart still trip-hammered in his chest, and his legs felt weak. He feared that if he stopped running, he would stumble, or fall, and that would call more attention to him than his headlong flight. The doors to the keep's chapel were open wide, as always, and he slipped inside, taking a moment to glance around and be certain that none had seen him enter. It wouldn't do to draw punishment for shirking his duties—he needed his freedom to carry out Father Kodesh's orders. Now more than ever he knew it would be imperative that there be no slip-ups.

There were no others in the small chapel. He slipped between the pews and around the altar, passing through a ray of scarlet and green light that filtered in from a stained-glass window above. His eyes were drawn inexorably upward, and he found himself staring into the accusing eyes of the Savior. That deep, sorrowful gaze traced his footsteps, pinned him to the stone floor like an insect on the tip of a dagger, trapped against a table top. He dragged his gaze back to the shadows beyond the altar and plunged through the doorway.

"Why have you come?" Father Kodesh asked immediately. "It is a bad time—a dangerous time—for you to be here."

"I have news of Santos," Ferdinand gasped, pausing finally to catch his labored breath. "I heard de Molay and de Chaunvier discussing him. They mean to push things ahead, to attempt whatever it is that Santos wants them to do soon."

"How soon?"

"They didn't say, exactly, but de Molay mentioned that Philip couldn't be more than three days away. He also said that he meant for this—thing—to happen before then."

"That is not such a surprise," Kli Kodesh frowned. "When else would they attempt it? I don't think Philip or his priests are going to want to join them."

"There is more," Ferdinand whispered urgently. "Santos showed him a head—some kind of disembodied thing. He told de Molay of its powers, and now our lord is more determined than ever that this is the way to save the keep. He is a man possessed, and somehow it rubbed off on de Chaunvier. They will gather again tonight."

Father Kodesh stood very still for a moment, lost in thought. If what Ferdinand said was true, then perhaps there was more danger involved than he'd imagined. He hadn't thought Santos capable of teaching so many followers so many intricate rituals in such a short time. He'd forgotten that there were adepts of other sorts among the Templars

...such a ritual was not beyond their scope. If the head were animated none would be beyond its power, not even Kli Kodesh himself. He had no fear of dying, but there were fates worse than death, even worse than a second death, and Santos would not hesitate to force them upon him.

"You have done well to tell me this," he said at last, "but you must go now. You cannot be seen here, and I have things to accomplish before the light fails."

Ferdinand nodded, turning slowly away. Then he stopped, glancing fearfully over his shoulder, "What is this thing Santos possesses, Father? What is it that is powerful enough to ward off an army?

It is not," Father Kodesh replied with a frown. "De Molay believes that it is, I think, but Santos knows better. The head is an oracle—it can provide information impossible to acquire by any other method—names, secrets. If Santos was to ask it for my true name, even I would be in peril. His only thought is of his treasures, his lost pride—we must be the ones to watch the larger impact of all of this. De Molay and his Templars are doomed—make no mistake that Philip will come, and the most that the head can do is to tell them how a few might escape, or how they might best prepare to die.

Santos has made fools of them all."

"Why didn't you tell them?" Ferdinand whispered, fearing his impertinent question would prove his last. To his surprise, Father Kodesh did not seem angry. There was an odd twinkle in his eye as he answered.

"It is more entertaining this way, don't you think?"

Ferdinand had no answer, so he turned away, ears burning and heart still slamming wildly in his chest. Entertaining? he thought. It was horrible.

As he was leaving the chapel, he heard Father Kodesh's voice float after him, and he hesitated.

"Santos can sense my presence, Ferdinand...but he is not yet certain where I am...they keep him isolated in the levels below. Find one who will be near to Santos, and mention my name. That is all that it will take. Just tell them to let Santos know that Father Kodesh sends his greetings."

Shuddering, Ferdinand left the chapel hurriedly, making the effort to slow his steps to a more normal speed. He knew he had to get to the kitchen before he was missed, but his mind was awhirl with so many questions and images that he could barely draw a normal breath. And who was he to tell? He certainly couldn't walk off to de Molay, or de Chaunvier, and confront them with his "message." If they suspected that Father Kodesh had any information on Santos, they'd confront him in a heartbeat, priest or not.

He stumbled around a corner, nearly crashing headlong

into a tall, thin man he vaguely recognized as a visiting cousin of de Molay's. The boy was near Ferdinand's own age, but he held himself with the haughty, aloof manner of a noble. He sneered down at Ferdinand, his hand drawn back as if to strike him for his clumsiness.

"You will pay more attention," the boy sniffed at last, holding his hand in check. "You nearly knocked me into this wall!"

"I am sorry, lord," Ferdinand said, his voice quavering and his mind working furiously. "I...I have an important message from the priest, but I do not know how to deliver it—I was in a hurry to seek assistance."

"Who is your message for?" the boy asked, drawing himself up imperially. "I'm certain I will know them, and I can pass it on for you."

"Santos. All he said was to give the message to Santos."

The boy's features grew pale, but to give him the credit due, he did not flinch. Instead he squared his shoulders and stared at Ferdinand carefully.

"How do you know of Santos?" he asked. "What have you heard?"

"I have heard nothing," Ferdinand replied carefully, "but I have a message for this Santos, if he is to be found."

"Tell me the message," the boy replied. "I will see him this very night, and I will be certain to pass on what you tell me."

Ferdinand hesitated, as though deciding whether or not he could trust the boy. He waited just long enough for his new "friend" to show signs of impatience, then he nodded, drawing himself up close to the wall and looking about furtively to be certain no one else would overhear.

"He said," Ferdinand whispered, "to tell Santos that Father Kodesh was here. Nothing more than that. He claims to have known this Santos for a very long time—he said nothing further would be necessary."

"Kodesh?" the boy repeated dubiously. Ferdinand nodded.

"Well, I will pass the message along, but to tell you the truth," and now it was the boy's turn to look about carefully before speaking, "from what I've seen, the last person Santos will ever seek out purposely is a priest."

Ferdinand would have loved to have asked questions, and he thought he might actually have gotten some answers, but just then Jacques de Molay rounded the corner, and the boy he was talking to snapped to attention as if drawn by strings. Ferdinand bowed his head and pressed against the stone of the wall, trying to make himself as inconspicuous as possible.

"You there," de Molay called out. "Boy." Ferdinand looked up.

"Yes, you. I want you to go to the kitchen and fetch a good jug of wine. I will be meeting in my chambers with Louis de Chaunvier, and we will need something to soften the edges of what we shall discuss."

Ferdinand nodded, turning and dashing away along the corridor. Behind him he could feel the boy's eyes burning through his back. There had been so much more that had been left unsaid—things that obviously weighed on the young knight's mind, and Ferdinand was sorry to have not had the opportunity to learn more about this "Santos" who had everyone in such an uproar. On the other hand, his message was delivered, and he was off the hook and out of the bright lights...better to be safe and find out about the stranger things in life after they were history.

No chance of that with Father Kodesh pulling the strings, but suddenly it seemed like an ideal to reach for. He wondered, suddenly, why it was that he'd never been satisfied with the world the way it was. Now that he knew it wasn't that way at all, he missed the security and normalcy of it all terribly. Still, the image of Father Kodesh (was it really Father, despite everything else he knew?) would not quit haunting him. The notion of eternity was new to him as a reality to those who still walked—and breathed? Did he?

Ferdinand scurried into the kitchen and prepared a tray with wine and goblets, as well as some bread and cheese, that he might carry back to de Molay. The last thing he wanted to do was to draw unwanted attention to himself through sloth or unsatisfactory service.

Kli Kodesh exited the chapel through a shadowed back doorway and began to ascend through the keep by a spiral stair that had seen little use in the last fifty years. It dated back to other clerics, other priests and other times. It was probably not a passage that Jacques de Molay would recognize, though he presided in name over the entire keep, and over the affairs of the Templars. It was a church secret, passed through the years, and Kli Kodesh was privy to many secrets.

He knew that de Molay's quarters would not be far from the top of that stair, and that if he made it into the passage beyond without being spotted, there was little chance of drawing attention to himself, or his access route. It was always a good idea to have some control over the environment that surrounded him. Less room for surprise, unless it came from him. There were other ways he could have accessed the Grand Master's Quarters, but he preferred to keep his status as priest at least questionably acceptable.

He stopped at the top of the stair and listened. The door was a smooth slab of stone that blended neatly with the stone of the wall. If it were not for the stairs ending directly against it, one might have concluded that the stairs led to nowhere, or to an unfinished trail. Kli Kodesh knew better. He extended his senses carefully. Nothing moved in the passage beyond. Nothing breathed.

He pushed on the stone and it slid inward without hesitation. He slipped through the opening that appeared and into the passage beyond, pressing the stone back into place quickly. He was two doors down from de Molay's quarters. Straightening his robes and pulling his cowl up over the wispy gray hairs that fluttered about his head like spider webs, he strode toward that door and knocked. No time for formality.

He could sense the two within, could hear their voices, lowered and muted. He also sensed that they did not intend to rise and open the door to allow his intrusion. Without hesitation he pressed inward on the door, finding it unlocked, and stepped inside.

De Molay rose instantly, his face darkening like the sudden

intrusion of a thunderstorm on a clear day. His mouth was open to curse whoever had the impudence to invade his quarters, but he clamped down on his lip, cutting off whatever it was that he'd been prepared to say. He might not know Father Kodesh, but he knew the robes of office, and he knew he faced a man of the Church. He had enough problems without including open sacrilege and blasphemy.

"Yes, father," he grated, gathering control of his wits quickly. "This is a very difficult time—I'm afraid I am too busy for confession."

"And I would not ask it of you," Kli Kodesh replied. "I think we both know that it would be far too interesting to waste on a single priest."

De Molay stopped, staring openly. What Kli Kodesh had said was as near to an accusation as anyone had ever dared speak in his presence, but somehow the tone in which it had been delivered did not carry the animosity one might expect.

"What do you want, Father?" he said at last. "I have little enough time to live, in all likelihood, and I have no time and little patience for games.

I am here to offer you hope," Kli Kodesh responded. "I have information that one comes to your aid you might not have expected."

"Unless he rides two days from here at the head of an army," Louis de Chaunvier threw in, recovering from his surprise at Kli Kodesh's sudden intrusion, "then he is too late and unimportant to our present dilemma."

"He needs no army," Kli Kodesh responded quietly. "His name is Montrovant, and he has supported and defended you— though you have not known it—since the days of Hugues de Payen."

"Montrovant?" de Molay asked, sitting back in his chair suddenly and staring blankly. Then his mind worked its way around the information that had just been presented, and that face transformed. First a slightly hopeful, interested expression, then doubt—then his features convulsed in anger and he rose again, slamming both fists down hard enough on the table to send the goblets of wine that had rested there flying.

"You dare to come to me like this?" de Molay cried. "You dare to mock me in my worst hour? Montrovant? A legend? A myth? You taunt me with heroes from a past that might or might not even have existed."

"Jacques!" Louis's voice was pained.

"No, it is only fair that he be skeptical," Kli Kodesh said, holding up a hand to silence de Chaunvier. "I would expect no less, and yet I tell you the truth. I have my sources, and they say that the man known as Montrovant is less than a day away from here, riding hard, and that he comes to your aid. Do not doubt the past," he added, moving close enough so that his face and de Molay's were nearly touching, nose to nose. "Your history defines you," he added, "and those who deny this truth are cursed to repeat the mistakes of their predecessors."

"No man is that old," Jacques whispered hoarsely. "You speak madness."

"Heads without bodies don't speak, either," Kli Kodesh replied, pulling back a bit and letting his face take on an inscrutable, impassive expression.

The two knights stared at him. De Chaunvier leaned forward, nearly standing, and de Molay's face had gone chalk white. Neither had the ability to speak—nor the ability to move. So they stared. After a long moment of silence, Kli Kodesh continued.

"Do not seem so surprised, Jacques de Molay. There are a great many things in this world that you do not understand. You seek answers beyond the realm of your knowledge, and in the same breath you deny as insanity other knowledge that could serve you just as well. Santos is not what he seems. Montrovant is not what you've heard. I am no ordinary priest. There are levels of reality, just like any other thing in life…yours is just one of many levels."

"Who are you?" de Molay asked quietly. "Who are you, and why have you come to me?"

"Be satisfied in knowing that I have," Kli Kodesh answered. "I am known in this time as Father Kodesh. I have known Montrovant and Santos longer than you, or your father, or your father's father have drawn breath. I say again, Montrovant is near, and he comes to offer his assistance."

"Should we wait, then?" Louis asked dubiously, uncertain where to go with the thousand questions assaulting his mind.

"You will do as you must," Kli Kodesh answered. "Know this. There is no love lost between Santos and Montrovant. They will not work together, so you have choices to make."

"Why now?" Jacques de Molay asked, rising slowly. "Why now, when everything is so close to ended that it seems an afterthought to offer us aid of any sort? Why would he come now, and not before? Santos came here even before we needed him, and he came bearing knowledge, teaching and power. Montrovant, if it is indeed the Montrovant you suggest, has abandoned us until our situation is so near to hopeless that even his legendary powers will seem pale in comparison to the threat. What can he offer? Will he battle Philip singlehandedly? Will he show us magic that will drive our attackers into retreat and save the lives of those who follow me?"

"You know as well as I that this is not an option," Kli Kodesh answered. "Montrovant is a powerful man, but he is not a god. He will offer you aid and answers, but none can stop Philip. Not Montrovant, not Santos. It is only a question of whose answers you will believe."

"What part do you play in this?" Jacques asked. "What do you stand to gain by telling us this, by filling our minds with false hopes and legends without substance?"

"I gain nothing," Kli Kodesh replied. "I am a priest of the one God. When you are ash and Philip has walked across your grave, I will preach the Gospel to others."

"You insolent dog." De Molay was out of his chair in an instant, drawing his sword, but de Chaunvier was quicker, and he grabbed his friend by the arms, holding him back.

"Listen to him, Jacques," he cried. "For God's sake, listen to something other than that madman in the cellars and the wine diluting your blood for just an instant and think! He is offering us hope! He is offering us an answer that doesn't rely on shadows and promises we can't even understand, let alone control. Will you not even consider his words?"

"I will not consider insanity as an option," de Molay bellowed. "For God's sake, Louis, listen to yourself. He is telling you that some fabled hero from our past will ride up and lead us to victory. He is offering us ghosts to replace something we can see in front of our faces. He is trying to lead us away from Santos and the truth, though I still do not see why."

"You would not know the truth were it to tap you on the shoulder and offer itself to you," Kli Kodesh said, his voice suddenly cold and distant as the wind across the desert. "You feed your imagination with images Santos fans into flames, and you trust him because you know that if he lies, you die. I tell you now, neither Santos nor Montrovant can save you, Jacques de Molay, but because you represent the lives of many it would serve you well to consider all your options carefully."

With that, Kli Kodesh turned to the door and opened it, slipping back into the passageway and pulling the portal closed behind him. Louis leaped to his feet and dove for the door after him, but by the time he reached the corridor beyond, it was empty. There were no echoing footsteps, and there was no sign of the priest who'd stood in their doorway only moments before.

"You should have listened," Louis said, turning back to the room. "Damn you, Jacques, you should have listened."

"Are you ready to spend our lives so foolishly that you would stand on the ramparts of the keep watching the horizon for signs of a dream?" de Molay asked his friend quietly. "I heard his words, my friend, and I would love to believe them, but I have seen Santos—I have felt his power—and all I have from this—priest—is words. I must go with what I know, not what I wish for."

"If you are mistaken?" Louis asked, turning to the window and gazing into the distance, as though Montrovant might ride into sight even as they spoke, ending the debate.

"Then we are dead," de Molay replied, bending to retrieve his goblet from the floor. He poured it full of wine once again and tossed it down in a single gulp. "We are dead, and he will say the last rites with a smirk on his face, damn his soul."

Louis continued to stare into the distance, not arguing. It was plain that his heart was not in the decision, but he did not argue further. He leaned over the sill of the window, and he kept watch. He felt as though he might stand that way until Philip arrived and parted his head from his shoulders, but it was not to be. De Molay downed yet another glass of wine, then called out to him.

"It is time, Louis. Santos will be waiting, the others will be gathering. We must go."

Reluctantly, Louis released the window and turned toward the door, his heart heavy and resigned. In the distance, too faint to be heard, the clip-clop of horses' hooves sounded through the darkness. The moonlight washed the keep in chiaroscuro grays. It was a night of destiny.

THIRTEEN

Montrovant had grown grim and silent as they continued their journey, but le Duc did not sense anger directed at himself, or at Gwendolyn. The old fire was in his Master's eyes, the old obsession back to haunt him. Montrovant saw the image of what he sought so clearly in his mind. Jeanne was still uncertain how possession of the ancient artifact could be so important to the Lasombra. He also had difficulty in understanding, particularly after the poor reception they'd received from Syd, just why Montrovant would want to do anything to help the others in his "family."

So many questions, pushed aside once more in the face of action. They covered many miles in the nights after leaving Holywell, stopping only to rest, and to feed. He noted with consternation that Gwendolyn did not join them in their hunting, nor did she seem to starve. She rode at their sides, and she watched them with a deep longing in her eyes when the blood-hunger overcame them, but she did not join in. Finally, it was too much for his curiosity.

"How is it that you ride with us, night after night, watching us feed, and yet you take none for yourself? I would be mad had I waited so long. You are no different than you were three days ago."

"It is Kli Kodesh," she said softly. "I wanted that hunger. I know you won't believe that. I didn't truly understand it myself, but now I know—now that it is too late for me. I lived a dull life, over-protected by a father who feared the one thing I yearned for each night. Passion. He kept me from any danger, but danger is the only thing that speeds my heart. "Alphonse, your father is Alphonse, yes?

Montrovant told me some of the tale."

"Yes," Gwendolyn smiled, "Alphonse. I saw his passion. I saw him in his hunger, though he was careful to distance himself from me at those times. I'm not really his daughter, you know."

"I wondered about that," Jeanne replied, "but I didn't want to contradict him," he nodded toward Montrovant, who rode a little ahead of them, scanning the road and the shadows beyond constantly. Jeanne knew that his master was probably aware of every word they spoke—perhaps of their thoughts as well, but he gave no indication of it. It was impossible to tell if he were listening, or ignoring them.

"He is my great-grandfather," Gwendolyn continued. "My great-grandmother still carried my grandfather, Alphonse's son, when Alphonse was Embraced. He managed to get away from them, to avoid drawing them into the shadows that had claimed him, but he returned. He followed the family, looked after them whenever possible. He caught me on the road, seeking escape. He would have taken me back to my mother, but I told him that I would just escape again. I thought I was strong enough to tempt him. I thought he would bring me to the shadows and passion I craved. I had more chance, it seems, staying with my mother.

"I became Alphonse's servant, his eyes and hands by the light of day. He kept me close, waking before the night could bring others near enough, and naming me his daughter if any asked. He watched me like a fussy old bitch with her pup. He very nearly smothered all that was left of my dreams.

"Then I saw Montrovant. I don't know why that was different, or what it was that led me to place everything on the line like that. There is something about your sire that is somehow less tame ...less controlled. I knew that there were reasons why few were Embraced, but I thought he might be the one to break those rules. I knew that Eugenio would keep my 'father' busy long enough, if only I could convince my dark one...Montrovant...to save me."

"But Kli Kodesh brought you that gift, or curse, instead," Jeanne concluded. "Is it so bad? Does it make such a difference?"

"The hunger never came upon me after I fed from my sire," she replied. "The darkness welcomes me, but I can endure the sun more readily than most of our kind. I have no family or clan save he who made me, though he was once Nosferatu, before the curse that changed him so long ago...binding him to unlife in ways I can't even fathom, let alone explain. He seeks final destruction more than any I've known, but it eludes him easily. To him I am nothing more than a tool—and possibly a short diversion from eternity. He gave me eternity, Jeanne, but he did not give me what I sought. Instead he gave me hell."

Jeanne grew silent for a moment then, considering her words. He tried to count mentally the times he'd yearned to see the sunlight. He tried to imagine the night without the hunger, Montrovant with anything but the predatory, cat-like gait that marked his power. Eternity to live. He'd never even considered the impact of eternity, and he'd had Montrovant at his side since his Embrace—he'd known no loneliness.

"I don't envy you your pain," he said at last, "but I would not so easily discount the magic of daylight, or the control your lack of hunger affords you. You may find passions of a different sort, if you set your mind to it. Kli Kodesh might be bored—he has lived long enough to use that as an excuse. For you, a world awaits."

She stared at him in silence, then a slight smile creased her face. "You sound like my sire," she said at last.

"Then perhaps he is wiser than you let on," Jeanne said, returning the smile.

Suddenly Montrovant reined in, motioning for them to do the same. He had his head cocked to one side, as if he were listening for something, but Jeanne knew that it went deeper than that. He was reaching out with his senses, seeking— something. Jeanne had detected nothing, but he didn't doubt Montrovant's ability. He'd seen it proven on too many occasions.

"We are near the army," Montrovant said at last. "We must be more cautious from here on out. No mention of the Templars unless we are certain we have found someone who will speak freely, and we must find ways not to draw attention to ourselves. I intend to get information here, but we must be on our way soon enough to get a lead on the army. We must reach de Molay before they do, or we have wasted our trip. The first of their guards are watching the road about a mile from here."

Closer than Jeanne had thought. Montrovant turned and started down the road again, not moving too fast. He didn't want to alarm the perimeter guards, who would no doubt stop and question them soon enough. Jeanne followed, and Gwendolyn rode at his side, a bit closer, it seemed. Jeanne smiled.

Jeanne detected the guards himself about five minutes before they drew abreast of the small stand of trees that concealed them. Montrovant had slowed his mount to a slow walk, and when a voice called out to them from the shadows to halt, he did so calmly, turning to watch the two men approach. "Who are you," the man asked gruffly, "and where are you headed?"

"We are traveling to the holdings of my cousin, Claude," Montrovant answered smoothly. "Is something the matter?"

"Philip's army is less than a dozen miles ahead," one of the two guards replied. "You will have to make your way around to one side or the other. None may pass except Philip's own men."

"And aren't we all Philip's men?" Montrovant smiled, sitting up a bit taller in the saddle. Nothing, not shadows or the silly smile planted on his face, nothing in the world could remove the regal, overbearing presence that was Montrovant. He towered over the two guards, and suddenly royal blood seemed to drip from his words. "I am certain that Philip would not appreciate your impertinence. This is the road that leads where I am going, and I am certainly not going to turn aside. Perhaps I can get a flagon of wine in your camp—some food?"

The reaction was instantaneous. The two men moved back a step, and the one who'd been silent spoke up suddenly. "No disrespect, Lord, but we were tasked with the guarding of this road."

"And you are doing an admirable job," Montrovant cut him off, "but I doubt that your orders were to make trouble for one of Philip's own nobles?"

The two shuffled uncomfortably. It was clear that they did not want to let Montrovant pass—and equally clear that they were going to do so. Jeanne smiled again, but he lowered his face so that they could not see.

Just then, there was a clatter of weapons, and the soft footfalls of approaching horses from the direction of the camp. Jeanne searched the darkness until he could make out two more men approaching slowly.

"Your reliefs?" Montrovant asked, dropping the venom from his voice as suddenly as he'd added it.

"Yes, lord," the first guard replied.

"Then your problem, and mine, are solved, are they not? You may escort us to the camp."

Straightening his shoulders haughtily, a movement that Jeanne didn't believe he could have perfected in a century of practice, Montrovant started on down the road again. The two guards moved forward as if to protest, but Gwendolyn was passing them and she gifted them with a sudden, brilliant smile. There was more power in that smile for a soldier on the road than in any amount of royal posturing on Montrovant's part. Sad and haunted she might seem, but Gwendolyn was beautiful, and the ancient blood that coursed through her veins only enhanced that beauty.

The three of them continued into the shadows. Jeanne could hear the four guards exchanging hurried words, then he heard the two moving quickly up behind them. It seemed that, despite Montrovant's desire to move into the camp without drawing attention, they were to have a personal entourage.

"Have you been on duty long?" Montrovant asked as the two pulled up to one side of him. He didn't turn to look at them, but his tone was friendly enough.

"Since sunset," the first man said gruffly. "It has been a long, thirsty night."

They rode in silence for a moment longer, then Montrovant spoke again. "I am more tired than I imagined." he said, faking a yawn. "Perhaps you would like to stop with us and share a drink? I've brought a gift of wine for my cousin, but somehow I doubt he'll begrudge us a drink on the road..."

The two guards looked at one another and shrugged. They were off duty—the road was no longer their problem, and free wine was never something to be turned down lightly.

"What are your names?" Gwendolyn asked. Her voice was an octave lower than normal, husky and sensual.

"I am Pasqual," the first man replied quickly, "and this rascal at my side is Thomas."

Montrovant smiled at them, reining in his horse quickly. "We must really stop and drink," he said. "I don't think I can ride another mile without some rest."

"Don't mind if we do," Thomas said, glancing at his partner to be certain he'd said the right thing. "It's still a ways to camp, and we'd have a fight on our hands to find a good bottle this late."

"Excellent. It's settled then," Jeanne piped in, speaking for the first time. "We haven't had a rest in hours, nor a drink. I for one was beginning to think that this saddle had become a part of my body. Fine thing that would be, trying to walk."

They all laughed at this, and what tension remained in the air was broken. Jeanne sensed the warm blood flowing through the veins of their new companions, and he steeled himself to ignore it. There would be time enough for feeding when they'd learned all they could learn, and it wouldn't do to take a guard on his way back to the main camp. They dismounted near a large, gnarled tree and Montrovant made a great show of rummaging through his backpack. He'd brought the wine from Holywell with just such a use in mind. There was no way for the two men to know that the three of them had no use for provisions. Sometimes the extra space in their baggage could come in handy.

Turning back, Montrovant held high two large bottles of dark red wine.

He set one aside and popped the cork easily out of the second with his dagger. The two guards eyed the bottle with appreciation. When they could, they stole sidelong glances at Gwendolyn. She watched them in amusement, smiling when she caught them staring—even winking at Thomas when he stared a bit too long. Montrovant was an imposing man—neither of them wanted to be too forward with his woman.

Sensing this, Jeanne spoke again. "You are remiss, Andre,"

he said, speaking directly to Montrovant. "You have failed to introduce yourself, your sister, or your companion. What sort of host do you suppose you will seem?"

"You are right, Antoine," Montrovant replied without missing a beat. "I am Andre le Duc Puy, third heir in line for a holding so small it barely qualifies as a holding—just this side of the mountains." He nodded vaguely back in the direction they'd come. Thomas and Pasqual paid little attention to his words. They'd perked up at Jeanne's calling Gwendolyn Montrovant's sister, and they were eyeing the bottle Montrovant waved about thirstily.

"This is my sister, Jeanice, and my traveling companion Antoine de Monde. And this," he held forth the bottle so that Pasqual could reach it, "is the finest vintage my father's cellars can boast. I hope that you'll find it to your taste."

Pasqual had already tipped the bottle up for a long gulp and handed it off to Thomas, who followed suit. The bottle then moved through Gwendolyn's hands—after a lingering touch of her slender fingers on the guard's hand as she took it. She held it to her lips, never letting her eyes leave Thomas's, tilted it but did not drink. She passed it to Montrovant, who followed suit, and then Jeanne took his turn. If Pasqual noted that little of the contents had disappeared before he had the bottle in his hand again, he made no indication of it.

"So," Montrovant said as the bottle passed to Thomas a second time, "Philip has finally had his fill of the Templars?"

Thomas barely noted that he had spoken. His eyes were locked on Gwendolyn, who smiled at him, letting her eyes drop to the ground coyly, then glancing up again. Pasqual watched his companion in amusement for a moment, then answered.

"There are rumors of dark things in de Molay's keep," he said softly. "Philip is not intolerant, but there are things that must not be allowed. I have heard from the mouth of one who walked the halls of that keep of strangers who rarely come out by the light of day, of strange chanting rising from the lower levels of the keep, late at night. He spoke of the worship of things unclean as if they were commonplace. The Templars, I think, have fallen from their faith.

I have known some of those knights," Jeanne offered. "They seemed steadfast, honest warriors to me, if a bit over-zealous."

"Oh, they are not all like de Molay," Thomas said quickly. "My brother and two of my cousins have taken that oath, and more honest, God-fearing men you could not find." He took another long swallow of wine as the bottle passed back to him. Jeanne watched the play of moonlight over the man's features. When the hunger was upon him, things that normally would not catch his eye came to new life. He could see the muscles working in Thomas's jaw, could sense the pulse of blood through his throat. The man's eyes glittered, and the scent of his blood was intoxicating. Jeanne clamped down on his senses, managing to nod at the appropriate pauses in the conversation to show his interest and attention.

"De Molay is said to traffic with demons. He has brought sorcerers into his keep. My friend told me," Thomas's voice lowered, as if the shadows might be listening to him speak, "that he heard that chanting himself, and that it was in no tongue of man. He speaks five languages, and none of them were a help to him listening to those voices. De Molay has called more upon himself than he realizes, I think."

He took another quick drink and upended the bottle, letting the final drop splash free. Montrovant smiled and reached for the second bottle. He had it open in a second and handed it to Pasqual, who had inched his way slowly around until he sat directly beside Gwendolyn, so close that their legs nearly brushed. Jeanne could feel the heat of the man's desire flooding through him—the rush of blood to his loins.

Gwendolyn glanced over at him and he saw a flash of something—hunger?—in her eyes. Then it was gone and she was whispering and giggling with the guard again. Jeanne cursed under his breath. She knew what the added heat was doing to him. She knew he hungered, and she teased him with it. Anger boiled forth, but as soon as it reached the surface of his mind he realized the ridiculousness of it and it transformed to sudden laughter. The sound burst from him in a wave of uncontrolled hilarity. Montrovant and Thomas stopped speaking for a moment to look at Jeanne in amazement. He couldn't help himself. He needed to release the tension building within him, and somehow the image of Gwendolyn, a drunken, foolish mortal hanging on her every word and motion, smiling across the clearing as she made the blood pulse faster through her companion, was too much for him.

"For...forgive me," he said, staggering to his feet and walking quickly into the shadows.

"He has trouble with wine," Montrovant said apologetically. Gwendolyn had turned away to prevent her own smile from following Jeanne's into gales of laughter.

"Ah," Thomas said, nodding in understanding. "Well, then, that much more for the rest of us."

"No more for me," Gwendolyn said softly. "I wouldn't want to act the fool."

Pasqual mumbled something soft and stupid into her ear—no doubt considering himself gallant—and Montrovant returned to the subject at hand.

"But these sorcerers," he said, somehow managing to sound truly puzzled, "where did he find them? France has no lack of magicians and charlatans, as we both know. Are these Frenchmen?"

"It is said they are not," Thomas replied, suddenly serious. He took another long gulp from the bottle. "There was one in particular, a short, dark man who rarely left the lower levels of the keep—this one bothered my friend deeply. He had the look of a Turk, or some other Saracen dog. Not a fit companion for holy knights, I'm thinking."

"Indeed," Montrovant replied. His mind was whirling. "Did this sorcerer have a name?"

"He did," Thomas replied, scratching his head with the bottom of the bottle as he thought. He'd forgotten completely about passing it to his companion, and Pasqual was so enamored of Gwendolyn that he'd forgotten completely why they'd stopped in the first place. "I'm not certain I remember what he said. It seems it was San something or other, like a saint, but this one is no holy man. He wears long robes that seem to be brown, but that ripple with shifting colors as he moves—no fabric like my friend had ever seen."

Montrovant had grown very still. "Could his name have been Santos?" he said at last.

Thomas sat bolt upright, nearly spilling the remaining wine and wasting the next few moments in making certain that he did not. "That is it," he said. "How did you know?" He looked slightly suspicious for a second, but then he remembered the wine in his hand and upended the bottle. The last of it slid down his throat and he stared at the empty container reproachfully, as if it had betrayed him personally.

Montrovant had turned away. His shoulders were tense, and Jeanne walked back around the tree, having recovered his control, just in time to see his sire turn back to the guard, reach out, and snatch the man out of his seat in one fluid motion. He clamped onto Thomas's throat, draining the hot blood from his veins, before Jeanne could gasp in protest.

Gwendolyn shrugged, slapped Pasqual hard across the face, and let him drop into her lap. She cocked her head to one side, smiling at Jeanne in invitation. He didn't hesitate. He couldn't imagine what Montrovant was thinking, but the hunger was too powerful to be ignored. There would be time enough to sort it all out when he had sated the thirst.

He fell on Pasqual, letting his head lean against Gwendolyn's breast. He felt her leaning in close, felt her lips close to his own throat as he fed. She was entranced. He knew she was reading his emotions—sharing the heat of the moment somehow.

He pressed up against her lips more fully, drawing Pasqual along with him. It seemed an eternity before he tossed the body aside. When he did so he did not move away from Gwendolyn, but lay shuddering in her lap. Montrovant had finished with Thomas and was up, striding back and forth before the tree, deep in thought.

As quickly as he could, Jeanne gathered his wits about him and untangled himself, rising. "What is it?" he asked. "What did he tell you?"

"It is Santos," Montrovant snapped. "That is why Kli Kodesh wants me there, why he sent you," he turned to Gwendolyn in sudden fury, "to drag me here. He couldn't get what he wanted from Santos before without using me for a decoy, and he thinks to do so again."

"I have no idea what you're talking about," Gwendolyn replied, rising at the sudden accusation in his voice and facing him. "I have done only what I was told, and I have traveled with you in good faith."

Montrovant grew calmer suddenly. "I know that. I have seen how Kli Kodesh treats his followers. I am only angry that I didn't guess what was to come sooner."

"Who is Santos?" Gwendolyn asked.

"He is ancient, and he is a guardian, that is the gist of what I know. You should ask your sire if you truly want more information. I intend to do just that when we reach de Molay's keep."

Montrovant stared down at his feet as if he'd just realized there were bodies there. "We must ride. We have half of this night left to us, and we have to reach de Molay in time."

They pulled the bodies behind the tree, obscuring them slightly from the road, and Jeanne drove the two guards' horses off into the night. They would find their way back to camp, riderless, and a patrol would be sent out—but in the direction from which they had come. Jeanne knew they'd be beyond range of the army the following night.

He thought briefly of Gwendolyn, of how she'd shared his hunger, of how it had felt to be so close to another besides Montrovant. He'd sensed the blood that flowed through her veins, as well—the ancient's blood—the curse. It had seemed intoxicatingly sweet. He also thought of Kli Kodesh. The old one would have enjoyed their trip so far—it had been nothing if not entertaining.

They mounted and, turning from the road, Montrovant led them off into the night at a gallop. The moon, still high in the sky, lit their way. The race was on.

FOURTEEN

De Molay and his followers drifted down into the lower levels slowly, men from different levels of nobility, different provinces and backgrounds, coming together under the cloak and mantle of darkness for a single purpose. They would save those above by any means possible, and if it meant the cost of their own souls, that was acceptable. Santos sensed this as they made their way into the chamber he'd prepared so carefully. Many times he'd felt the energy rising and the desire flowing from man to man—but this was different. Always he'd been the focus, the power bending each soul to its task. De Molay, weak as he as he was, malleable and naive in the ways of power, was their focus.

Somehow he would have to lead them all through everything that was to come without compromising this basic principle. De Molay was a savior in their eyes, the leader who would see them through to safety. These were not simple men, but leaders—rulers who'd forsaken their own titles and lands to follow a greater cause. These were men with lives resting on their decisions, on their integrity and their faith. They would not be the easy tools Santos had made use of in the past. They were their own men, and he had to keep this in mind as he molded them into a single cohesive force that could bring him the answers he needed. He had to hold them together long enough to meet his own needs. It would be a challenge, and after so many years of having things exactly his way, a challenge was something he looked forward to. He watched as they poured through the doors, and he smiled. Soon. He would know soon if he was wasting his time.

De Molay took his customary spot near the front, de Chaunvier at his side. They moved in silence, forming the circles—concentric binding rings that would become their protection and their focus in what was to come. Something was wrong almost immediately. One of the younger men, one whose name Santos couldn't even recall, was moving toward the front, away from his normal position. Cursing inwardly, Santos moved instantly to cut him off.

"I mean no disrespect," the young man said, the words spewing suddenly from his mouth as if he'd kept them there, poised on his tongue and suppressed until just that moment. "I have come with a message, a message that I was to bring to you, and to you alone."

Santos stopped short. A message? Who, other than those gathered, would know who he was? His mind began to race, and the anger he'd suppressed for so long began to boil and rage in his stomach. Before the boy spoke, he knew the words that would follow.

"I was to tell you that Father Kodesh is here. He said you would understand..."

Santos was trembling. He struggled with the heat of the anger, the flames of rage that threatened to blaze outward from the black pit that had once housed his soul, and scorch them all to cinders. Closing his eyes and backing away, he came to rest against the stone wall of the chamber, beside the altar that held the head, and he grew silent.

The boy, horrified by the reaction his message had brought about, backed away hurriedly, crashing against the gathered knights and drawing cuffs and curses from all sides. None paid too much attention to him, though—all eyes were turned to Santos. It was several moments before the small man's eyes blazed open once more, and when they did all those present pulled back and away. His eyes glowed with a horrible light, and his features twisted suddenly into an expression never meant for a human face.

"Prepare!" he grated harshly. His voice was magnified and distorted, echoing eerily through the chamber. All fell to their knees, heads dropping to the cold stone of the floor and hearts beating rapidly. Whatever had happened, whatever the name Kodesh had meant to him, it had brought forth the truest glimpse of power Santos had released in their presence.

The chanting rose as if from a great distance, and though they knew that it was Santos, this knowledge did nothing to calm the fear in their hearts. Worked into the words he spoke, blended with staccato rhythms and impossible pronunciations, they heard words—names—that called out to them. Each of them heard a different name, felt a different tug at his soul. They did not raise their heads, but as the pulsing darkness of the chant filled them, their voices rose to join it—drawn by the words, the names they could not recognize and yet could not escape. The names that were their very essence, drawn forth and stolen, feeding Santos's growing strength.

As the rhythm took control, they began to rise, slowly, as if from a deep sleep. They stumbled against one another, wobbling in place as their heads dropped back in unison, eyes still closed but pointing skyward. As the chant continued, changing tone and picking up intensity, they grew steadier. The circles tightened, and they began to shuffle slowly forward, one body so close to the next that it was impossible to tell where each began or ended, their robes flowing together and flapping about them at each step.

Santos seemed oblivious to them, staring through them and beyond, his features still contorted horribly, his voice booming forth as if he spoke into a long, echoing chasm. The name Kodesh had launched him into a frenzy that could only be released through the flame of power, flowing up from deep within him. He needed to feel that energy, to experience the joining. He needed to know that it was too late for those above, that he would succeed where he'd failed once before, and that he would have Kodesh groveling at his feet as he'd dreamed on so many dark occasions. He needed to feel his power, and the best way to ensure that he did was the chant.

Each of those moving through the dance was joined in turn to Santos. Each of their energies would be turned toward the single task of reviving the head—of seeking the answers that would lead him to his goal. They all knew that they were seeking answers, they just didn't know those answers would be directed only to Santos's questions. They didn't realize the totality of their servitude.

He could see de Molay leaping past every now and then as the circle spun a certain way. The man's eyes were sunken, hollow and empty—haunted. Others had different ways of coping but the end of it was the same. Deep in their hearts they knew that Santos ruled them more surely than de Molay ever could. They knew that they would never achieve the freedom they sought, nor would there be an answer to Philip and his army. The end of the Knights Templar as they had known them was in sight, but even closer and more easily spotted was the means of their personal destruction.

The level of their combined voices rose and fell with the rhythm, and Santos felt the energy in the room expanding. He closed his eyes, letting the sounds wash his thoughts of revenge and his concerns for the completion of their task from his mind. He reached out to the power that hovered above and around them and began to channel it through himself, letting it renew and cleanse him. He felt his legs launching into the intricate steps of the dance, though he'd not directed that action, and he screamed in release.

Whirling from his place at the altar he launched into the midst of the others, taking a place in the circle and matching them step for step, his voice rising and falling within the backbeat provided by theirs, his words more quickly spoken and complete. He wove in and out of the sound, the melody to their harmony. None but he knew the meaning of the words, but all felt the power behind them, the power that grew around them and filled them, the power that promised the answers they sought.

He knew it would not reach the required level—not so soon— but he felt the tension, the hunger to succeed that permeated the hearts of the others who danced. He knew it could be done, and soon. Increasingly it appeared that if it were not accomplished soon, it would fail again, and that was a turn of events that he wasn't ready to face even the remote possibility of.

They danced, and he chanted, and the hours passed slowly

through midnight toward dawn. At some predetermined interval, though it would never be a point that any of the others could be certain of, the ritual ended. Limbs returned to the control of those born to them. Voices, hoarse from too much and too harsh use grew silent. Without speaking to one another, they filtered out, moving stiffly through the stone doorway into the passage beyond and on toward the stairs that would lead them to their chambers, strong wine, and beds long overdue.

Santos stood in the shadows, watching them go. They did not glance in his direction. For them, he did not exist, certainly not at that moment. He was a tool, a means to an end. That was what their minds repeated over and over, fighting to convince their aching, God-starved souls that it was true.

De Molay was one of the last to leave. He stopped for a moment, turning back, and stared at the altar. His eyes seemed to bore into the vacant, unseeing eyes of the head where it rested. The flickering light of the candle flames danced along the walls and the smoke from incense and offerings swirled about the base of the altar, lending it an air of otherworldliness. Finally, he dropped his eyes and turned away. Santos wondered if the man might actually have felt something, been gifted with a passing vision. Whatever the case, he seemed satisfied with what he'd seen.

Santos watched him walk off into the darkness, but he did not move to follow. Instead, he turned in a different direction altogether—toward the door on the side of the chamber that led to his own quarters. He had to sit and gather his thoughts—there was work to be done, and he would need all of his faculties to complete that work. He was not immune to the rigors of the ritual, merely more accustomed to them. It had drained his own strength as well as that of the others, and what he'd borrowed from them he'd channeled back out again, feeding it to the head, using it to support the requests he made with his mind. He was not so much the final goal of that stolen power, but the redirecting force.

He sat and crossed his legs, then his arms, letting his head drop forward against his chest. Emptying his mind, he floated free, letting himself cast off his physical form and drift as his thought directed. Shut down and bereft of input from his mind, his body could recover more quickly. Free of the physical, he could seek answers to different questions. He could seek the other—the missing link. Kli

Kodesh was a thorn in his side, but rarely did he do his own work. The ancient Cainite slunk through the shadows, watching and smiling just out of sight, praying for something of interest to blossom from the ashes of a world gone too cold—too distant—to warm what remained of his heart.

Santos knew such despair well—but he had his own way of dealing with it—more direct. He lived for a purpose, a focus, and that focus called to him across years of denial—years when he had been unable to fulfill the tenets of his geas. He'd been charged to guard and protect certain relics, objects of power his creators had deemed too dangerous, too important, for the lot of mortals and immortals alike. For over a century he'd kept that pledge—adding some secrets, learning more of those he'd been entrusted—always secure.

Now those treasures, and their secrets, had been wrested from his grasp, his heritage denied. Inadvertently, Kli Kodesh had renewed Santos's will to survive. The challenge had proven immense, the fear, the uncertainty, all of it had blended to bring levels of energy and intensity to his thoughts and actions that the centuries had stripped away. He might feel grateful for it, once he'd recovered that which was his—without the challenge he might have withered into shadows and left his charges to fate and history. Now it was personal.

He slipped into the Shadowlands, letting reality fade behind him. The familiar gray and black wash of decay engulfed the stone walls, dust and debris littered the passages, and the dim brilliance that permeated day and night in those lifeless lands poured in from above. The stone of the floor was ravaged by time, large chunks of it missing entirely. He let his spirit float upward through the cracks.

The keep was a ruin, the walls crumbling and fallen, the gates nothing but skeletons of stone and rotted wood. He let his senses range beyond the keep, searching. Somewhere he believed he would find them. Whoever, whatever Kli Kodesh had called to his aid was out there, waiting to be discovered and vanquished. He felt the death to come—the decimation. It wasn't far in the future. All around him, in the shadows and beyond, the restless dead waited, some with slave chains, others watching for glimpses of the living. They, too, could sense what was to come.

He moved toward the main gate and passed across a patch of scorched earth with a wooden stake protruding from its center. The wood was charred. Dust swirled around its base in a breeze that seemed to come from every direction at once, and to dissipate the same way. Santos hesitated. Something important would happen here—someone important would die. He considered for a moment the notion of waiting to see if he might discover the source of the ashes, but his mind told him that those ashes lay beyond his own goals—in the days to come.

As he moved across the land he saw remnants of Templar robes, red crosses faded and torn, caught in the limbs of trees and blowing across the road. There was no trace of the flesh that had carried them—no indication of life—or afterlife—save those who waited in the shadows. They ignored him, and he them. He had nothing to share with the dead. There were always secrets to be learned in their company, but this night he required only their world.

He moved across the land to where Philip's army was approaching. He could move much more swiftly in this state, and the miles flowed away beneath him rapidly. The camp appeared on the horizon, dim light from the fires flickering against the eerie illumination of the sky.

He moved among them. Seated around the fires were men with their faces half-eaten by decay, others missing limbs and with horrifying wounds that already festered with decay. They joked and laughed with others who would survive the days to come, unaware of the fate already etched across their death-tainted forms. Santos ignored them. He reached out with his senses, seeking something that didn't belong, something beyond their mortal world of blood and death.

Once or twice he thought he detected a slight trace of what he sought. The essence of his past called out to him, and he could not discern whether his own mind created the sensations, or they were real. There was no concentration of the sensation, just ghost whispers that tantalized, but could never satisfy. The agitation of his inability to narrow his search to a particular area ate at his control, and he knew he must return. His physical shell was vulnerable when he was disembodied, and it would take a certain amount of time and effort to make his way back if something were to go wrong. Montrovant might well be waiting in the shadows, watching and laughing, but there was no time to dwell on it.

With a sigh of release, Santos slipped back across the miles. It was not like the slow, concentrated passage he'd made to reach Philip's camp. He snapped across the distance, one world to the other, darkness and shadow to the flickering light of torch and candle—numb spirit gave way to the cool, damp recesses of the lower levels of the keep. The stone was back in place, solid and seemingly impervious to time or destruction. Santos smiled thinly as it all came back into focus.

Rising, he made up his mind. He would have to bring matters to a close quickly and certainly. He'd felt the level of energy during the ceremony—more than adequate to his needs. All that remained was the final, driving force—the desire of his servants, and that he could accomplish in only one way. He would have to go to them, and he would have to lie. De Molay was in a particularly bad position to doubt Santos's word—he needed a miracle. All that remained was to promise it to him, and to turn that deceit to his own favor.

Santos strode purposefully through the passageways, reaching the main stair and starting up without hesitation. They'd not seen enough of him on the upper levels, it was time to make an entrance as only he could do. It was time for closure.

Ferdinand just managed to slip back behind the pillar as Santos's short, robed figure emerged from the stairs leading to the lower levels. He wasn't certain why he ducked—something deep inside his mind called out to him and he obeyed. He slammed himself against the cold stone of the wall, his heart hammering madly, and Santos slid past him as smoothly as a snake. Somehow the man did not look to his side, did not see Ferdinand quivering in the darkness—or did not find him important enough to acknowledge.

For a long moment after he was alone in the passageway, Ferdinand did not move. He felt trapped, as though a thousand eyes watched him, the combined weight of their stare pressing him against the wall. His mind told him that he was safe—that he'd not been spotted, but his mind could not control the fear, and the fear had latched onto his heart.

Finally he pulled free of the wall. Looking both ways up and down the passage, he drew in a deep breath and turned to follow in the direction Santos had taken. He didn't want to follow. He wanted to turn and to run as fast as his legs could carry him away from what was to come, but he could not. Father Kodesh would want to know—would need to know—what was about to take place. Santos never left the lower levels, and it must be an important event indeed to cause him to do so. Nothing of this magnitude could be ignored.

As he began to move, his courage returned. There was no sign of his quarry, but it wasn't difficult to guess where he might be headed. Only a few nobles had quarters on the upper levels. The direction Santos had taken was a direct path toward de Molay's private chambers.

Something was happening, something important. Ferdinand wanted more than anything to bear the news of whatever it was back to Father Kodesh, to win his trust. Too many things beyond the scope of reality as he'd grown to understand it had lured him to the shadows. He needed to know what Santos had planned, and he needed to know that, when it was all over, there was at least a chance that he would still be involved—that the boundaries of his existence might be extended. He wanted to know if he would be more than a momentary tool, granted the darkness that Father Kodesh strode through so boldly, or whether he would be cast aside and forgotten.

He rounded the last corner slowly. De Molay's door was just ahead, and he peered around the corner, making certain that the passageway was empty, before sliding from the shadows and approaching the door. This was the true test of his courage.

It was one thing to slink through the shadows, another to be out in the open. Though it would not be odd for a servant to wait outside de Molay's door, this fact did not wipe away the fear.

He moved cautiously forward until he was a single pace—a second—away from the door. Too close not to commit. He took the last couple of steps and pressed his ear to the door. At first he could hear nothing but the pounding of his own heart, but as he stood waiting the fear receded a bit, and he became aware of the voices beyond the wooden door. The first was as familiar as his own voice. The Templar lord was excited, and his voice carried more easily than it might have otherwise. "Tomorrow? So soon? But Philip will not be here for at least three days—why now? Just yesterday your vision guided us to wait."

"I have had—visions." The voice that followed de Molay's was slippery, almost too soft to be heard, but Ferdinand concentrated, and he found that, soft as they were, the words were clear and sharp. "I have seen this keep in ruins, the skeletons of your followers strewn throughout, and a great scorched patch of earth in the main courtyard, surrounding the remains of a wooden stake. There is less time to spare than you think, Jacques de Molay. The time to act is now. Our faith must carry us through the moment—nothing less will suffice."

"How do we know you have seen any vision?" a third voice cut in angrily. It was Louis de Chaunvier. Ferdinand recognized the harsh tones of the big knight's voice instantly.

"You are not the only late-night visitor we've had these past nights," de Chaunvier continued. "A priest—though for the life of me I can't think him such, came to us and told us others were approaching. He said that powers from our past would return— do you believe that, Santos? Do you believe the past can return to make itself known in the present?"

"Montrovant." The word was out of Santos's mouth before he could bite down on it, and the reaction that one word brought to the two knights' faces confirmed his suspicion.

"You knew?" de Molay breathed. "He is truly coming, and you knew, and you did not speak—told us nothing?"

"The Dark One may indeed come," Santos said at last, his voice carefully even and controlled. "There is nothing he can do for you except to watch you burn and to sift through the ashes Philip leaves behind. He is but one man."

"As are you," de Chaunvier cut in.

Ferdinand's heart caught in his throat as he considered the reaction such a statement might draw. Santos was no ordinary man to be spoken to in such tones.

The expected explosion did not come. There was a long moment of silence, then Santos continued as if he'd not heard the last outburst at all.

"You have no idea what you face, or what you have in your favor. There are other powers at work here than those we seek to invoke—ancient, powerful beings who will grind you beneath their boots to serve their own ends, or for the sheer enjoyment of it. To them, you are less than dust. If you choose to trust them, that is what you will become. You have but one chance, and that chance lies with the power of the oracle that awaits below."

"And you?" de Chaunvier insisted. "Among these ancient powers, serving only themselves, what master do you serve?"

Only silence followed for a matter of several moments, and Ferdinand was certain that the Templar lord had gone too far. Miraculously, there were no screams of horror or pain.

"I am not here to debate with you," Santos answered softly. Though his voice was low and subdued, the venom was apparent in his tone, and the words carried with a power that went beyond mere sound. "I am here to warn you, and to offer you a way to continue your pitiful existence. If the situation were not so dire, and if it did not threaten my own safety as well as yours, I'd kill you very slowly, my friend, and as you died I'd remind you that you are a pitiful, weak mortal man—and that I am not. You may believe that, or not, as you choose. Do as you will in what is to come, just believe this—I will survive."

Ferdinand backed away from the door. Something told him the interview was over, and he did not want to face whoever might be the first to depart the chamber. He had nearly backed into the shadows when the door suddenly slammed open and Santos emerged.

Miraculously, Ferdinand had slid into the shadows in time once more. Santos was angry, and he spun away with a short step moved down the passage quickly.

De Molay's voice floated after him from within the chamber. "We will be ready. We will come tomorrow after the sun has set."

Ferdinand had grown brave from his success at evading Santos twice, and he did not hesitate as long before following as he had on the lower levels. He wanted to know if there would be other stops, or if Santos would disappear into the dungeons again. He wanted a full report to give him reason enough to see Father Kodesh.

He slipped along the stone wall, keeping back far enough that Santos's shadow would just turn a corner before he would follow, keeping his eyes peeled for any turn that might divert the shorter man from his return to the shadows below.

He saw Santos round the final corner and he hurried his steps, wanting to be certain he caught the last glimpse of the dark, mysterious stranger as he ducked out of sight. It was that haste that was Ferdinand's undoing.

As he rounded the last corner, a strong hand whipped suddenly out of the shadows, taking him by the throat and pinning him roughly to the wall. He tried to cry out, but his air was cut off.

Santos watched him as he might a bug he was contemplating bringing his heel down upon. He bored into Ferdinand's mind and heart with eyes no more human than those of a stone statue. Ferdinand tried to struggle, but it was pointless—the strength of the man's grip was incredible, and his feet barely reached far enough to brush the stone floor as he was lifted like a child.

There was an odd, tingling sensation, and Santos eyes blazed with sudden light.

"Kodesh," he muttered. Nothing more, just that one word. Without further hesitation, the man dragged Ferdinand free of the wall and continued on toward the stairs. Ferdinand struggled, but it was pointless. He was dragged behind Santos like a child's doll, banging painfully off the stone of the floor and stumbling down the steps. Santos continued as if he weren't dragging a grown man behind him, paying no more attention to his captive's efforts at escape than he might a recalcitrant puppy.

As the darkness swallowed him, Ferdinand reached out with his mind—crying out to his master for help. He didn't know if his message would get through, but he knew he had to try. As the two passed onto the stairs, the passageway returned to its silence, and all grew still. Only the muffled sound of feet on stone stairs indicated that anyone moved through the darkness, and that sound faded slowly into quiet.

FIFTEEN

As the horrible weight of the sun's rays lifted from the Earth, Montrovant and le Duc rose from their safe-haven in the cellar of an abandoned home and moved toward the surface in silence. They were less than two hours' ride from de Molay's keep, and their silence reflected their tension. It was a moment of fates tilting, balanced on a thin wall of uncertain knowledge. Just before he mounted the final step into the growing shadows, Montrovant stopped, halting Jeanne with a hand hard against his chest.

Jeanne shook off the last vestiges of lethargy that clouded his mind, willing his senses to become fully alert. He'd noted immediately that Gwendolyn was not with them, but this wasn't a rare thing—she did not fear the sunlight as strongly as they did. Though it could burn her, and destroy her, she could bear it for longer periods than they. She seldom required rest.

The sound of voices floated down from above and he strained to make out the words. One of the voices was Gwendolyn's, and though she sounded agitated, he didn't believe it was from fear. Nothing in her tone spoke of immediate danger, but who could she be talking to? The other voice was softer, but somehow more powerful. Jeanne could feel it shivering through him, carrying easily despite its subdued tone.

Jeanne turned to Montrovant, but before he could form his question, the tall vampire was up and through the opening, diving to his right and coming to his feet in a crouch. Not knowing anything else to do, le Duc followed suit, taking the opposite direction and rolling to a halt behind a small bit of crumbling wall.

The conversation beyond the door stopped, and the night fell to silence. Jeanne noted several things at once. Gwendolyn stood in the clearing beyond the cellar stairs. At her side a man stood, thin and gray, his hair whipping about him like a white mantle. Jeanne's mind put the image to a name at the same instant Montrovant voiced it.

"Kli Kodesh."

Nothing more was said for a long moment, then, with a suddenness that nearly caused Jeanne to launch backward into the shadows, the ancient threw back his head and began to roar with laughter. His frame shook, and he doubled over insanely. Montrovant stood, glaring coldly at his antics, and Gwendolyn stepped back a pace, but Jeanne could only watch in amazement.

Montrovant moved slowly forward, but Kli Kodesh didn't even acknowledge his advance. He was still doubled over, convulsing helplessly in gales of unchecked mirth. Jeanne searched his sire's features and saw the anger building. He moved forward himself then, to intercept if necessary. Anger would not be enough to bridge the gap in power between the two.

Montrovant spoke first.

"Why have you come, to gloat?"

Kli Kodesh raised up a bit, regaining control of himself slowly. Montrovant stood, waiting, as a parent might over a recalcitrant child. Looking up, seeing him towering above, Kli Kodesh reeled to one side, shrieking hysterically and falling into another fit of laughter.

Montrovant moved to follow, but Jeanne was at his side, and he held him back with a hand on one arm. The older vampire turned back swiftly, as if to strike his follower aside and continue, but when their eyes locked, he hesitated, then stopped. The anger did not dissipate, and he was clearly not pleased by Jeanne's interference, but he made no further move after Kodesh.

"What is the meaning of this?" he demanded, turning to Gwendolyn instead.

"I did not call him here," she replied. "He would not have come had I done so. He does as he pleases.

As do we all," Kli Kodesh tossed in, choking on the effort to form the words. "As do we all. You in particular should understand that, Dark One. You will forgive my outburst, I hope." He was still grinning inanely, but his voice was coming under control. "You were so dramatic, leaping from the shadows to catch me—doing what?"

"I am trying to understand just that," Montrovant grated. "I understand that you've dragged me across the miles once again. I understand that you sent me into the mosque of al Aqsa on a fool's errand, full aware I would not come out with what I sought, and that I might not come out at all. I understand that you played me against Santos toward your own end without a second thought for how it would affect others. Am I missing something? Are there other reasons I should despise you, or have I covered my ground well?"

The ancient's laughter, as well as all traces of humor, dissipated like so much dust, swirling away in the wind. He stood straight and silent, his eyes boring into Montrovant's, but the Dark One did not flinch.

"You don't know everything you believe you do," Kli Kodesh said, finally breaking the silence. "You are so certain you have the answers, all of them, and that your plans will lead you to the glory and dreams you've set aside for yourself."

"And you are certain that the world is but a huge entertainment set aside for your own amusement," Montrovant retorted. "At least I don't slink through the shadows while others carry out my plans."

Kli Kodesh stiffened, but again he didn't reply. Jeanne kept expecting the ancient to snap under the barrage of insults and accusations, but he held his ground.

"We have no time for this," Kodesh said at last. "For different reasons, we have come to the same road once again. It might have been a thousand others, but it was not."

"Perhaps our roads have crossed by chance," Montrovant replied, "or perhaps you led us here." He was unable to let the antagonistic tone drop from his voice. Jeanne had rarely seen his sire so angry, and never in a situation where he could not vent that anger without ending his existence.

"I admit that I brought you here," Kli Kodesh said softly. "I sent the message with Gwendolyn to warn you of what was taking place, and to let you know that what you seek is very near."

"The Grail is in that keep?" Montrovant nodded in the direction of de Molay's grounds. "Is that what you want me to believe? If de Molay has such an item in his possession, then why would he need help against Philip?"

"I did not say that de Molay was in possession of anything. I said that what you seek is very near."

"More riddles. Always the same, old one, your words, your actions...what will I do to amuse you now?"

"I'm not asking for you to amuse me," Kli Kodesh replied softly. "I'm asking for your help. Santos is here."

"Santos..." Montrovant's already angry countenance darkened yet again. "Santos. I had hoped he'd returned to whatever dark little hole he crawled out of."

"It is not that simple," Kli Kodesh replied. "Santos did not become what he is in the same way we have been Embraced. He was created, and that creation bore a purpose. He is the guardian, and he will stop at nothing to find that which has been entrusted to him. He seeks revenge, as well, but the thing that eats away at his mind and whatever blackness now represents his heart, is his failure to live up to his responsibilities."

Montrovant was not convinced. "What could I do for you that you could not do for yourself, old one? Die a second and final death?"

"He has someone—close to me." Kli Kodesh replied, averting his eyes. "He has a follower of mine, one with enough of my essence within him to give Santos power I cannot afford. I would go after him myself, but I fear he might have the advantage."

"So you want me to do it for you," Montrovant replied, spitting violently. "You are afraid—you—and you want me to take the risk."

Kli Kodesh was standing across the clearing in one instant, and nose to nose with Montrovant in the next. Neither Jeanne nor Gwendolyn were aware of the motion until it had been completed, and even Montrovant was only able to move scant seconds before the ancient's flesh would have contacted his own.

"You presume too much," Kli Kodesh hissed.

Montrovant held himself steady, and Jeanne was amazed by his control. The tension in the air was thick enough to have sliced with a blade, but Montrovant would not back down.

"You may destroy me, if it is your wish," he replied coldly, "but I will speak my mind. For one coming in search of aid, you have a strange way of presenting yourself."

Kli Kodesh backed off a pace, but his eyes still blazed with cold fire.

"Who does he hold?" Jeanne asked, trying to break the aura of anger and venom that poisoned the air.

Both Montrovant and Kli Kodesh turned to him as if they'd been slapped. They'd apparently forgotten that they weren't alone.

"His name is Ferdinand," Gwendolyn said at last. "He is a servant in de Molay's service. Father Kodesh here has been using him as an informant."

"He is Embraced?" Montrovant asked.

"No," Kli Kodesh said, turning away, "but I have foolishly shared too much with him. Knowledge can be as dangerous as blood in the wrong hands.

And so you fear Santos," Montrovant replied incredulously. "After all that has happened, after we sent him scurrying into the shadows, you still fear him."

"Do not make the mistake of believing that because Santos was driven from Jerusalem he is not a great danger to you," Kli Kodesh continued. "He still retains the head, and from the reports Ferdinand was able to bring to me before he was— taken—it is this very night that the oracle head will speak again. You and I both know the consequences that could bring."

"He knows you are here, obviously," Montrovant mused, "but what danger is there to me? He has no idea I'm anywhere near here."

"You underestimate his anger and capacity for revenge. When the oracle speaks again, he will ask after you. If you were a thousand miles away, still he would ask about you. It was you who took away his purpose...his reason to exist. It was you that led de Payen to him, and the Church, and it was you who chased him from the Holy Land, his tail between his legs."

"So what can we do?" Jeanne cut in. "If what you say is true, we must act, and now. We have no access to that keep, and Santos is too powerful for a direct assault to do us any good."

"You have an advantage," Kodesh replied. "I have spread the news of your arrival—you are somewhat of a legendary figure, Dark One. At least one of de Molay's close aids is awaiting your arrival. Louis de Chaunvier is his name, and he is de Molay's closest confidant. He doesn't trust Santos, though he's agreed to support de Molay. If you can reach him before they move to the lower levels you might be able to find a way in—a way to disrupt what is to come. Once broken, the circle of power that Santos will use to reach the oracle cannot easily be restored. Not in time to do any of us harm."

"And what is in this for me?" Montrovant asked. "You have given me your usual riddles, but there must be more. If I am to ride to battle in your name," he paused at this, sneering slightly, "then I must know what it is that I'm fighting for. When will you reveal the location of the Grail? As soon as your henchmen have had a chance to move it?"

"You will have your answers," Kli Kodesh replied.

"I have no reason to withhold them—not after Ferdinand is freed."

Gwendolyn moved closer. "Freed, or killed? Why must we free him?"

"He amuses me." Kli Kodesh dismissed her with a toss of his thin, snow-white locks. Jeanne watched her eyes as they dropped to the ground and read the disappointment in her expression. She was the old toy now, it seemed. Kli Kodesh had already moved on to new amusements.

"It would be safer to kill him," Montrovant threw in. "Easier, as well. It is one thing to get in and strike swiftly at the source of the danger. Making it back out of that keep with a prisoner is another matter entirely."

"I've told you," Kli Kodesh smiled thinly, "they nearly worship your memory. You will have all the assistance you require once Santos's hold over them is broken."

Montrovant stared at him without speaking, trying to read the inscrutable lines of the ancient's face. Kli Kodesh returned that stare until Montrovant, at last, looked away.

"I have never been so tempted to risk my existence for the chance at another's blood," he said at last. "Your words entice me, but my heart tells me you serve no other but yourself—ever. You speak in riddles, telling each of those you meet what he wishes to hear, but all that is given in return are more riddles, and then betrayal. I do not want to help you, and yet that choice, as well, you have removed.

"I sense that you are truthful in one thing: the Grail is near here. If the treasure you snatched from beneath my very nose in the Holy City was not near, then Santos would not be here either. If you won't give me the location, what choice do I have but to seek that answer in the only other place I might find it?

"I will go after Santos, and, if it amuses me," here he hesitated, taking a step closer and staring intently into Kli Kodesh's ancient eyes, "I might release your servant. Make no mistake, I will eventually find what I seek. I will hold it in my hand, and I will drink from those depths, and I will feel that power. Your games and lies and trickery will not matter then more than leaves dropping in an autumn breeze."

Kli Kodesh merely stood and watched him, expression unreadable. He did not look away, nor did he flinch at the insults. He watched Montrovant patiently, waiting for him to finish. Angry as Montrovant was, he was wasting his words. Kli Kodesh had come to them with a purpose in mind, and that purpose would be served. He was content to stand back now and watch to see what would transpire. Jeanne read it in the ancient's stance, in the casual set of his shoulders. It reminded le Duc of a parent's patience with a stubborn child.

"We must move now if we are to reach de Chaunvier before he leaves his chambers," Gwendolyn cut in. "They will wait only until the moon has reached the center of the sky to start, and they will be in their places in Santos's chamber before that."

"I will need you with me." Kli Kodesh spoke the words softly, but their impact on Gwendolyn was sudden and intense.

She spun, her eyes wide and her mouth falling open. She backed up a step toward Montrovant, her arms raising from her sides. "But…I have come with them so far, to leave now…"

"Your place is with me. Have you forgotten this?" Gwendolyn's head dropped to her chest and the fire left her voice. "No. Of course not. How could
I forget?"

"She has been a great help to us," Jeanne cut in, aware as the words left his mouth that he was overstepping more boundaries than he could imagine. He pressed on. "She knows the inside of the keep better than we—would it not be better if she stayed with us until this was complete?"

"I cannot risk another so close to me with Santos," Kli Kodesh replied with cold finality. "You must go on your own. We have other tasks to complete."

"If I find," Montrovant said, ignoring the exchange, except as it affected his own plans, "that you are spending the time while I am doing as you bid me in betraying me again, it will be a final mistake. There are things which you fear, and there are other powers on this Earth than yourself. I will track you, and I will destroy you. On that you have my word. Take the girl if it means so much to you, but remember your promise."

Without another word, Montrovant turned and walked away through the shadows. He made no move toward the horses—there was no time. It was him and le Duc against the night, Santos, and whatever demons that ancient might possess. The time for worrying over being spotted doing something supernatural was past. If he failed in the moments and hours to come, then the knights would be nothing but a faded memory—whether it was Santos or Philip who made it so, it would happen. None who might see him this night was likely to see another.

Besides, if what Kli Kodesh had told them was the truth, they would not be looking for Montrovant the man, or Montrovant the knight. They would be looking for a dark savior, a power to flash from the shadows and drive Philip screaming into the night. He did not want to disappoint any who might actually be watching.

They flashed across the landscape, leaving Gwendolyn

and Kli Kodesh to stand in the shadows and watch as they disappeared into the distance. Montrovant was the swifter, but le Duc managed to keep him in sight, following his sire by the sound and scent as much as the sight of his darting, shadowy form. They both knew the way to de Molay's gates. The aroma of hot, fresh blood was in the air, drifting to them from the walls of the keep and the halls and chambers beyond.

Montrovant moved as if he were oblivious to that scent, but le Duc had no such strength. The hunger was eating at his concentration. He fought it back, focusing on his sire, and on the landscape before them. There would be time enough for the hunger and the blood when the night's work was done.

He reached deep inside for the familiar red haze, felt the world slowing, his motions becoming smooth and fluid. He did not so much hear and see the landscape as it passed as he felt it—became one with it. He remembered the haze from his mortal days in battle, remembered the sensation of seeking and ending the lives of others. He felt it in the air, sensed it in his sire as he flashed across the land in the Dark One's wake. It would be a night to remember. He moved to the laughter of the fates, and de Molay's keep loomed above them, tall and imposing, entrapping them like a huge spider's web.

As Montrovant and le Duc sped off into the darkness, Kli Kodesh stood watching, as though his will could drive them more swiftly to their goal. At last he turned to Gwendolyn, whose eyes were still focused on the ground at her feet, her shoulders drooping in despair.

"Come," he said softly. "You will see them again soon enough. For now we have others to meet. There are more things afoot tonight than de Molay and Santos know—more than Montrovant suspects. We must not hesitate, or it will be too late." Gwendolyn nodded. She did not appear cheered by his promises, but neither did she hesitate to do as he bid. If she opposed him, it was certain she'd never see Montrovant again, and that was not a thing her heart could bear.

Kli Kodesh and Gwendolyn streaked into the darkness, moving on a line parallel to the keep. The night returned to its silence—the moon watching them all with her solitary, glowing eye. In the darkness ahead, Gwendolyn suddenly sensed a group of others—all Damned. She nearly pulled back, certain that it was a trap, but Kli Kodesh only quickened his pace. With a small cry she followed, wondering what deception she'd be dragged into next. Wondering if Montrovant would believe that she'd known nothing about it. Wondering. Suddenly the night that had seemed so short loomed like an endless, painful dream.

SIXTEEN

Gwendolyn quickly became aware that Kli Kodesh was not heading for the keep, as she'd supposed. Despite his brave words to Montrovant, it appeared that perhaps he did fear Santos. At least he seemed not to wish a direct encounter. It wasn't until she sensed the presence of others that she truly understood.

It had all been planned. Down to Montrovant's dramatic departure, the speeches and call for aid—none of it was true. Not completely. Kli Kodesh had led them all down trails of falsehood carefully laid for the purpose of diverting their attention from his true purpose. She should have suspected. Ferdinand was only a servant. He might well have more knowledge of her sire than he'd had before

Gwendolyn left, but that did not mean he was a danger. He did not have the Blood, and he did not have Kli Kodesh's true name—without one or the other of those things there was no particular danger that Santos could pose without being face to face with Kli Kodesh. At least that was the way she understood it.

The two of them moved around a small copse of trees and she saw another waiting for them. He stared straight into her eyes from a very long distance, and she knew him in that instant. Nosferatu. Gustav. She'd met him only once before, but the experience had been so intense that she'd never shaken his image from her mind. He was powerful, not so much older than she, but a leader where she preferred to be led.

Gustav's own followers spread around him, shadowed by the darkness, a circle of red glowing eyes. Those eyes traced the progress she and Kli Kodesh made, progress that was much slower than it had to be—as if for effect.

"You have called, and we have come," Gustav said without hesitation. "What is it that you would have us do—where are the treasures?"

"They are safe enough, for the moment," Kli Kodesh said, reaching out a hand to place it on the Nosferatu lord's slender shoulder.

Gwendolyn was amazed again by the translucent quality of the vampire's skin—the way that her sire's blood had twisted even the horror of the Nosferatu to a thing very akin to beauty. Gustav was tall, emaciated, his head completely bald and his nose resembling a beak more than any appendage born to a human face, and yet he was not ugly. He glowed from within, a light that could not be extinguished, and it shone on certain hidden angles of his face, enhanced the expressive quality of his eyes, until features that would have seemed hideous under any other circumstances transformed themselves into a thing of power.

"You have done well," Kli Kodesh continued. "Montrovant has charged ahead, as I knew he would, to launch himself into the jaws of the demon. He was never one for the waiting game. We have a full day until Philip arrives, and with the confusion that will soon take place within the keep, we should be able to be in and out of the tomb without causing a stir. We must be gone before the dawn."

Gustav nodded, but the questions in his eyes remained.

"Why now?" he asked quietly. "Why not wait until Philip has his way with de Molay, and the area has returned to peace? Why take the chance of being seen, caught, or worse? Why draw the attention of others, of Santos or Montrovant, when there is no need?"

"Need?" Kli Kodesh replied, grinning slyly. "There are a great many levels and intensities to such a thing as need. We will act as I've said we will because it pleases me. There would be no point to this if it did not complicate—have you learned so little of me over the years, Gustav?"

He hesitated for a long moment, studying the elder Nosferatu's features carefully.

"Surely you know that the only purpose to such actions is the value of the entertainment?"

Gustav didn't reply, but Gwendolyn detected no amusement in those cold, gray eyes. He merely nodded and waited. She waited as well. She had no real idea of what was to come—this was the closest her sire had ever come to revealing intimate information in her presence. She knew that Gustav and his followers had played an important role in the ancient's past—a role that somehow continued into the present and expanded with the events of the time.

She couldn't imagine what could have brought the thin, aristocratic Kli Kodesh into partnership with such horrors as the Nosferatu, but it was obvious that there were a great many things she could not imagine that it might be better if she could. She had to wonder, knowing what she did of the various families of the Damned, if her sire were not Nosferatu himself, prior to the curse...if she did not have that twisted blood in her own veins...held at bay by his own special taint.

Too much depended on what would take place in the next few hours. She needed to listen, to concentrate, and when the opportunity arose, she needed to get away and take that information to Montrovant. She knew that the Dark One did not trust Kli Kodesh, that he had probably anticipated the treachery, but still she had to do what she could.

She could barely restrain herself from glancing to the skies...Montrovant had his own ways of following. There was no reason to believe he would take her sire at face value, though the ancient would no doubt detect such surveillance...and would it matter? The runes had been cast...what remained was to determine their meaning, and to act accordingly. It would not be easy. Kli Kodesh's control was masterful and complete, and he was not alone. All it would take, once she made her break, was for one of his followers to casually mention her absence, and it would be over. He would summon her back and she would obey. No matter the call of her heart, the call of the blood would win the battle, and there was no way of knowing how he would react after such treachery.

The Nosferatu gathered more closely about Kli Kodesh and

Gustav, and she drew herself into the shadows, watching. They were speaking in very low tones, and though she could catch small snatches of words, half-sentences and slightly raised tones, she could not put enough of it together to make sense. They continued to mention a tomb, and treasures, but nothing specific that she could grasp. Whatever it was that consumed their attention, it was not her. She continued to pull herself farther back into the darkness, not letting her gaze waver from the small circle that surrounded Kli Kodesh. If one of them turned, or if her sire shifted his attention toward her for even an instant, she would fail. If she failed, she would not get a second chance.

Her nerves fluttered but she held them in check with every bit of her will. If she bolted, they would see her. She needed to be far enough away before she made her break that none would catch the motion in the periphery of their senses or vision. She kept moving, thinking all the while that it was happening too easily, that it was as though they were letting her go, but unable to stop now that she'd committed herself. She wondered briefly if Montrovant would trust her even if she did manage to break away.

When she could only just make out the group standing in the distance, she turned and let herself stretch out—moving so quickly across the landscape that she blurred to a shadow. She moved in tense anticipation of the rude jerk that Kli Kodesh's control could apply, but it did not come. She disappeared around the far side of the keep and made directly for the wall, not hesitating as she reached its base, but leaping against the stone, moving so quickly she seemed to glide upward. She scaled the wall as if there were steps and handholds cut into the stone and slipped over onto the top of the wall gracefully.

Two events occurred in rapid succession then. There was a strangled cry from her left, and she sprang. Even as she'd come to rest on the wall she'd sensed the guard—too close not to notice. She had no time to spare for worrying over who might see her. She was in the air again almost the second her feet touched the stone, and she snapped the man's neck in the next instant, strong hands closing over him and smashing him down against the stone. The scent of his blood was pleasant, but it did not draw her. She let him fall, turned to check back the way he'd come, and followed the wall toward the nearest stair.

Now that she was in, she wanted to draw as little attention to herself as possible. She needed to reach Montrovant quickly, and she could not do that if she had a group of angry mortals chasing her, or any other such diversion.

She stretched her senses, seeking Montrovant's mind—calling out to him. She knew such a call was dangerous. It might attract Kli Kodesh's attention, if he were looking for her. She knew that if he truly wanted to find her, the effort would be less than that of a mortal swatting a gnat, but she wanted to believe she'd won freedom without his notice—at least for the moment. The thought that even this bid for freedom was tied to his devious plans was more than she could stand.

There was no immediate sign of Montrovant's presence, so she scrambled down a curving stair to the courtyard of the keep and picked her way through the gardens, sliding from tree to tree, shadow to shadow, eyes and mind alert for any who might notice her passing. There was no movement outside the confines of the keep itself, and few lights burned within. Fewer than she would have expected.

There was an odd vibration in the earth beneath her—an energy that seeped up to caress her obscenely. She hurried her steps, not wanting to maintain contact with the ground beneath her—forcing motion. She felt the call of that energy, felt it searching her soul for—something. She drew her thoughts deeper into her own mind and concentrated.

She slipped along the inner wall until she came to a door, and thankfully it opened. Security, for the moment, seemed concentrated on the outer wall. That would change when Philip drew near. For the moment she took advantage, entering the dimly lit passage beyond the door and heading straight for the central passage of the keep. She knew the inner layout well enough after the time she'd spent there with Kli Kodesh before he'd sent her away. Those times had been less tense, Philip's edict only a distant rumor, and she'd had free run of the keep.

She headed straight for de Chaunvier's quarters. That was

where her sire had sent Montrovant, and that was where she assumed he'd be, if she weren't too late. Otherwise they would all be below, and Montrovant would be forced to follow, hoping to disrupt the ceremony before it was too late. If he failed, it would be too late for them all—Santos would have the answers he sought and there would be nothing to stop him. Nothing.

She reached the upper level and made the turn toward de Chaunvier's quarters, stopping short as she rounded the corner and drawing herself quickly back around into the shadows. Voices floated down the corridor—the steady pounding of booted feet. She sensed Montrovant, le Duc and one other immediately. It had to be de Chaunvier. She'd met the man only once, and briefly, at mass. "Father" Kodesh had been speaking on the sin of pride—she'd not seen him look to the floor during the moment of silent prayer. He'd stared ahead, instead, fierce, proud eyes that bowed to no one.

She knew that Montrovant would know she was there, but at the same time she understood that it would not be a good thing for de Chaunvier to know. He would be caught up in the moment, walking in the presence of legend—of the sort of history one never expects to see validated. Montrovant had been instrumental in the formation of their order, even though the knights he'd known had predated the actual Templars by several years. The stories had grown from even the magical, unreal reality to mythic proportion. Now the myth walked the halls of Jacques de Molay—the only real question was whether he could prevent the mistakes of his predecessors from recurring, and the future from swallowing himself and the knights irrevocably.

Gwendolyn managed to find an alcove she could press herself into before the three passed. Their voices became clearer as they approached, then passed.

"Santos is a snake," Montrovant was saying. "He seeks nothing that will not aid his own particular cause, and to believe for even a moment that he has your interests in mind as well is folly. He will spit on the ashes of this keep and worm his way into Philip's confidence without the slightest guilt. He cares for nothing but revenge and the recovery of what he believes to be his own—treasures and powers that belong rightfully in the hands of the Church."

"The head?" de Chaunvier asked. "Is the head such a treasure?"

"The head is a power unto itself," Montrovant intoned. Gwendolyn would have smiled at the purposefully ominous tone of his voice, had the situation been anything but what it was. "It is not a part of Santos's charge, but something he acquired through association with the Cappadocians. He is an extremely learned scholar in all of the dark arts. The head is the key to his power—the answer to his questions. If Santos possesses your true name, he can control your soul. The head can provide that name—even mine. That power cannot save you from Philip, as he claims, unless of course you have some way of forcing him to use that power on Philip himself...which I doubt. The damage he can do once it is his again is beyond description."

"What do we do about Philip, then?" de Chaunvier asked, his voice rising an octave. "If you don't come to aid us, why should I listen to you?

There are worse things than dying at Philip's hand," Montrovant replied evenly. "Much worse. If you believe that the short years of your life are the only ones that can matter in your existence, you have not been paying attention to what Santos has told you. There are powers you do not understand, issues that hang in the balance this night that you could never comprehend. What is important is this—Santos must be stopped. Jacques de Molay must be stopped. He has been drawn in too deeply. He may even know that it is wrong, but still he will go through with this because he sees no other alternative. He is not ready to give himself for the good of the many. He will have it all or none, and that is when Santos is at his most dangerous. He will suck de Molay dry, and he will take you all along with him. He has no soul left to lose—that is the difference."

There was silence for a long time after that. Gwendolyn waited until she heard them descending the stairs before she slid from the shadows and followed, keeping herself pressed tightly against the wall and carefully back from the group descending ahead of her.

Once she caught le Duc glancing back over his shoulder. His eyes met hers unerringly, their minds linked—just for that second, and he nodded. Then the contact was broken and she was following at a distance again—separate, but knowing they were aware of her presence. The energy she'd felt seeping up from below was growing in intensity—driving up through stone and brick to grasp at her with ghost-fingers of unclean desire. She sensed that what was sought was not herself, but the blood that flowed through her veins. Kli Kodesh's blood. The blood that could lead Santos back to her sire and be the force behind his revenge.

There wasn't enough behind the groping assault to be effective, but it was an insidious reminder of how much was at stake. Her mind reeled, and in a sudden moment of clarity, she saw that there was no way that Kli Kodesh had not foreseen this, that he had not let her go full aware she was leaving. How could he not be aware? The only questions was, why had he allowed it, and what did he expect her to do now that she was within the keep? What possible entertainment value could she provide that would be worth the risking of his blood?

She followed them to the main level of the keep, and moments later, de Chaunvier in the lead, they disappeared down the stairs that led to the lower levels. She moved to the head of that stair, but hesitated. There would be no turning back from this. She didn't know why she was drawn after Montrovant as she was, but in the end the reasons did not matter. She slipped onto the stairs and melted into the shadows along the walls. There was no movement below save the three she followed, but she could sense that something was growing—something deep and resonant that shook the walls and vibrated through the stone of the floor and up through her bones.

It had begun. She knew, somehow, that de Chaunvier's presence was necessary to the completion of the ritual, but they had not waited for him to begin it. Santos was no fool. He would not hold off his plans for one mortal—even if the lack of that mortal might cause him to fail entirely. His life was in little danger, comparatively. It was his new followers who fought for their lives. It gave them an energy and power that they would not otherwise have had, and perhaps—despite de Chaunvier's treachery—it would be enough.

The chanting was loud enough to be heard clearly from where she made her way along the wall, but she could not make out the words. They were in no language she was familiar with—not even in a language that sounded remotely human. The syllables were too rough—and at the same time too complex—for human speech. Instead it reminded her of an odd, rhythmic melody—a dirge. There was no real tune to it, but the patterns of sound were unmistakably musical in nature.

She felt a rift growing between Montrovant and de Chaunvier. Apparently the Templar lord had gone ahead, entering the chamber as he was expected to, leaving Montrovant beyond the portal. The chanting shifted subtly, new tones adding themselves into the mix and others melting to different notes as if whatever had shifted in the energy that flowed through the tunnels and chambers had been made complete. De Chaunvier. He'd added his voice to those of the others.

Somehow Santos seemed unaware of the intrusion of Montrovant, le Duc, and herself, but it did not ring true with stories Kli Kodesh had told her of events in the past. If he was not aware, then something else was taking his full attention, and if he was aware, and just unconcerned, then it was worse yet. She knew that if anyone was an unexpected twist in the mix it was her. Montrovant knew she was there, le Duc as well, but de Chaunvier did not, and it was his mind that Santos had drawn into the chant.

Gwendolyn doubted that the Templar lord had the strength of will to keep any secrets. If Santos didn't yet know he was in danger, he would know soon enough. The question was whether or not de Chaunvier could reach Jacques de Molay in time to warn him, and whether that warning would be taken well. Santos might be evil, but de Molay still believed him the only answer to their dilemma. It would not be easy to sway the man from this belief, even less easy with Santos's spells weaving their way around them all.

She pressed as close to the wall as she could and slid forward. The doors to the chamber itself were still out of sight, and she wondered where Montrovant was hiding, or if he was hiding. There was no way to predict what he might do. The only thing she knew for certain was that they could not let the ceremony reach completion. She could only imagine what kind of danger that might bring as Santos anger burst on them full bore; not to mention the bulk of the Templars, who would see their intrusion as sacrilege.

She glanced around the corner and took in the passage beyond in a second. Montrovant and le Duc stood poised on either side of the doors to the chamber, as though they were waiting for something, a sign from within, or the last moment when concentration would be furthest from the possibility of interference.

She slithered around the corner, making no sound and willing her mind to silence. It was not enough. Montrovant looked up from where he stood on the far side of the entrance to the chamber, met her eyes, and stopped her cold. She had never seen such resolve—such intensity—in a single pair of eyes. He nodded toward the door almost imperceptibly, then held up a hand to warn her back.

Something was happening. The energy, which only moments before had circled them, permeating the air, was coalescing and sliding inward. She could feel the circling of force, like an invisible vortex, drawing everything into that chamber of shadows, drowning out separate sounds in a single cloak of confusion and darkness.

She reached her own hand out toward Montrovant, but before he could react, a scream arose from within the chamber. It rose like the mournful cry of a banshee—the wailing of a tormented soul. A shiver sliced through her veins, and she knew the voice in that moment as de Chaunvier's.

The energy crackled and rushed out of control—no longer focused, but still powerful. At that moment, Montrovant leaped through the doorway into the chamber, le Duc at his heels, and, knowing nothing else to do, Gwendolyn rushed for the entrance after them with her head lowered and her mind reeling. For better, or for dead, there was no turning back.

SEVENTEEN

Jacques de Molay was only aware of Louis's arrival on the very periphery of his senses. He knew that things had changed, that something formerly lacking in the chant had shifted and grown more powerful. He felt it as it coursed through him, entering and receding in waves that drained each of his thoughts as they came to him, taking with it his energy, his resolve. He stood and he danced. His lips moved and he knew that the odd, incomprehensible words of the chant were pouring forth in waves, but he had control of none of it.

He was beginning to wonder if there would be anything at all left of him by the time it was over—part of him hoped there would not be. The sensation was of such completion, such wonder and power, that to become a part of it for eternity did not seem such a bad end. Not as bad as being burned alive by Philip and his fanatics, or betrayed by the very Church he'd sworn to serve.

Santos swayed before the altar like a serpent, sleek and hypnotic. When Jacques looked he did not see the short, slight man he'd spent so many hours listening to and studying under, but another altogether. This being was tall, emaciated and powerful. He waved his arms and threads of energy that Jacques had not previously been aware of were spun through the air like a giant tapestry, crackling with energy and leaping wildly toward the walls. The pulsing energy behind those threads was blended with the rhythm of the chant—with the patterns of the dance. It was woven into his own mind and soul, a part of him as he was of it. Magic.

How many times had he dreamed of that word—that notion.

Magic that he could control. Magic that would open doors to things unknown and solve problems where his own mind came up against stone walls. This was an impossibility, all of it, and yet he danced, and he sang, and he watched the lifeless face glaring down on them from the altar, heart in his throat for the miracle that would save them all.

Now the magic flowed around him like water in a raging river and he had no control over it whatsoever. He wasn't certain if he'd even survive it, and the notion that the prancing demon by the altar cared for the salvation of his soul, his people, or his order had passed through fantasy to the totally surreal long before that moment. Santos was not human. He walked and talked as a man, but Jacques knew that what he saw now was much closer to the reality—the rest was a clever facade. These thoughts and others slipped in and out of his mind, but he wasn't able to grasp them or give them coherent consideration. They were snatched away and replaced with the thoughts he was supposed to add to the spell.

He sensed that the magic was not all Santos's doing. He felt each and every one of his followers in that force, felt them draining away toward the altar in the same fashion that he felt his own strength fading. It didn't affect their ability to prance and leap to the rhythm of the chant, or to keep the words pounding loudly from throats that should have been dry and sore. That strength was being focused back through them by Santos. He was taking their essence and distilling it through himself, using it to work them like marionettes.

Suddenly Louis was at his side. His friend's features faded in and out, wavering from shadow to grim visage and back again with each pounding of the energy that forced the blood through his veins. He concentrated, gripping the final strands of his dissolving mind. Louis. He had to try to warn him—to let him know what was happening. He had to force his lips to form coherent words.

In a sudden instant of clarity he was able to make out his friend's eyes. They were panicked, bloodshot. Louis was fighting the same fight within his own mind, clawing his way through the others toward Jacques. He was trying to say something, to snap free of the power that bound him.

Jacques saw this, then he saw Santos rise to an impossible height above them—or seem to—and he saw him snare Louis with a glance. Waving his hands in a new pattern, not part of the rhythm, but running in syncopated time to it, Santos reached out toward Louis and Jacques saw his friend lurch, stricken, nearly dropping to his knees. The energy surged, threatening to break free, but suddenly Louis was back on his feet. He spun past Jacques, dipping and leaping with a perfection his limbs could never have attained on their own. His eyes flashed past Jacques, and they were dead. Where there had been a strong will battling for freedom there was dead, unseeing darkness.

It was too much. The weight of the responsibility he'd carried for so long roared down on Jacques like a landslide, crushing its way straight through to his heart. He let his head fall back and he forced the scream that rose from somewhere deep within him to slash through the sound, disrupting the chanting and flying at Santos like a weapon.

"No!" He forced the word out, and though it was strangled and garbled, it was heard. Santos spun toward him, raising his arms again, but it was too late. "Enough!" Jacques cried. "Enough. It. Will. Stop. Now."

All around him, the others dropped like flies. The energy had sustained them while Santos was directing it, circling it back to them and draining it free again. Now the flow had stopped, and there was nothing to keep them animated. Jacques staggered, but did not fall. Somehow he held himself steady, keeping his gaze directed at Santos.

Santos quivered with rage. The power rippled through and around him. There was a greenish haze rising from the altar, surrounding the head, but it sat as dead and silent as when Jacques had first laid eyes on it, and somehow he knew that it would continue to do so. Santos took a step forward, then another. His eyes were blazing now, and his hands were in motion once again. His lips were moving—mumbling something so low that the sound did not carry. Jacques felt the hairs rising on his neck, and he knew that he'd made the last mistake of a long life. As surely as his mother had borne him, he was going to die.

Then the world exploded around him for the second time in only a span of short moments, and strong arms grabbed him from behind, dragging him away. He had no opportunity to resist, nor did he have any way of knowing who it was that held him. It didn't matter. They were moving back through the fallen bodies toward the door, and others were moving as well. A huge, dark figure had materialized in the door as Louis screamed, dark hair flying about his head as he dove into the chamber with impossible grace and speed. A second shadow flitted across that opening, not so fast, but with purpose, and he caught the glitter of a blade drawn.

Then there was nothing to do but lower his head and force the remaining energy in his tortured frame toward his feet. Whoever held him supported him a bit, but it was obvious that they were not much stronger than he.

"Damn you, Jacques," Louis's voice snapped in his ear, "stand up and run, or as God is my witness I will kick you through that door and all the way up the stairs. We have to sound the alarms—these men need help, and we are in no condition to offer it."

"Who?" Jacques managed to grunt. "Who has come?"

"Montrovant." Just that one word, but it slammed through Jacques like a stake hammered through his heart. He'd been warned. He'd been told that the Dark One would come, and he'd chosen his own path—the wrong path. Now good men lay at his feet as he ran for the sake of his own doomed life. He didn't know if any of it could have been avoided, but he knew that the fault for it lay on his shoulders.

They ducked through the door and into the passage beyond, expecting at any moment to feel the familiar tug of Santos's mind dragging them back, but the attack never came. There were cries from the room at their back, sounds that neither Jacques nor Louis could identify, or cared to.

A woman stood in the hall, just outside the door, and Jacques tried to stop and warn her, to let her know of the danger that lay within, but Louis dragged him onward. Jacques nearly broke free, but then he saw her face—met her gaze. She was not frightened, but there was a dark beauty about her that defied description, a luminescence to her skin and a depth to her eyes that he'd never before experienced.

He met that gaze for only an instant, then Louis was dragging him away again, but the image of her features embedded itself in his mind. Then there was the gray stone of the walls and the sudden added difficulty of forcing his drained body up the stairs toward the levels above—toward the world he'd known all his life and forsaken, toward those he'd doomed. He owed them this last effort. He owed them anything that was left to him, but still he could not erase the woman's image from his mind. He swore to himself that, should he live through the night, he would find her—would test the hunger in those eyes and know her mind.

The sound of dark, maniacal laughter floated up from below, and they redoubled their efforts to climb free. Louis was calling ahead of them, trying to attract the attention of guards, or servants, anyone who might roust the others from their bed. They might all die when Philip made his way to the castle, but they would fight one battle before then, and in this they could not fail. The laughter continued to mock them as they fled.

EIGHTEEN

Le Duc sensed that Santos was aware of their presence, but he was equally aware that de Molay's sudden outburst and treachery had not been expected. The room was a chaos of cries and bodies slamming against one another in a frantic effort to escape something that could not be seen. Santos stood in the midst of it, swaying back and forth like a confused serpent, sweeping his gaze around the room.

Montrovant was moving, and Jeanne followed his sire's lead. There was enough movement in the shadowed chamber to disguise their motion and give them a few more seconds. Jeanne felt his mind slipping away, felt his hand groping for the blade he wore at his side, as the tense lines of his face melted into a grim smile. The haze was descending, the red madness of battle that had been his mantle since the days of his youth, that had led him from his home, to the Holy Land, to the Templars, and finally led Montrovant to him. He welcomed it.

There might be nothing Jeanne could do in the conflict to come, but if he died the final death it would be as he'd always known it would. He would die a warrior, clawing at his enemy's throat and watching as the red blood spilled, his or the other's. It mattered little, in the end. All blood spilled eventually. Santos was a worthy foe, and it was as good a day as any to meet Death a second time.

He rolled nimbly in the opposite direction from the one Montrovant had taken, sliding through the milling bodies like quicksilver, using them as shields and gliding through shadows when there was no other cover available. Always his eyes were focused on Santos. The man paid no attention to him, but he did not trust things on the surface as he trusted his heart. His heart told him to tread lightly.

He saw that the small, thin man had spun away from him, saw his shoulders tense and his hands come up to spin and weave in some sort of intricate pattern that left wisps of light hanging behind his fingers in the air. Montrovant rose from the darkness across the room, moving toward Santos and the altar before which he stood so swiftly that he appeared to glide. His eyes glowed brightly and his lips were drawn back in a snarl.

Jeanne watched for a second, fascinated, as his sire moved toward Santos. There was no effort to pull away on the smaller man's part, no evidence of fear. A soft chant drifted across the room, and Jeanne realized that he could hear it over the cries and moans of the others, who were finally finding their way toward the door in their panic. He concentrated, but he couldn't make out the words. He thought he heard the name Montrovant, but he couldn't be certain, and it galvanized him into action.

He moved forward as quickly and silently as possible. He could not tell if Montrovant had seen him, nor could he be certain that Santos was not aware of him, but it no longer mattered. There was no other enemy in sight, and the battle madness demanded blood. He kept close to the floor and locked his gaze on Santos's slowly swaying form.

Behind Santos, a mist formed of incense and residual energy clouded the features of the head. Jeanne's concentration slipped. The head was as dangerous as Santos—did they dare to ignore it in such a moment? The ritual had not been completed, but who knew what properties it might actually possess, or how they might be released? Who knew how close they were to a destruction they could not understand or combat?

Santos took a step back, and Jeanne stopped, standing tense but very still, watching. Montrovant's leap had brought him in a long, slow arc toward Santos's throat, soaring across the chamber like a giant bird of prey. Santos held his ground, and at the last second he lashed out with one arm almost contemptuously. Montrovant drove into the smaller man, but was knocked aside, deflected by the impossibly powerful blow. Santos staggered but was not toppled, and Montrovant rolled to one side, out of sight.

Jeanne moved. He leaped at the altar, taking the head by the wispy gray hairs that clung to its scalp and swinging it up into the air like a club. He saw the eyes, dead and lifeless, spinning up over his head, then he saw nothing but his target.

Santos spun, eyes blazing, but le Duc was beyond thought. With a scream of rage, he brought the head around in a wide arc, crashing it against the side of Santos's skull and driving him back. The hair held, and Jeanne swung the head up again, intending a second blow. Santos, recovering swiftly, swept out with one leg and knocked Jeanne's feet from beneath him deftly. The head swung up and flew into the shadows.

In the second that Santos's concentration was broken—as he turned to watch the head fly across the room and mouthed a negation that never made it to full sound—Montrovant sprang again. This time Santos didn't even see him coming, and the two of them tumbled to the ground in a blur of darkness. Jeanne moved forward, his sword raised, but he couldn't get a good glimpse of who was on top at any given moment. The speed of their movements was uncanny, the strength of their blows enough to be felt through the stone floor of the chamber. Jeanne danced about nimbly, waiting.

He heard a strangled cry, recognized it as Montrovant, and moved closer, but he still couldn't be certain that if he attacked he would not strike his sire. With a curse he drew back his blade, ready to swing it with all his might—to hell with the consequences. The blow never fell.

Gwendolyn materialized from the shadows with sudden fury, screeching madly.

"Let him go!" she cried. "It is not the Dark One you want. It is the blood of Kli Kodesh, and I tell you now it stands before you. Kill Montrovant and you will never see it spilled—never know that name that has haunted you through the ages. This I swear."

Santos heard her, and her words struck home. He did not release his grip on Montrovant's throat, but he raised his head to stare at her. His head was cocked oddly to one side, like a dog that has heard something it can't quite figure out. In that instant Jeanne struck.

He put every ounce of strength granted him in his second life into that blow, slashing at a slight upward angle with his blade, driving it in beneath Santos's chin and slicing cleanly through the skin of his throat. One moment the ancient stared at Gwendolyn, the next his head seemed to leap from his shoulders, following the arc that the other head had taken short moments before.

There was a garbled, unintelligible bark of sound as his larynx gave way, then nothing. Silence. Jeanne and Gwendolyn watched numbly as the head took flight and Montrovant rolled free, tossing the dried husk that had been Santos's body aside in distaste.

There was no blood. There was no moisture at all. Santos had disintegrated into dust, leaving the pungent odors of spice and musk in the air. What remained of his frame couldn't support the weight of his robes, and they crumpled to the floor. Montrovant rose to stand beside le Duc, staring at the remains.

"What was he?" Gwendolyn asked softly. "What manner of being crumbles to dust at his death?"

"I do not believe we can count on his death any more than we can understand his power," Montrovant answered. "We have won. For now that must be enough."

He turned toward the doors that led to the keep above.

"They will be returning shortly. I will have to speak to them, de Chaunvier and de Molay. I will have to explain why I am here and pray that they know where the treasures are being kept—that they know of the Grail. We have very little time."

"How do you know how much time remains?" Jeanne asked, still dazed from the battle madness. "Do you not hear them?" Gwendolyn asked, turning her enigmatic smile full upon him. "De Molay's men are on the stairs, calling out as they come, and the name of Philip is on their lips. They come to rescue you, but only because they fear Philip more than the broken power of Santos."

Jeanne did hear them, once he concentrated. Feet were pounding on the stairs, and the clatter of armor and weapons drew nearer.

"The head," Montrovant said quickly. "We must get it and

remove it from this place. It is too powerful to fall into Philip's hands, or those of the Church. It must be taken far away where it can do no further harm."

"I will take it," Gwendolyn said softly. "I will take it down the back wall of the keep, where the mountain and the ocean meet. There is no way that Philip, de Molay or any other could follow me there."

Montrovant stood very still, gazing into her eyes, trying to read whatever emotion or deception might be behind her words. Satisfied, he turned away.

"We will catch up with you when this has ended," he replied. "We have to go after the Grail.

Wait," Gwendolyn called out as he headed for the door.

Montrovant turned, standing tall and proud, his eyes glowing brightly.

"They mentioned a tomb," she said softly. "Kli Kodesh, he has others nearby—Nosferatu. They are outside the gates of the city."

"I knew I couldn't trust him," Montrovant spat. "It is well. We will deal with de Molay and his men, and then we will deal with the ancient and his treachery, one way or the other. He shall have his entertainment this night, I think...more than he has bargained for."

"He thought that you and Santos would destroy one another," Jeanne said softly.

"No," Montrovant replied. "He knew that one of us would survive. He knew, as well, that the conflict would buy him time. Let us pray that it has not been enough time."

He turned to the door and was gone as surely as he'd stood before them scant moments earlier. Le Duc stole a last glance at Gwendolyn, trying to read the inscrutable expression on her face and failing. Then he spun to follow Montrovant to the upper levels. Nothing mattered now but to see it through to the end, and the haze had not departed so completely that he could resist the draw of battle. If Philip were truly approaching, and if Montrovant was planning to support de Molay, or even to win his way free, it was likely that Jeanne's blade would drink deeply at least one more time before the night was through. As he hit the stairs at a run, he prayed that it would be so. He had been too long at peace. The scent of blood, the taste of it permeated the air, driving him further toward the red. He could not stop to feed, not now. But soon.

He could not hear Montrovant on the stairs, but he could sense the trail his sire had left, and he followed that familiar tug of blood to blood, letting himself be drawn onto the main level and ignoring the stares of those around him as he bounded through them and headed for the stairs.

His first thought was that Montrovant had returned to de Chaunvier's quarters, but as he rose through the keep he realized that it was not so. They had bypassed that level and headed up toward the wall and the towers beyond. Montrovant was climbing toward the open air, and Jeanne doubled his pace, racing upward in pursuit.

He was vaguely aware of Gwendolyn gliding along behind him. She kept her silence, but he could sense the tension that drove her onward. Any moment Kli Kodesh could call out to her. She might want to support Montrovant, her "Dark One," as she'd dubbed him, but it was not fully her decision. The only hope she had was that her sire was too involved in whatever subterfuge he'd entered into with his Nosferatu followers to bother with her. The other possibility was that, independent as her actions seemed, they were exactly what Kli Kodesh expected of her. Jeanne knew he would have to watch her, along with whatever other responsibilities and burdens fell to him. Montrovant would ignore her as insignificant; Jeanne could not afford to follow suit.

He reached the top of the stairs and flew toward a squat wooden doorway at the end of a short hall.

He could feel the night breeze slipping in through that opening, and he could hear footsteps running, voices crying out—the voices the others had heard from below. He knew his own senses were not what they might be. He was younger in the blood than they. He knew, also, that he had other talents, other strengths, that they might not even suspect. He could sense the pounding of blood through many sets of veins—the pumping of endless hearts. For a second he reeled from the sudden impact of seductive sensation. He stumbled against the wall of the keep and the impact jarred him back to the moment.

Below he could feel them surging forward, hundreds—thousands strong. He could hear their cries. "Sorcerers! Heathens! Death to de Molay!"

So many strong hearts pumping delicious blood, so many thoughts floating on the breeze, confusing his already weakened control. Jeanne forced himself to slow his steps, taking equal control of his thoughts and reaching out to Montrovant for support—or at least for direction. He'd slammed into the wall so quickly that he'd lost track of his sire, and the last thing he wanted at that moment was to be abandoned on the wall of a castle full of mortals out for blood. They did not know him as they knew Montrovant. They would remember if they checked the books, the records—his name would be present—but it would not be enough.

He staggered past two guards who were rushing along the wall, eyes intent on the mob below. He watched as they reached out for the topmost rungs of a ladder he'd not even seen, shaking it violently, then pushing it outward with a cry. He heard those who'd climbed cry out in anger, then in fear, as they tumbled into the darkness, armor and weapons weighing them down mortally. The crashing, screaming, and moaning from below attested to the good aim—or fortune—of the guards. They'd taken out more than those dropped.

Jeanne saw Montrovant ahead. The Dark One had leaped to a point on one corner of the wall, standing like a huge specter against the backdrop of the sky, glaring down at those massed below. His head was thrown back, fangs extended and eyes glowing pits of hatred and anger. He looked less like a man than at any moment since Jeanne had first seen him...more like a demi-god, paying no attention to the arrows whistling by his head. He stood immobile for what seemed an eternity, and Jeanne had just managed to get himself moving again when Montrovant dove back onto the wall and retreated toward him rapidly.

"We have to get below," he said quickly. "There is something wrong. The Church is with Philip, but it is not just the

Church—there are others. I can't tell for certain who, or what, they have traveling with them, but there is an aura of old power hanging over us like a shroud. We have to move to be certain that shroud doesn't settle over us."

Le Duc hesitated. "You mean we are leaving?

Unless you feel a sudden urge to die for the order you left so long ago," Montrovant grated, "then I would suggest we leave, yes. What we seek is not within these walls, I would sense it if it were, and Santos would most certainly have had it in his possession. If we stay, we will almost certainly never leave under our own power."

The matter-of-fact way Montrovant outlined their probable fate drove like a well-honed blade through the battle-madness that had engulfed le Duc's consciousness. Gwendolyn appeared suddenly at their side, but Montrovant barely spared her a glance. He turned and headed back toward the stairs.

Jeanne followed, grabbing Gwendolyn by the arm. He wanted her as close to him as possible so he could watch her. She didn't resist as he dragged her back toward the stairs, but she did look perplexed. "He says they have someone—something— with them. We have to get out. Now."

"But..." Gwendolyn looked back over her shoulders. The guards had successfully repelled the attack. Below they could hear the sound of retreating boots and the clatter of horses' hooves and weapons. For the moment, Philip was drawing back. The keep would not be taken so easily, it seemed. Not this night.

"There is nothing we can do. We are not enough, not with what they have brought against us. We must go."

She nodded suddenly and followed, and Jeanne released her arm. Montrovant had already disappeared into the depths of the keep, and the two of them rushed down the stairs like a strong burst of wind, charging explosively onto the lower level. Jeanne hesitated, but suddenly Gwendolyn grabbed his arm and yanked him forward again. He might have lost track of Montrovant, but she had not. He followed her lead, and he found that they were returning toward the lower levels.

Everyone they passed stared, but none questioned their

passing. Montrovant dropped to the lower level like a stone through water and wound his way down the passages, passing the chambers where Santos and the head had threatened to destroy them all only moments before. The battle was up and beyond the walls; none had the energy to concentrate on a new threat from below.

Jeanne wondered what the purpose of returning to those vault-like chambers might be. Santos was dead, or gone for the time being—there was nothing of value left below, unless Montrovant was after the head, and that was difficult to understand. If that had been the case, why leave it in the first place?

They did not stop at the room where they'd encountered Santos, however. Montrovant flew past that entrance without so much as a glance, running full tilt down the passageway beyond. The floor had begun to slope upward again by the time that le Duc suspected there was another way out. He came to a halt behind his sire's back, directly in front of what seemed to be a solid wall blocking their progress. Without hesitation Montrovant moved forward, ran his hands across the stone surface, and pressed quickly in a sequence of indentations. The stone slid aside easily, not even a soft grinding sound to note the passing of tons of stone.

Turning with a quick, dark smile, Montrovant said, "I saw one of the knights enter this way earlier...knew I could find the latch if I looked closely. I didn't think we'd need an escape route until I sensed what awaited us out there."

Another mystery. There had been such doorways and passages in Jerusalem, but Jeanne had never had the opportunity to broach the subject, and now was certainly not the time.

Montrovant launched himself into the darkness behind the portal he'd opened, and Jeanne followed. He felt Gwendolyn moving close at his side, and was suddenly glad she was there. The stone closed behind them, as though on some sort of timed mechanism, and they were plunged into total blackness. The lack of light calmed Jeanne's nerves, and he found himself moving smoothly and confidently again. Ahead he sensed the movement of cooler air—freedom—or Philip? Only the next few moments could tell.

NINETEEN

Beyond the main battle lines, the bulk of Philip's army had begun the task of entrenching themselves for a siege. There was little hope that their initial surge would overwhelm the defenders of the keep. It might be days—even weeks—before they could breach the walls and bring down the gates. It didn't matter. Time was on their side—time, hunger, thirst—all the weaknesses of mankind.

Philip's own tents were set far back from the front line, and beyond these there was yet another grouping—smaller, but very elegant for such travel. The tents were of scarlet, and there were as many servants rushing here and there between them as there were guards patrolling the outskirts of the camp.

Brown robed figures stood stoically by the entrances to these tents, weapons that looked only slightly more out of place than the men who bore them hung in plain sight from the belts that bound their robes.

In the central tent, a tall thin figure sat quietly, his thoughts turned toward his own mind. All of his concentration was inward. He couldn't afford even the slightest spark of his true being to slip through the walls of his control. His mask of humanity had to remain complete and compelling. There were other enemies than Jacques de Molay present, and none of them could be taken lightly. He'd sensed the passing of the guardian, Santos, among others. The fleeting ghost-touch of Kli Kodesh's ancient essence flitted about the shadows, but never quite made itself known. He couldn't be certain whether the old one would detect him or not. It was even less likely that he would be able to guess at Kodesh's reaction to his presence. Best that none knew he was there, for the moment, and that he assume it to be so.

The brothers gathered about him closely, and they all knew of his "condition." He could not travel in the light of day, but had to sleep—at times to be borne upon their shoulders, or hauled in a cart. It was a penance, so they believed. He had traveled thus for hundreds of miles, and as each of those miles passed, the danger of suspicion grew, and the tales of his devotion to his Lord, and to the

Church, multiplied. It would have to end soon, or he would have to leave—possibly for good. There was no way he could let the truth be known.

He wanted to call out to the others, to join them. The road had brought longings he'd not known he still had—a desire for open road and bright stars shining down on a road to new lands. It had been dead within him for so long, this urge toward adventure and the open road, that it suddenly made him feel very alive. He smiled at the thought.

The tent flaps were pulled wide, and Bartholomew, one of his followers, made his way into the interior of the tent. He did not speak, but instead stepped forward, nearly dragging the cowl of his robes on the ground he bowed so low. In his hand he held a bit of paper, and this he placed on the floor before his master's feet. He backed away without a word, sweating profusely and breathing shallowly.

Glancing down, the thin priest read the words on the message quickly. It was in Philip's bold, arrogant script.

"We have them trapped like rats. Soon the Church will have the opportunity to cleanse them. We ask your blessing in the coming siege. The men are restless—it could mean the difference of days or weeks."

As representative of the Church it was his duty to bless. He was to sanction the spilling of blood in the name of God, and this message was Philip's way of asking that he bestow that blessing this very night. There was time. The sun was hours from the horizon, and it had been too long since he'd walked among men freely. Another foolish urge, he knew, but another that made him smile as well.

Rising, fighting to maintain the inward concentration that

would allow him the control he needed for the blank-faced, stoic guise he wore in mortal company. It was his shield against detection, as long as he was able to maintain it. He strode purposefully to the front of the tent and pushed the flap aside, stepping into the night beyond. The monks at the door looked at him in surprise, then returned to their silent vigils. There were other matters within that required their attention.

Leaving them behind, he strode through the camp. His dark red robes glistened like black liquid in the darkness, and the whisper of silk against his thighs as he moved was rhythmic and hypnotic. He moved with a grace that would have shamed a dancer, and he moved directly toward Philip's tent. No time to waste, no reason to do otherwise.

He came to a halt just outside, and the guards were already scrambling back through the door as they sighted him striding from the shadows. In truth, though they respected the Church very much, Bishop Eugenio made them nervous. He could feel their fear trailing behind them as they fought to be the one who would enter the tent to announce his arrival—and to not be the one left outside to greet him as he arrived. He drank in their fear and was surprised at how much the sensation pleased him. "Your Eminence," a bulky young swordsman spoke up, stepping forward and kneeling in the dirt, head bowed.

The tent flap opened, and suddenly the opening was filled. Philip stood there, untired by the day's journey or the evening's battle. His eyes were alight with the thought of victory after so long on the road, and his spirits were high—undoubtedly aided in this by the fruit of the vine. He stepped from his tent and knelt quickly, if not overly reverently, reaching out to take his visitor's hand and bring it to his lips.

"I thank you for coming," Philip said. "It is a grand day, or will be when the sun rises upon it. It will be a good thing to face it with the blessing of our Lord."

"I am not certain how our Lord truly perceives all of this violence," he answered, drawing Philip back to his feet easily, aware that the man was astonished by his strength. "I will offer my blessing, nonetheless. We must end this, and soon."

"That much we agree upon Your Eminence," Philip replied.

"War sounds so much more pleasant when the bards wrap their tongues about it than it seems when one is caught up in the middle of it. I'll be as glad as any to return to my castle, and my wife, and spend a few weeks—maybe years—deciding the fate of battling cattle herders."

"Let us do this. Let no more blood be shed without the proper invocations and blessings. Let this be a battle for all that is godly and righteous.

Of course," Philip said curtly. "How could I wish it otherwise? If it were not for the atrocities involved, I certainly would not be standing here before the holdings of Jacques de Molay, nor, I'm certain, would I find myself in such fine company." Turning back to the guard who'd first noticed their visitor arriving, Philip barked his commands quickly. The young man stumbled over himself to get away and spread the word. All those not injured or on the front line already were to assemble.

It had been a short conversation, much as expected. Philip was as intimidated as the others, as uncomfortable as any. He attributed his fear to God, to the tenets of Church and faith, to his upbringing—to a lifetime of supporting a Faith that rarely supported in return. The Church was fast becoming an agent of fear, another road to power for those not graced with royal blood.

None of that would matter in the moments to come. What could inspire fear on the one hand could inspire greatness on the other. He would bless their weapons, put the words and power of God behind the deaths they would cause, and they would go to the battle with the glow of faith burning from their eyes and lending its strength to their arms. It had been so through the crusades, through the pages and histories of the Bible, warped as those were becoming over the years.

He had seen too many such battles, too many tragedies attributed to a force for the greater good, to put any faith in powers beyond his own. Fortunately, in all the centuries of his life, his own had never proved lacking.

He strode through the gathering ranks of Philip's men purposefully, looking to neither side, but concentrating on the air a few feet above the heads of those directly in front of him.

He didn't need to watch where he was going. His senses were keen enough to guide him, and they were scurrying to get out of his way, in any case. He fully believed that the superstitious cretins would move tents or cut down trees to prevent them blocking his passage if they thought it would aid their souls on the road to "Heaven."

He could hear the sounds of the battle in the distance. Small fires had cropped up all around him, some with the aromas of food wafting from them, others merely warding against insects and adding to the illusion of size the army wanted perceived by those on the walls of the keep.

He could make out small figures scurrying about on those walls, shadows against the dim light of the moon. The closer, brighter light of the campfires, and the deeper red of the fires near the siege engines, the tar and pitch that would be slung over the walls, clinging to walls and men alike, burning them to ash.

"Praise the Lord," he muttered.

"What, Father?" a soldier standing nearby asked, fluttering around him like a nervous bird. "Is there something I can get you? Is something wrong?

Nothing." He brushed the man aside and continued along the rapidly forming line to what passed as the center, wondering if he could, after all, bring himself to mouth the meaningless words that he knew he must utter to pacify them all. Somewhere out there, Montrovant and the others were waiting, seeking what could not be found. There were matters much more important than the coming battle, or the lives of a few knights—even that of a king—in the balance.

Philip motioned that he should approach, and he did so, though nothing in his manner or gait suggested that it was due to any desire to be near the monarch.

"There is a great evil loose upon the land," Philip cried out. "An abomination before the Lord. Men worshiping idols, forsaking the God of their fathers and their father's fathers for the promise of dark powers. We move to put an end to this—to drive that evil back to the darkness from which it arose. We walk in the shadow of the Lord. We act in the name of His

Church. This night we will receive his final blessing, and soon, very soon, we will prevail in the task lain before us."

Turning, he locked eyes, then he continued.

"Bishop Scarpocci will administer the sacrament."

Stepping forward, Eugenio lowered his head and began to pray loudly and without passion. All around him the heads of those gathered dipped as well. Silence dropped over them quickly and completely, and his words echoed off the distant walls of the keep, so powerfully did they carry. They were words of praise—promises of victory and assurances of divine strength. They were tightly fabricated lies and deceptions, wound into the fabric of belief that had once held the Templars themselves so tightly to their cause.

TWENTY

Kli Kodesh and Gustav conferred in the shadow of one of the larger tombs. They hadn't counted on Philip being quite so prompt, and there were other things happening that were outside the range of their plans.

Gustav did not like things to be outside the confines of closely regulated boundaries, and though he couldn't exactly sense what it was that was wrong, he knew that his master was only too aware.

"There is something—someone—with Philip," Gustav said at last. "I cannot tell for certain who, but they are old—powerful."

"I know him," Kli Kodesh answered impatiently. "He will not cause us problems. He is here as an emissary of the Church."

"The Church has never been our friend, and that would seem to give him license to act the same."

"I am telling you, Eugenio will not pose a threat. We must move our cargo out of here now—this very night. Montrovant might be distracted, but he is not stupid. And there is the bitch to consider. She has told him by now what we plan."

Gustav stared at his master for a long moment, trying to gauge what he saw in those ancient, gray-flecked eyes. He did not believe that Gwendolyn had escaped on her own. He didn't believe, for that matter, that he himself could have done so. He didn't answer. Not for the first time he was forced to try to weigh his own importance in the ancient's eyes. Not for the first time he was less than happy with the result.

"If Montrovant is aware of us," Gustav said at last, "then moving the treasures would be playing right into his hands. If we leave them in place, we could make a run for it, distracting him."

"We will move them tonight," Kli Kodesh replied without hesitation.

"He will catch us."

"Do you fear him, then, Gustav? Have you so little faith in me that you think one so young can take something we do not wish taken?"

"I fear nothing. If I did, I would not follow you and your endless…entertainments."

There was a tense moment of silence where things might have gone either way. Gustav waited, motionless, for Kli Kodesh to decide his fate. The time for dancing and foolishness was past. Those around them had ceased all movement at the first raising of Gustav's voice.

Kli Kodesh's face cracked suddenly, breaking into a helpless gale of mirth. He fell to the ground, doubling his thin frame over and letting his snow-white hair dangle to the ground before him. His frame shook uncontrollably and he banged his head violently into the earth, as if trying to shake loose the humor of the moment and return himself to his senses.

Gustav did not move. He wasn't foolish enough to think that this was truly a vulnerable position for the ancient, nor was he ready to challenge such power with his life on the line. He stood, his followers gathered at his back, watching in silent fascination, until Kli Kodesh regained some measure of control and raised himself to his knees, looking about himself in bewilderment for just a second. The next his eyes were clear and bright again.

"Pack everything up, Gustav. We leave within the hour."

There was no point in further argument. Turning away in silence, Gustav gestured for the others to begin moving the stone from the door of the tomb. Others were already moving closer with a small horse-drawn cart. On the cart sat several wooden crates, banded in steel. They lay open and empty, their interiors dark patches in the silvery moonlight. Kli Kodesh stood back and watched, still trembling from the fit of laughter that had claimed his senses only moments before. He watched, but his mind was far away—scanning—planning against possibilities only he could see.

Eugenio should not have come. He should be tucked safely away in his monastery, where he was happy. He should be ignoring his progeny's odd quest, leaving them all to their amusements, and yet here he was. There had to be more to it than a simple desire to help Montrovant. The call of blood to blood was a strong one, but the risk of exposure in Eugenio's position was phenomenal. The Lasombra had far too much to lose for it to be a simple rescue of his progeny.

What then? Brow furrowed, Kli Kodesh continued to concentrate, watching the darkness that surrounded them as the Nosferatu quickly packed the contents of the tomb onto the cart and prepared to take off. Damn Eugenio, anyway; what did he want?

Jeanne pressed himself to keep up, and Gwendolyn moved easily at his side. Montrovant had launched himself through a lighter patch in the shadows ahead, and Jeanne saw an instant later that it was a doorway. The light he saw was that of the moon, and they'd come out just beyond the walls of the keep on the opposite side from Philip and his army. To their right was a sheer cliff, dropping away to a rocky beach. The crash of waves on those rocks was rhythmic and hypnotic, but Jeanne's concentration was on Montrovant.

The tall vampire had stopped short, turning his head first one way, then the other, as if confused. Jeanne let his own senses expand, searching for whatever was the cause of Montrovant's confusion. He felt others out there, powerful presences. One was familiar enough: Kli Kodesh. There was another, though, achingly familiar and nearly as ancient. He couldn't put a name to it, but as he came nearer, Montrovant did so for him.

"Eugenio."

Jeanne hesitated, grabbing Gwendolyn again and holding her back. He had to be certain he'd heard what he thought he'd heard, and he had to be certain how Montrovant would react. Eugenio? Here? Why, after all this time, and what did it mean for them?

"We must move quickly," Montrovant said suddenly, turning to them. His eyes burned with intensity. "Eugenio has come—he is with Philip. I have no idea how this has come about, or why, but if he were here to aid us he would have made his presence known before now. If he were not my sire I would not have known him just now—his mind is powerfully shielded."

"Kli Kodesh is near as well," Gwendolyn cut in. "I can feel him nearby—he is...disturbed by something."

Montrovant paused for an instant. If Kli Kodesh were distraught, then apparently there were others whose plans had been complicated by this new twist. Then the moment passed and he spun away, disappearing so quickly into the night that he was nearly out of sight before Jeanne was able to launch himself in pursuit, cursing.

They moved along the edge of the cliff, heading on a straight line away from the keep itself. The fires on the other side shone around the edges of the stone structure, silhouetting it in rose and magenta against the deep ebony of the sky. De Molay and the others could not hold out for long. The Templars' days were numbered, it seemed. They would die, but the Dark One lingered.

As they passed beyond the cleared area that surrounded the keep, a short, squat stone structure loomed on their left. A church. Jeanne wasn't certain exactly how he knew this, but there was a feel to the old place that reached out to him. It left him cold, cold and empty as the church itself must have been for the last fifty or more years. Half the walls had given way to time, and the windows were wide open and overgrown with vines. The small tower that had once housed the bell lay toppled to one side, and the moon played off it in eerie, shadowed streaks. Beyond the church was a gate that was no longer attached to the fence decaying on either side of it, and it was through this that Montrovant sped. He paid his companions no more attention than he might have an annoying insect that flitted about his head, and for a moment Jeanne considered just stopping, pulling Gwendolyn to a halt beside him, and letting the fool get himself killed. It would solve a lot of problems, he knew, but there were other, worse dangers—and one of those might be waiting behind them. If Kli Kodesh was not interested in doing them in, Eugenio almost certainly had other than their best interests in mind. Even if neither of them were concerned with a couple so young to the Damned, the fallout from whatever they did have in mind was likely to require all the craft and strength they had between the three of them, just for survival.

Montrovant was moving with a bit more stealth. Jeanne relaxed somewhat as he and Gwendolyn caught up. He didn't slow his own progress until he was nearly abreast of his sire, not wanting the other to put on a burst of speed and leave them behind. Whatever was coming up next, they would all be a part of it, and he wanted to be close enough to follow Montrovant's lead. Gwendolyn seemed content to let him lead the way, and he was grateful that she didn't question him. She certainly had the right to, but it would have served no purpose at that moment but to slow them down.

The impression that they were not alone grew stronger each second. Jeanne could feel the weight of eyes boring through him, from the front, back, sides. He ignored the nagging mental itch and concentrated on more practical senses...sight, sound—touch. He knew that Montrovant, or Gwendolyn, for that matter, was more likely to detect trouble than he, but his instincts were different from theirs. His were the instincts of a born warrior, without the burden of careful thought or devious planning. Things that might not register in Gwendolyn's mind would alert him in an instant. Montrovant couldn't be trusted not to ignore such warnings. That left Jeanne.

The graves surrounding them were overgrown and crumbling, with a very few exceptions. Apparently whoever had once cared for the cemetery had long since given up that responsibility. A very few monuments were cleared well enough that the inscriptions could be read. It seemed if one did not have surviving family, there was no one left to maintain the grave... or to mourn the dead in this desolate place.

"Where are they?" Gwendolyn asked at last. "I can feel them, Kli Kodesh, the others, but I cannot tell where they are watching us from."

"We are surrounded," Montrovant replied softly, "but it is a ruse. We are meant to concentrate on the imminent danger of those left behind while others make off with what we seek.

They circle us to confuse our senses. The rest of the party is moving—there."

He turned suddenly and pointed along the ragged line of the cliff. Jeanne frowned, In that direction the drop to the ocean below was even more steep and cruel than that beside the walls of the keep. Access from that direction would be impossible for any invading force, nearly so for a single very talented man. It would pose little challenge to one such as Kli Kodesh, but how could they escape once they made the descent? Something was not right. "It is another trick," Jeanne exclaimed suddenly. "There is no reason they would risk us catching up to them on that cliff, and there is no way they could escape with any sizable cargo unless they plan on destroying us here."

Montrovant spun, surprised, but then he nodded. Concentrating, he smiled. "If they plan on ending us here, Kli Kodesh himself will have to do the work. There is none other among them powerful enough."

"Then Gustav is not here," Gwendolyn cut in. "He was old to the Blood when he first fed from Kli Kodesh. He was here when I escaped."

Montrovant nodded in agreement. The ancient Nosferatu was nowhere nearby, and that was reason enough to believe that Jeanne was correct. Somehow he was moving in another direction, and they were shielding that movement.

"We can sit tight and wait to see what they have planned," Montrovant said softly, "or we can try to outguess them and follow Gustav."

"I have no stomach for waiting," Jeanne replied.

"I want to leave this place," Gwendolyn agreed. "They are driving me insane, and too much of eternity stretches before me to face without my wits." Montrovant smiled. Jeanne knew he'd never planned on truly offering a choice. More likely he was concentrating, trying to determine where Gustav might have gone. Jeanne could sense nothing but a confusing mess with one powerful splash to their left. That splash was Kli Kodesh himself, and suddenly he knew what they had to do.

"It is the ancient who shields him," he cried. "He is moving around the flank of Philip's army."

Cursing, Montrovant dove into action, leaping straight at Kli Kodesh so suddenly that he was gone before Jeanne and Gwendolyn could react. They followed as best they could, but even with proper warning neither was match for the Dark One's passion or speed. There was a cry from the shadows, a loud curse.

Jeanne slid around the corner and skidded to a stop. Montrovant was kneeling, his entire frame trembling with the effort to rise. The anger and hatred blazed from his eyes, which glowed like hot coals in the darkness.

Standing over him, Kli Kodesh held one hand out, palm down, as if physically pressing his assailant into place on the ground. The ancient's eyes glittered, as well, but with madness and mirth, not anger.

"No," Gwendolyn cried. Jeanne reached for her, but again he was too slow. She leaped past him, screeching in rage and diving at her sire's eyes with her hands outstretched like talons. He looked up, half dazed, half-amused. His eyes locked with hers, and she fell to the ground, her legs collapsing beneath her and her head dropping so that her face pressed into the damp soil. Kli Kodesh started toward her, his smile washed away in a sudden burst of rage. As he moved, he neglected Montrovant for just that second.

Jeanne saw the Dark One poising to spring and he launched himself into the fray, knowing it was a foolish and probably final gesture, but unable to stop himself. Montrovant had no chance against one so ancient, none at all, but if he were to have the opportunity to test this he needed a distraction. "Leave her," Jeanne cried as he leapt from the shadows. "Leave her and face me, old one. I've had enough of your damned games."

Jeanne's blade was in his hand, though he did not recall drawing it, and the rage rushed through his veins, shutting down rational thought. This grinning madman had played them all for fools again and again, and now he stood there, mocking them, controlling them like so many marionettes in a show. It was too much.

He swung his sword in a wide arc, aiming it for Kli Kodesh's throat. Of course, that throat was not there when the blade passed, but neither was Kli Kodesh closing in on Gwendolyn any longer. A huge shadow materialized from the right, crashing into the old one and driving him to the ground. Jeanne tossed his blade aside and leaped after them. No way Montrovant could hold him, but the three of them? What then?

He crashed into the rolling heap of bones and muscle and managed to make out Montrovant's dark hair, blowing wildly about his head in the night wind. Grabbing Kli Kodesh's legs, he held on, praying that Montrovant had something in mind besides just attacking and dying. Gwendolyn was beside them now, and she'd latched onto one of her sire's arms, holding it in place.

Looking up, Jeanne could see that Montrovant had Kli Kodesh's throat gripped tightly between strong fingers and was holding that ancient, graying head tightly against the ground.

"Where is it?" Montrovant screamed. "Where have they taken it? You will answer me, or by all that is holy your blood will spill for the final time this night."

The ancient went suddenly limp in their arms, but none of them released their hold. Jeanne knew it was too easy, and moments later, when their captive's emotions shifted yet again, driving him into gurgling, hissing spurts of laughter, he knew the truth of it. They were the playthings of a madman.

Montrovant's anger grew and the ancient's mirth followed suit. The ancient rolled back and forth on the ground, beating his hands against the earth despite the hold Gwendolyn had on one arm, kicking his legs in seeming glee as Jeanne held on grimly.

As the haze released his mind slowly, Jeanne became aware that they were not alone. The Nosferatu. Montrovant paid them no more mind than he might have a swarm of insects, but Jeanne leaped to his feet, locating his blade in an instant and bringing it to the ready. Gwendolyn stood as well, but she made no move to attack or defend, only watched coolly as the disfigured, ethereal band circled them slowly.

Then, almost casually, Kli Kodesh pressed his hands against the ground and levered himself upright, despite Montrovant's grip, finding his balance and lurching to his feet. Montrovant did not release his hold, and the two of them stood now, the elder grinning up into the face of the younger, whose face was so suffused in rage that Jeanne began to worry he might have lost his reason.

With a sudden violent heave, Montrovant actually lifted Kli Kodesh off the ground and flung him to the side, where he crashed into the stone wall of a tomb. Looking a bit surprised, the ancient regained his feet once more, brushing the dust calmly from his robes as the Dark One approached him once again.

"You really are wasting your time, you know," Kli Kodesh spoke at last. "I've sent the treasures out of here with Gustav, and if you don't catch him by sunrise, he will be long gone."

Montrovant stopped and stood very still. Jeanne could feel the emotions warring in his sire's mind, could feel the turmoil. Another chase, more lies, more likely than not, and this grinning madman stood there still, mocking them. Tantalizing Montrovant with first one, then another bit of the puzzle, but never enough to keep up with the new pieces being cut.

"Why should I believe you, old one?" Montrovant replied at last. "Why, when you have twice sent me to near-certain destruction, both times for the dual purpose of distracting your enemies and providing sick, personal entertainment for your ancient, putrid mind? You tell me why I should believe you, because my instincts tell me you are lying to me once again, and I'm tired of being toyed with."

"So," Kli Kodesh replied, still smiling. "You will stay and threaten my existence, will you? Surrounded as you are, powerful as I am, you would rather fail to kill me than pursue your dreams? I'd thought better of you than that, really I had. I have to say I'm a bit disappointed, Dark One." On those ancient, mocking lips, the name seemed empty. It was obvious which of the two had seen the deeper darkness.

Suddenly there was a stir among the Nosferatu, and both Kli Kodesh and Montrovant turned to the outer ring, as though they'd heard something far away. Moments later, the steady creaking of wagon wheels approached them, and the shuffling of feet. Many feet. The Nosferatu drifted back into the shadows, and Jeanne could feel their fear, though as of that second he didn't know the nature of their danger.

Montrovant stood like a statue, waiting. The ancient stood beside him, a few feet away, and for the first time since his earliest encounter with Kli Kodesh in Jerusalem, Jeanne saw an expression of bewilderment blanketing those inscrutable features.

A tall thin figure made his way through the graves, and behind him a group of others, huddled close together and shuffling in step, followed. As he drew closer, the man tossed the hood back from his head, letting his long hair blow in the wind and the bright glitter of his eyes burn forth.

"Eugenio," Montrovant muttered under his breath. "Wha...?"

"I thought it was about time I came and saw what was happening for myself," Bishop Scarpocci's voice boomed out. "I see that there are more forces involved here than I was led to believe."

Kli Kodesh was grinning again, and he stepped forward a few feet. Jeanne could sense the power emanating from this new figure, could feel the call of blood to blood that drew him more strongly, even, than Montrovant's.

"Now this is entertaining indeed," Kli Kodesh cackled. "This is better even than I could have planned it. Both of you here at once. How jolly."

"You see," Eugenio said softly, "I knew you would not be able to resist having a hand in all of this. I knew I would find you here, and, if I did, I would find what Montrovant seeks, as well."

Kli Kodesh smiled again. "You have found your whelp," he said, ignoring Montrovant as he would a child, "but that is all you have found. There is no treasure for you here, no Grail or holy object, Bishop. You'd better run along back to your little stone prison and stick to things you understand." Montrovant started toward Kli Kodesh again, but Bishop Scarpocci held up a hand, motioning him back. With a smile that matched Kodesh's own, he motioned to those behind him. They moved slowly forward, and the creaking of wagon wheels resumed.

Seconds later, a cart rolled into sight. On the driver's seat, bound in chains, sat a robed figure.

Jeanne stared at the wagon, then turned back to Eugenio, and finally to Kli Kodesh. Kli Kodesh had gone silent, and his jaw had dropped. He spoke a single word.

"Gustav."

"The entertainment," Eugenio said softly, "is just beginning."

TWENTY-ONE

Jacques staggered down the main hall of his keep. There were screams all around him, women sobbing in corners and young people rushing about, gibbering in fright. His men held the walls, but barely. Philip had redoubled his attack, and somehow Jacques knew that his moments were numbered. His mind reeled with the events of the past few hours. So many things he might have done differently…so many others he need not have dragged down with him.

Now he wandered, stumbling into walls and cursing as he went, toward his chambers. There was nothing left to do. He would sit back in his chair, the same chair he'd sat back in for decades. He would pour himself a large goblet of wine, down it, then pour another, and he would continue that process until there was nothing left of his mind. No pain. No images of men burning, falling from the walls of his keep trying to keep out a ruler who fought with the same Church at his back that Jacques had sworn to defend. No accusing glances or cries of fear. Red wine to wash away the red blood that stained his hands.

He staggered onto the stairs, climbed. It wasn't until he was nearing the top step that he felt a strong hand clamp onto his shoulder, pulling him back. He lurched forward, trying to keep his balance and not go toppling back down the stairs. The motion dropped him to his knees, cracking them painfully on the stone of the floor, and anger blossomed suddenly, overcoming the melancholy that had stolen his sense only moments before.

"Damn you, I…" he turned, and he fell silent. Louis stood there, one hand still gripping his shoulder, staring at him with such reproach and disdain that it stole his courage in an instant.

"It has to end, Jacques. We can't slink off to drown our sorrows as these people who trust us die. By the God I still deem holy, I will not let it happen."

Jacques didn't answer immediately, and Louis shook him insistently. "Do you hear me? We must do something...now. This very moment."

"And what would you have me do, Louis?"

Jacques asked, shrugging free of the other man's grip and turning to face him fully. "Would you have me wade out into the attacking horde and beat them off with the strength of my arm and the courage of my soul? Would you have God intervene? Should I ask him, do you think? What is it that you think you and I might do to set things right? Tell me now, for I am without words or thoughts on this!"

Louis's reaction was sudden and violent. Jacques barely had time to realize his friend's arm was swinging back before the fist connected with his jaw and sent him reeling backward. He pinwheeled his arms, trying to recover his balance, but it was too little too late. He crashed into the stone stairs with stunning force, cracking his head on the wall. Before he could cry out Louis was on him, holding him down by the throat.

"Damn you," Louis grated, his eyes blazing inches from Jacques's own, "You will get up and you will come with me and we will find a way to end this. I have followed you, listened to you, and it is possible that I have given over control of my soul to you and that demon you keep below. I will not see you drag the others down that same road so you can spend your last hours clutching a bottle of wine and crying in your room. You will stand like a man, or I will kill you now and save Philip the trouble."

Jacques blinked once in confusion; then his eyes cleared. He rose shakily, Louis still gripping him by the arm, waiting for an answer.

"You are right, of course," he said, brushing his friend's hand aside. "I have no right to give up, though my soul is forfeit. I think, perhaps, that it is time for you and I to pay Philip a visit, or to welcome him to our halls."

"You will repent?" Louis asked.

Jacques returned his friend's gaze levelly. "I will not. I have failed in what I sought, but it does not change the loss of my faith. With creatures such as Santos in the world, how can one have faith in higher powers?"

"That is the difference between us, Jacques," Louis replied. "With such powers as Santos loose in the world, I cannot help but pray to a higher power."

Jacques clapped him on the back heartily, the smile returning to his face for the first time in so long it felt strange. He started back down the stairs, bellowing for his armor and his sword, and Louis fell in behind him. The time for waiting was at an end. They were knights, after all, and when there was trouble, there was one way they met it best: together, swords drawn and minds free of all else. Perhaps if they'd remembered that, they might not have been dragged so far into the darkness.

The air in the keep seemed charged with energy. Knights and servants ran crazily about, gathering weapons, slipping into armor. Jacques had called them all to the courtyard, and rumors flew in all directions of what he had planned. Some believed de Molay would lead them in an attack, spending their lives in one last, insane charge. Others believed he would surrender and put himself at Philip's mercy. Still others said that he'd found a way they might all slip past the army waiting beyond their gates and escape to fight again another day.

One thing was certain, he was going to act. That was the best news they'd had since hearing of Philip's edict. There were no new rumors of the dark stranger in the dungeons of the keep, but it was whispered that things had changed. It was also apparent that their lord had not returned to those lower levels. There was no more talk of devils and black magic. Jacques was storming about like a man possessed, but he was alive with the spirit of the Templars, and it was a familiar spirit.

It took a remarkably short amount of time to gather the majority of them into the courtyard, and Jacques wasted no time. He jumped to the top of a wagon so that he could be seen and raised his hands for silence. In that moment, standing as he was, looking down on them from above, he looked every bit the

Templar lord. He wore full armor, his eyes flashed fire—he was the Jacques de Molay of old.

"I have called you here to give you a final choice," he cried. "I have led you into a position that could cost your lives, and I am sorry for that. I would not change anything that I have done, except that I would have done what I have done on my own. I have cost you all a great deal, and for that I hope you—and God—can forgive me."

There was a rumble of whispered words, but the sound died away quickly when he continued to speak.

"Philip stands outside our gates, the Church at his back, ready to put to death any who will not renounce the vows we have sworn to live by. He has proclaimed to the world that all that we are, all that we stand for, is darkness and evil. He has said that we are the servants of Satan, and for this he and his followers have declared that we must repent or die."

Here he paused, looking around at those gathered in silence, searching their faces carefully.

"I would not make that choice for any man. Our order will not die here today. You know we stretch beyond the boundaries that Philip controls, beyond even the boundaries set forth by the Church. There are places you can go—ways to continue in the service we have set forth. These roads I open to you. You may go, renounce the order, renounce me—and save your lives. It was not your choice to risk them—but I will make it your choice to keep them."

"What of you?" a tall knight cried out from the very top of the stairs leading back into the keep.

"What will you do?"

"My time here is ended," Jacques declared stoically. "Philip will not accept my repentance, even were I to offer it, and I shall not. I have lived too long as I am, too many bridges have burned behind me. I will not tell you all of the things I've done, nor the things I've seen," He swept his gaze over them quickly, as if expecting them to challenge his words. "I will say only this—there is more to our world than meets Philip's eyes, or even those of the Church. Do not let them close yours. Leave here as free men, and find your families—your homes. Keep our secrets alive in the world. Too many great men have come before me for you to allow me to end it here."

The murmuring rumble of voices rose quickly, and Louis de Chaunvier stepped up to stand at Jacques's side.

"I will remain, as well," he cried. "Any among you who would stand with us as brothers may remain. We will send word this very day to Philip that he might let those who wish to repent leave in peace.

"Know this—if you remain with us, your lives are forfeit. Philip will put us to the flame—he has no choice. The minions of Rome swarm around him like insects waiting for their turn at a rotting carcass. There will be torture, pain, and no easy deaths."

Small groups began to cut off from the main pack. Jacques stood quietly watching as many moved toward the keep, some to retrieve their belongings for a journey, others to retrieve their weapons in the hope of dying cleanly before Philip took them and burned their lives away. There was nothing more he could say. His future lay in the shadowy shapes flickering through the flames just visible as a glow above the walls of the keep. In the clashing of weapons and the cries of an enemy he'd once called brother.

Louis clapped him on the back once more.

"I will go now and organize those who will leave. They will need the provisions worse than we—and I think it will take some doing to get them out of here quietly."

Jacques nodded. He was nearly beyond words, but he managed to voice a final question.

"Where is he, do you think, Louis?
Philip?"

"Montrovant. The Dark One. He was here when we needed him most, but now it is as though we dreamed it all. Do you think he watches us still? Do you think he approves?"

Louis pondered the questions for a long moment, then shrugged. "He did not seem to judge us, Jacques, only to warn us. This is not his fight—not any longer. We should be thankful he returned in time to grant us our souls."

"Did he?" Jacques turned away and strode toward the

stables, his shoulders squared and his steps strong and even. He did not turn back.

Louis watched him go, then, turning to the nearest knight who'd remained at his side, he barked out orders for a messenger to be sent to Philip, and for others to gather what remained of the supplies. He would have to get them packed and distributed quickly, or it would be too late. Once Philip took the keep, all would be forfeit, and it was unlikely, though he might be willing to spare the lives of the "repentant," that he was going to be generous with food, medicine or other supplies. His men had been too long on the road.

In the distance he heard the clatter of hoofbeats and the cries of the awaiting army. It was, he decided, a good night to die.

TWENTY-TWO

Jeanne saw Kli Kodesh stare at the wagon for a long time, not meeting Gustav's eyes. There was no defeat in his stance, no backing down or turning away. Jeanne's mind began to work over the possibilities swiftly. What more could he have planned? The Nosferatu he had gathered about them, with Gustav in chains, were no match for Eugenio, nor for Montrovant, for that matter. Kli Kodesh might destroy them all himself, but not without a price, and not without the risk that he himself would be taken down. Protected as he might be from the final death by his curse, his blood was under no such protection. Jeanne could feel the draw of it himself, and he knew that the potential flowing through the ancient's veins called out to Montrovant and the bishop even more strongly.

"We will see what we do and do not have," Eugenio said softly. He gestured to the monks gathered at his back, and they moved toward the cart. Gustav glared at them, but he was helpless to prevent them from searching the cart, and he knew it. Jeanne watched in fascination.

Kli Kodesh made no move to prevent them from doing as the Bishop had bid them, and that was strange, as well. Something was itching at the back of Jeanne's mind. Something they were forgetting. The monks pulled back the cloth coverings on the wagon to reveal the large wooden chest that lay beneath. Montrovant strode forward suddenly, leaping to the side of the wagon and pushing the monks out of his way. They didn't resist, scurrying this way and that at his approach. Eugenio didn't say a word, only watched.

Montrovant didn't hesitate. He grabbed the lid of the chest, and, though it was locked securely, ripped it back so that the wood around the hasp gave way and it slammed open with a thud. He stood that way for a long time, gazing at the contents of the chest. Jeanne wanted desperately to know what was in that box, but he knew better than to interrupt the moment.

Suddenly Montrovant plunged one hand into the crate and drew it forth with a long, thick chain of pure gold dangling from his hand. Beneath his tightly gripped fingers an ornate cross spun lazily in the moonlight. It was old, and there was something more. Jeanne could sense a power emanating from it—a presence. Montrovant held it for a long moment, then threw it back into the box in disgust. Leaping back to the ground, he called out to Eugenio.

"It isn't here."

"Not here? What do you mean?"

"I mean," Montrovant replied, "that we have captured the wrong treasure. There are objects of power in that chest, things I doubt that mortal men have held or felt the magic of in hundreds of years, but there is no Grail."

Eugenio turned back to Kli Kodesh, who watched them with a mocking smile planted on his ancient features.

"Did you truly believe that I would send such an object away protected by only one? Even one such as Gustav? Did you think I would hand it over to you so easily?"

"Where is it?" Montrovant growled. "What have you done with it?"

"What makes you think I ever had it?" Kli Kodesh replied shortly. "In fact, what makes you think that what you seek is a cup? What makes you believe that the vessel that contains the blood you seek has ever been something so simple?"

"You speak in riddles," Montrovant replied, his anger returning hot and sudden. He took a step toward the ancient before regaining control of his temper. "I am so very tired of playing that game." Jeanne was listening to the exchange, but only with the periphery of his mind. There was something waiting to form that he knew would be important, and he had to shut out his surroundings enough to grasp it. Gwendolyn had noticed his frown, and she'd moved closer, shielding him from the ancient. He didn't know why she would make such a pointless gesture, but in seeing it his last reservations about their new traveling companion slipped away. She might not be of any use against her sire, but it was not because she didn't hate him. It hit him at last with the subtlety of a herd of wild stallions. The others. He had completely forgotten those who were scaling the walls of the cliff toward the ocean below. Both he and Montrovant had been so certain that the group was a decoy that they'd pushed them from their minds. The dawn wasn't far away, and there was little time in which to act.

"Boats!" He cried out the word before he could temper his reaction with caution. Montrovant spun on him, ready to take the frustration the ancient was building in his mind out on someone less powerful. Something in the word "boat" sank in. Jeanne saw the light of comprehension flash across his sire's face, and the equally confused look that passed Eugenio's at the same moment.

"The cliffs. Damn you," Montrovant spat at Kli Kodesh, "you sent it to the cliffs!"

The Dark One sprang for the shadows, but Kli Kodesh was faster. Jeanne knew they had guessed rightly in that instant. His plans undone, the ancient wasn't ready to have them broken up by Montrovant, or anyone else. The two went down in a heap for the second time that night, but Eugenio was by their side in an instant, dragging them apart.

"So," Kli Kodesh spat, "you would challenge me?"

Eugenio reached beneath his robes and pulled out a small pendant. It was an Egyptian symbol, an ankh. He held it up before him and began to chant in a language Jeanne couldn't understand. The light in Kli Kodesh's eyes flashed from anger to concern and he backed away slowly.

Montrovant didn't hesitate. He leapt toward the cliffs in the distance, and without a backward glance, Jeanne followed. He knew Gwendolyn was with them as well, but he couldn't stop to look back and be certain she was keeping up. Behind them the chanting continued, and he could hear Kli Kodesh responding with curses and odd phrases of his own. The power that had flooded that area was astonishing—beyond anything Jeanne had ever experienced, even in the presence of Santos.

He didn't know how long Eugenio could hold the ancient at bay, but shortly it wouldn't matter. They would either head off the Nosferatu at the cliffs, or they would be too late. There was little, at this point, that Kli Kodesh could do to stop them. He might follow and destroy them, but they would know whether they were right, or wrong.

Jeanne didn't truly care about the Grail in the way that Montrovant did, but he was beginning to get the fever. It had never seemed as real to him before as it did in that moment, and the implications, even to one not impressed by affairs of the Church, were staggering. He'd seen the power of other objects, and his heightened senses had granted the ability to perceive how much strength faith could lend to a mortal. How much more powerful, how much greater the aura, of an object like the Grail? And what had Kli Kodesh meant when he'd asked Montrovant how he knew it was a cup that held the blood he sought?

Too many questions, and none of them as important as keeping up with Montrovant, who flew across the miles like a storm. He paid no heed to his followers, nor did he appear to take note of anything they passed. He angled straight for the cliffs, and Jeanne was beginning to fear that he would be over the cliff and out of sight before Gwendolyn and himself even reached the edge.

When he reached the cliff's edge, Montrovant didn't hesitate. He leapt into the night sky, forcing the transformation, stretching his arms, even as they shriveled and re-formed, beating them wildly at the air until the leathery skin stretched out and drew him aloft once more. He circled once and dove.

Jeanne had no such ability. He gazed down over the cliff at the pounding waves below. There was no sign of a ship, and nothing moved on the small, sandy coast at the foot of the rocky drop-off. Nothing.

Gwendolyn appeared at his shoulder then, pulling him back from the cliff's edge, and he pulled away from her angrily.

"Montrovant is down there," he grated, "and if we don't find a way to follow, and quickly, he will be gone."

"He will not go far," she said urgently. "Something is happening back at the keep—something important. Kli Kodesh has left the bishop and the others behind. They are leaving as well. All of them are headed for de Molay's keep."

"What does it mean?" he asked her. "Why would they return to that place?"

"I don't know," she replied, "but I sense none of the others— if the Nosferatu were here, they have found a way to escape from here long since. We cannot catch them before the light."

Jeanne leaned back over the cliff, but he still saw nothing. He stretched his senses, searching for the Dark One, and he detected nothing but a faint glimmer of his sire's essence, high above and moving away rapidly.

"I will wait here, and when he returns, we will go to the keep and see what has happened."

"I will wait with you, but the dawn will not be long in coming. You cannot wait beyond that. Montrovant will return, with or without that which he seeks, and he will find shelter. He has walked this Earth much longer than we, and we must trust him to watch out for his own safety."

"There is the tomb," Jeanne replied. "We can return to the tomb and wait there, if he doesn't return. He will certainly go there, if only to find out what transpired between Eugenio and Kli Kodesh." Gwendolyn nodded. She turned, then, following his gaze out across the waves, and Jeanne glanced at her sidelong, wondering how much she knew—how much she could see and feel beyond his own abilities. She cocked her head, as if listening to a sound across a great distance, but she held her silence.

Philip had sent members of his personal guard in search of Bishop Eugenio Scarpocci as soon as the messengers arrived from the keep, but the bishop was not to be found. It didn't matter. After so much time on the road, so many days of marching and sleeping in damp, chilly tents and eating slop, they were about to be vindicated. The Church was a part of this victory, and he wanted the bishop there to witness and bless his victory, but he would not wait indefinitely. There would be plenty of time the following evening, when the Bishop's "condition" allowed him to exit his own quarters, for prayers and blessings. Perhaps it was proper that this night should be his alone.

The messengers themselves, two young knights barely old enough to ride and carry a full-weight blade, sat atop their mounts, trembling in fear. He left them that way as he savored the moment. He had no intention of harming them, nor did he plan on a mass slaughter of those within the keep, but there was no reason to tell them this at such an early point. No doubt his reputation preceded him, and he rather enjoyed their squirming and posturing.

Finally, he decided he'd waited long enough. He gestured to one of his guards, who led the two mounted men forward, and he stood, waiting for them to gather the courage to speak. They did not do so at once, instead keeping a close eye on the armed guards that flanked them. Finally, the older of the two raised his eyes to meet Philip's.

"Your highness," he began, his voice shrill and ill-controlled, "Jacques de Molay, Grand Master of the Order of the Poor Knights of the Temple Solomon, has asked that I relay the following request to you. He wishes to open the doors of his keep, and to allow those who feel the need to repent, as you ask, to go. He further requests that, should this happen, no harm come to those he releases."

"No harm will come to any man who repents his sins in the name of God and swears allegiance to Mother Rome," Philip answered grandly. "You must return with this answer, but you must add the following. Tell Jacques de Molay that the lives of all who repent will be spared, but that the lives of those who do not will be forfeit. Tell him that we will find the truth behind the tales of his evil, and that the Lord will have his retribution. We have come not in my name, but in the name of the one God, and no work of Satan will be allowed to flourish in any land where I have sovereignty."

The second lad's head popped up at these words, and there was surprising courage etching the young lines of his face.

"Jacques de Molay serves no evil," he said slowly. His companion had turned to regard him in what amounted to abject terror, but the boy paid him no heed.

"The knights have supported the Church from these shores to the Holy Land and beyond. They have supported the monarchy in times of trouble, both financial and in battle. It is a sad day that we have come to this."

"Who are you, lad?" Philip asked.

"My name is Antoine Cardin," he replied proudly. "My father served in the order, and his father before him. My great-grandfather served under Hugues de Payen himself."

"That is a grand history," Philip replied, "and one to be proud of. You are not a blind man, though, so you may see what has happened. The order you serve is not the order Hugues de Payen foresaw. Idol worship. Sorcery. Putting one's self before the Church. These are sins that cannot be ignored, and all of these and more have been reported within these walls. I urge you, Antoine, to reconsider what it means to you to serve the Church, and to reconsider as well the value of your life. If you do not recant your vows, you will forfeit your life, and I will watch you burn before the sun rises tomorrow." Cardin didn't speak, but he wheeled his mount and started for the keep without looking back. His companion, nearly panicked, turned and followed the younger knight at a gallop. Philip stood and watched them leave, deep in thought.

He wondered how a man like de Molay could inspire such fanatic loyalty. His own men, he knew, would abandon him in a second in the face of such a hopeless cause. He couldn't blame them; no man wanted to die. He wondered what it would be like to care about something deeply enough to consider it worth his life. Shrugging, he turned back to the camp and began to bark orders to his commanders as he made his way to his tent. He could ask his questions of de Molay himself, once he'd rested and the keep was theirs.

He disappeared between the flaps of his tent and the preparations began in earnest for the evacuation of the keep. The sun was just cresting the horizon.

There was no sign of Montrovant, and the pain of the sun was finally too much for Jeanne to stand. Gwendolyn stood silently at his side, waiting for his word. He knew she would get him to shelter, knew as well that she didn't require it as soon as he did—but that this day she would wait with him. He wondered, not for the first time, about the blood that had given her this gift, or curse, dampening the burning fear of the sun, and taking the hunger that drove him, day and night.

"He will come," she said softly. "We must get you out of the light."

Nodding, Jeanne let her lead him away from the cliff, and the sudden release of the concentration he'd focused on the horizon, where Montrovant had disappeared, allowed the pain and the immediacy of his danger to flood his senses. The pain lanced through him and he cried out, setting off for the cemetery with every ounce of strength left to him. He felt the hunger building, but there was no time, or way, for him to feed, not with the sun rising and an army camped only a few short miles away.

Gwendolyn was at the tomb even before he flashed into the small clearing. There was no sign of the others—only footprints and the ruts where the wagon-wheels had plowed into the earth remained. He had no time to wonder what had happened. He slid into the soothing darkness of the tomb with a groan, and Gwendolyn entered after him, pulling the stone seal back into place easily and shutting out the light. The pain slipped away almost as quickly as it had come, and the darkness called out to him.

"I..." he began.

"Shhhh..." Gwendolyn soothed. "Rest. When the sun has departed once more, we will talk, and we will go to the keep to see what has happened. The Dark One will return...he is not so easily evaded, no matter what Kli Kodesh or the bishop believe."

As Jeanne slipped into darkness, he thought he heard screams and the clatter of weapons, but they faded into shadow. Long after his mind had shut down, Gwendolyn sat at his side, staring at the door and listening to what happened beyond. She was listening when the doors of the keep opened and Philip's army rolled in. She was listening when those who would survive trudged wearily out onto the road and began to make their way to homes and families far away. She was listening, still, when Jeanne awoke.

The first thing he noticed was that the door was rolling aside, and that Gwendolyn was nowhere near it. The second was the sound of screams, and the acrid smell of smoke and soot.

Montrovant stood framed in the doorway, haggard and worn, though his eyes blazed with incredible intensity. He spoke a single word, "Come," and turned away. Jeanne rose, and he followed. The edges of the shadows were illumined by the glow of distant flames, and with Gwendolyn at his side and Montrovant striding purposefully ahead, they returned a final time to the keep of Jacques de Molay.

TWENTY-THREE

They followed Montrovant for a few moments in silence, neither willing to be the one to drag him from his reverie. Finally, without turning to acknowledge them, he began to speak.

"When I leapt from the cliffs," he began, "I could sense them, barely, against the horizon, and I thought that there might be time—just enough time—for me to reach them. I knew you could not follow, but there was no time to explain. One lost moment and I'd have had no chance at all."

"You found them, then?" Jeanne asked quickly. "No. The sun rose, and I knew that, even if I made it to the ship, they would deny me shelter and I would be destroyed. I followed as far as I dared, and I memorized the course they were sailing, but

I could do no more.

"I barely made it back to the shore, and not near here, before the light burned too brightly for me to continue. I found a small cavern just above the rocks, and I crawled as far back into it as I could. There I stayed as the sunlight burned and the ship moved farther and farther out to sea. When it grew dark, I flew over the sea once more, but there was nothing. Not a sign, not a glimpse. I came straight here then, though I knew Kli Kodesh and the others would be gone. I'd hoped to find you here."

"What is that smoke?" Jeanne asked, not wanting to change the subject, but unable to contain his curiosity.

"They will burn the heretics at the stake this night," Montrovant replied matter-of-factly. "Those who have not repented their vows to the Templars will die."

"Who would be foolish enough to die for such a cause?" Jeanne asked. "Why would they not pretend to capitulate, then leave and regroup?"

"Because they do not think like you, my friend," Montrovant said, smiling for the first time since he'd returned. "Jacques de Molay will die, and also his friend, de Chaunvier, I believe. There are others, some fanatics, others fools. All will die before the Earth has fully cooled from the sun."

Gwendolyn shivered, clutching her arms about herself. To live after death did not mean that one lost the fear of it—the acidic, heart-stopping terror that oblivion could muster. Fire was as dangerous to the three of them as it would be to de Molay, and Jeanne wondered fleetingly if they were truly safe. Certainly Philip could not harm them, not on his own, but Eugenio had still not given up the secret of what had dragged him forth from his monastery—his safe-haven. Kli Kodesh had not made his presence known, either, and both of them were still nearby. Even Jeanne could feel them.

The two ancients were keeping their silence, and Montrovant ignored them, moving closer to the keep with every passing moment. They could see the glow of flames in the distance, and as they neared the cleared area before the keep, the light grew brighter. Voices materialized from the silence, cries of pain, cries for mercy...cries of glee from those who looked on. The stench of burning flesh filled the air, reminding Jeanne briefly of feasts and tournaments—days long denied him.

They reached the outer ring of those gathered, and Montrovant began, slowly, to work his way forward. He kept to the shadowed area along the wall, preferring to be behind the stake—beyond the point where all eyes would focus. He didn't want to call attention to himself, but he had to know—had to see.

Jeanne wanted to see as well. He had been one of these men, had worn the white robes of the Templars and ridden at their side. He'd known Hugues de Payen, tall, proud founder of the order, and he'd lived through the first of the hundreds and thousands of conflicts that had besieged them. Though he was beyond such concerns, it was difficult to let them go completely.

They worked their way through the crowds, and eventually they broke into the front ranks. One man hung from a stake in the center of the clearing, half-charred as flames licked at his legs and torso. He screamed, but no one listened—not to his pleas for help. They listened to his pain, to the screaming, but none cared for his well-being. They had not come to see him saved, but to see him destroyed.

The man was Jacques de Molay, and Jeanne felt a moment of pain, a hint of loss, that was difficult to explain. The Templar lord had made poor choices. He'd nearly sold them all into a slavery much worse than any punishment Philip might mete out, and that included death. He'd been willing to sacrifice them all—everything—for answers to questions he would never have fully understood. Still, he was Grand Master. It was not a position held by the unworthy.

Jeanne thought that the end must be somewhere near, but suddenly the man's features returned to their lucidity. Though the flames licked and crackled about him, engulfing all but his head and shoulders and setting his hair ablaze like a flaming halo, he smiled, and against all the laws of nature, or of God, he began to speak.

"Are you ready to repent your sins?" a voice boomed out. Jeanne turned in shock. Kli Kodesh stood a pace beyond the circle of wide-eyed spectators, and at his side was Bishop Scarpocci. Ko-desh wore the robes of a priest, and none in the circle seemed dismayed by this. Jeanne had forgotten that the ancient had stayed in the temple under the guise of a priest.

"There is time to save your soul, if not your life," he continued. "What say you, Jacques de Molay? Will you burn now and forever for your sins, or will we welcome you into the arms of your God?"

"I burn," de Molay croaked, forcing the words through parched, crackling lips, bending over with the effort. "I burn, but you will follow, Philip. You and the coward you call Pope will join me before the court of God Almighty before a year's time has passed. This is my promise to you. The Knights of the Temple will not die...but you shall."

As he spoke his eyes pierced the shadows, ignoring Kli

Kodesh, bypassing Eugenio, and driving their full weight into the rapt gaze of King Philip. The monarch met that gaze, but looking more closely, Jeanne saw that there was a tremor in Philip's stance.

De Molay's jaws still moved, but no further sound emerged. Jeanne tried to read those crackling lips, to know who else was cursed, but there was no hope for it. The flames rose, engulfing de Molay's body and charring him to ash.

"Ashes to ashes," Montrovant whispered, as if mocking Jeanne's thoughts, "dust to dust."

Montrovant turned away, and moments later, Jeanne followed. Gwendolyn turned as well, but stopped suddenly, and Montrovant stiffened in that moment. He'd felt the same tug that she had, and he turned quickly, taking her by the arm, pulling her close, and guiding her out through the gathered warriors, knights, servants and onlookers. Kli Kodesh was calling to her, but it seemed that the Dark One was not quite ready to let her go.

He held Gwendolyn's hands tightly between his own, and turned quickly to Jeanne.

"Go to them," he said. "Tell them that she is with us, now, and that we will continue our quest. Tell them that it is over for now."

"And if they will not listen?" Jeanne asked. "Then return, if you can," Montrovant finished, "and if you do not, I will come after you. I think our friend," he gestured at the grinning, flaming skeleton engulfed in flames behind them, "would agree that it truly is a good night to die."

Jeanne made his way back through the crowd quickly. He had little patience for those gawking at the spectacle of men being burned alive, and he pushed his way roughly through the crowd, ignoring those he angered. The two "priests" had moved back from the front ranks for the moment, probably until the next victim was brought forth to the slaughter.

Jeanne meant to find them before that happened.

He saw the colors of the Church flying above one of the tents, and he made straight for it, sweeping his eyes over those who scurried about the camp and watching for any sign of

Scarpocci or Kli Kodesh. He sensed them both before he saw them, and Eugenio met him at the flap of the tent, one hand dropping in a calming gesture onto the shoulder of the guard Jeanne was about to cast aside to gain entrance. He realized that they must have known he was coming, possibly from the moment Montrovant commanded it.

"So, the Dark One has sent his whelp," the bishop said suavely. "Enter, Jeanne le Duc, we have much to discuss. It is always good to welcome—family."

Jeanne felt the rush of anger that threatened to overcome his thoughts and battered it down. He was here for a reason, and that reason did not involve tossing away his existence in a futile attempt to retaliate against Eugenio. He lowered his head and entered the tent as the bishop held the flaps open wide. They slipped closed behind him, and he found that he now faced both elders.

"Why is he here?" Jeanne asked, the words leaping forth before he could regain control of his thoughts.

Kli Kodesh smiled and rose from where he'd been sitting.

"The bishop and I have come to an agreement of sorts," he said suavely. "I think your sire will find the arrangement—entertaining."

Jeanne bit his lip to keep from responding. He'd had enough of the ancient's "entertainment" to last several lifetimes, but now was not the time to tell him so. Not before he had what he'd come for.

"Arrangement?" he prodded.

"It seems," Bishop Scarpocci joined in, "that 'Father' Kodesh has slipped his treasures through our grasp another time. I take it from your presence that Montrovant did not reach the ship in time."

"No," Jeanne replied simply, "he did not."

Then it is settled," Scarpocci said with finality, turning to nod at Kli Kodesh. "We will bring the matter before the Church upon my return, but you may take my word that they will agree. I am not without influence in Rome."

"I don't doubt you," Kli Kodesh replied. "You have been closed up in that monastery so long that I was beginning to wonder if you'd ever break free, but your influence is not to be questioned. Your name is spoken in places much farther from Rome than this, and with respect."

"Enough of your words," Eugenio snapped. Jeanne watched the two carefully. Apparently things were not quite as civil in the seclusion of the tent as they'd first appeared.

"Your order will guard the treasures, maintaining constant contact with the Church, and with Montrovant. These are the conditions. I will set the Dark One up in a stronghold not far from the mountain in question, and you will have your followers contact him there. A representative of the Church—unless things have changed since my departure, Bishop Santorini—will keep tabs on both Montrovant and the order. He is not quite aware of my nature, but he knows enough to fear me. I trust Montrovant will have no trouble in earning the same level of 'respect.' The first indication of treachery, and it is ended."

"Agreed," Kli Kodesh said, a faint smile dancing across his lips.

"Order?" Jeanne cut in.

"You will remain silent until I speak to you again," Eugenio lashed out. "You will take the instructions I will give you to Montrovant, and you will convince him to follow them, or I will have you, and he, on the very pyre that took de Molay this night. Is that understood?"

Jeanne gazed at the bishop calmly, though the anger raged just below the surface of his thoughts. He did not acknowledge the bishop's words, nor did he deny them. He gazed silently into those ancient, timeless eyes, and he waited.

"Tell the Dark One I will meet him on the walls of my monastery in two weeks' time. Tell him to prepare himself for the task of building a new Order, a new breed of knight. Tell him that not everything is as it seems, and that he must do as I say—just this once—in all the long years of his existence. Tell him to search his heart, and to trust me. I will speak to him when I can—soon. Can you remember that?"

The words were etched into Jeanne's mind, but still he hesitated a moment. Despite his obvious disadvantage, he wanted to be certain that fear did not show on his features. He wanted this arrogant, ancient vampire to know that things were indeed not as they seemed; that though it might appear to be so at the moment, he did not have every advantage. Finally, as if in afterthought, Jeanne nodded. "It is well," Eugenio said softly. "Go, and deliver my message. You must take yourself from this area swiftly."

"What of Gwendolyn?" Jeanne asked quickly. "She wishes to accompany us, but," he hesitated, turning to Kli Kodesh, "that choice is not entirely hers."

"She may go as she wills," the ancient cackled. "I will see her again. I will see you all again. I will see you all as dust, and there will be new entertainments."

Jeanne turned, not acknowledging the ancient's taunting words. He slid through the flaps of the tent and headed off into the shadows. Behind him, mocking laughter floated through the night. A single word filled his mind, floating out from the interior of the tent to haunt him."Dust."

TWENTY-FOUR

Montrovant's eyes narrowed dangerously as Jeanne relayed Eugenio's message. He spoke quickly, not commenting or embellishing the words. The central point was that their search was over. Not only had they not acquired the Grail, but they would now be expected to maintain contact with Kli Kodesh's Nosferatu, never truly knowing if those had it or not, and unable to act. It was a bittersweet moment, and when he'd finished, Jeanne stepped back a pace, watching his sire's features.

A world of emotions and a longing that stretched up from his very soul crossed the Dark One's face.

Years—centuries—a lifetime. He'd dedicated them all to this singular purpose, and for what? To become a watchdog for the Church? A guardian of guardians, only in place because he was powerful in ways the holy men were not?

Finally he spoke.

"It would seem that, for now, our traveling days are numbered, Jeanne," he said softly. "I don't know whether Kli Kodesh ever had the Grail, but if he has it, we can't afford to turn aside from this. You say that Eugenio told him treachery would end our bargain?"

Jeanne nodded.

"Then our course is clear. We will go to this mountain, we will watch them as we are bid, and we will find a way to incite them to treachery."

With a sudden laugh the tall, gaunt vampire clapped Jeanne on the back heartily.

"Will you join us, milady?" he asked, turning to Gwendolyn and offering her his arm.

Smiling, she took it, offering her other to Jeanne. There were several hours before morning, and suddenly he felt the urge to run—to run and not look back—all cares forgotten.

As if in answer to his wish, Montrovant took her hand, turning and streaking off into the night. Gwendolyn ran easily at his side, and Jeanne watched as they took off, smiling softly. He lifted his eyes to the moon, feeling that silvery light wash over him, and went in pursuit.

A sudden dizziness shifted through him, and he stumbled, smacking his chin on the ground painfully. Something was happening—something new—and he was having trouble orienting himself.

The Moon called, and they answered. Behind them, smoke rose over the keep of Jacques de Molay...dark, bitter, and final.

EPILOGUE

Beneath the keep of Jacques de Molay, in a silent room of damp stone, the head lay forgotten in a corner. The dust that had been Santos shifted. At first the movement was slight—barely a shifting of air—a whispered promise in the dark stagnancy of the dungeon. Then there was more. Energy coalesced about the area, and the spirit that had been Santos reached out—sought—found maggots, wiggling and squirming in one of the damper corners. He dug deeper, found their name—vibrated the air to form the sound. The change was slow—excruciatingly slow. What passed for consciousness nearly left him, but then he had experienced the change.

Slowly he crawled across the floor, sightless, using his other senses. He didn't have the strength to seek a larger form—a more complex name. He slid across the cold stone floor until he came up against the solid mass of the head, and he began to slither upward. He didn't stop until he'd found the ear, and, with a supreme effort, he toppled inside. Once there he crawled deeper as quickly as he could. Exhausted, he rested.

All thought, all function, closed down. He would wait. He would endure. He would return. Nothing mattered but that he return to his geas…his duty. If it took a year, or a century, such things mattered little to him. A final thought—a name—flashed through his thoughts as he passed into darkness.

"Montrovant."

As he passed into the void, gray-flecked eyes mocked him, and dark laughter pressed around his soul.

About the Author

DAVID NIALL WILSON has been writing and publishing horror, dark fantasy, and science fiction since the mid-eighties. An ordained minister, once President of the Horror Writers Association and multiple recipient of the Bram Stoker Award, his novels include *Maelstrom, The Mote in Andrea's Eye, Deep Blue,* the Grails Covenant Trilogy, *Star Trek Voyager: Chrysalis, Except You Go Through Shadow, This is My Blood, Ancient Eyes, On the Third Day, The Orffyreus Wheel,* The DeChance Chronicles, including *Heart of a Dragon, Vintage Soul, My Soul to Keep, Kali's Tale* and the stand-alone spinoff *Nevermore – A Novel of Love, Loss & Edgar Allan Poe.* His novels in the O.C.L.T. series include *The Parting, Crockatiel,* and the novella *The Temple of Camazotz* He is also the author of the memoir / cookbook *American Pies: Baking with Dave the Pie Guy.* David can be found at http://www.davidniallwilson.com and can be reached by e-mail at david@davidniallwilson.com.

Curious about other Crossroad Press books?
Stop by our site:
http://store.crossroadpress.com
We offer quality writing
in digital, audio, and print formats.